MW00944156

Companion Pieces

Stories from the Old World and Beyond

Melissa F. Olson

OTHER WORKS

The Old World Series

Dead Spots
Trail of Dead
Hunter's Trail

Boundary Crossed
Boundary Lines
Boundary Born

Midnight Curse
Blood Gamble
Shadow Hunt

Bloodsick
Boundary Broken (Coming 2019)

The Nightshades Trilogy

Nightshades
Switchback
Outbreak

Also by Melissa F. Olson

The Big Keep

TABLE OF CONTENTS

Sell-By Date

Author's Note: This prequel story takes place a few months before Dead Spots.

I.

Westwood Village, snuggled right next to the UCLA campus, is an adorable little mecca of nice restaurants, tolerant coffee shops, timeworn bars, and great movie theaters. Because it's right next to the city's biggest university, it's also vampire paradise. Especially if, like me, you look *maybe* old enough to be a college freshman.

It was a Sunday night in May, and I was leaning forward on my bar stool in Roberto's Cabana, trying to get the human bartender to look my way. I was here to hunt, but I wanted a prop drink, something to help me blend in with the large crowd of twentysomethings. The bar was surprisingly packed for a Sunday night, but I knew that the students were in the middle of finals and had probably come to blow off steam and/or get wasted with their study groups. Wasted, transient young adults in good health, who are prone to low inhibitions and frequent blackouts? Like I said, vampire paradise.

The sole bartender was in his late twenties, with a bit of that wild-eyed look universally shared by grad students who are grading papers and writing their own at the same time. He also had dark hair that was starting to silver prematurely and an endlessly put-upon expression as he focused on the customers clamoring for drinks at the other end of the bar. He was ignoring the few customers on this end, and finally I gave up for the moment and spun my stool around, leaning my back against the bar so I could survey the crowd for adequate prey. I didn't actually have to feed tonight, since I'd fed the night before, but…well, what else was I going to do? I was the goddamned immortal undead. At this point I fed just to pass the time.

There were plenty of potential blood donors, but the problem was culling one from the herd. Students were gathered in tight, excited clumps, talking or complaining or arguing about their exams. The human emotions were running high tonight – you could practically taste it on the air. Some of the kids seemed truly upset, while others were triumphant, beaming with some kind of relief I didn't really understand. After a quick initial scan I glanced at the blonde co-ed next to me, who seemed to be at the bar alone. She was staring morosely into an empty glass that had once contained a cranberry-vodka, or something equally pink.

As I watched, a twin trail of tears erupted from her eyes, making their slow way down her round cheeks, dripping onto the scarred wooden bar. She made no move to wipe the tears away, and I frowned with distaste. Honestly, who goes to a bar to cry alone? She was alone, though, so I looked her over a little more speculatively. The girl was cute rather than pretty, probably a size eight, which was actually considered overweight in this shallow town. The extra fifteen pounds she carried were distributed mostly in her hips and not at all in her bra, but then again, sexual attractiveness wasn't important in my food. As far as I could tell, the sex-and-feeding thing was something my kind only did in the movies, or when they thought they were supposed to behave like vampires in the movies. I mean, when I was human, and my mother made me wring a chicken's neck to be our family's dinner, it wasn't like I made out with it first.

Before I could decide whether she'd make a good meal, though, the bartender finally remembered the total length of his bar and began making his way down to my end. Smiling beguilingly, I leaned way forward, letting my cleavage spill onto the bar. I waved a 10-dollar bill and called brightly, "Yo! Silver Fox!"

The guy completely ignored me, which was surprising in itself. Then he actually beelined straight for the sad co-ed, lifting her empty glass away and wiping the table underneath it. "You okay, hon?" he said, as quietly as he could over the sound of cheery Spanish salsa music and arguing students.

The sad blonde looked up, startled to see the bartender in front of her. She wiped at her cheeks with the heels of each hand, putting on a bleary smile. "I'm sorry, yeah, I just totally bombed this final" –her voice broke, and her face did that weird crumple thing that happens to women on nighttime soap operas, only not as pretty. "And I'm worried about my scholarship…" She trailed off, and the bartender just nodded sympathetically and put a clean pint glass in front of her, filling it with tap beer. "On me," he said in the same low voice.

For some reason, that only seemed to make the co-ed more upset. "Thank you, I–" she paused and let out a wrenching sob, one hand fluttering near her face like it might fan her off. "I can't," she wailed. She rose from the stool and fled toward the bathroom.

"I'll take it," I said happily, dropping the ten on the bar and reaching out to grab the pint. As I pulled it toward me, though I felt the bartender's hand close firmly on my wrist. I looked up at him in confusion. Had he not seen the money?

"I don't know how you got in here," he yelled to me over the music. He was scowling now, and looked at me like I'd just urinated on the bar in front of him. "But I don't have time to fuck around with fake ID's right now. Get out of here or I'll call the cops."

A flash of anger hit me like a lightning bolt through my usual fog of detachment. I had been turned into a vampire at the age of seventeen, which at the time was old enough for me to get married and start a family. Now, though, I couldn't even get a friggin' pint without a hassle. Silver Fox turned to go, taking the forbidden beer with him, but I reached out with vampire speed and snagged his hand. Surprised, he paused and met my eyes again. He opened his mouth to shout at me, but it was too late.

Fixing my eyes on his, I opened up a connection between us so I could press his mind. I have no idea how this actually works, mind you, but it's sort of like glaring at someone with your brain: you focus on them as hard as you can and mentally push your will into their brain. As vampire party tricks go, it's my personal favorite.

"You've seen my ID," I said, keeping my voice as low as I could and still let him hear me. "You feel terrible about accusing me of being underage. You've decided to buy a round of drinks for everyone sitting at the bar, out of your own pocket."

The guy nodded, his face slack, his eyes eager to please me. "Now," I commanded, and fear dawned in his eyes as the guy actually knocked over several glasses in his rush to do my bidding. I smiled. Some humans should learn a little fear.

Yeah, okay, it wasn't exactly the bartender's fault that I looked like I should be picking out a prom dress instead of a tap beer. And I don't make a habit of pressing minds in public - it's kind of a no-no, what with the ironclad "don't let the humans find out about us" business, but the guy had pissed me off. I'd worn my nicest, most adult clubbing outfit: a light green cashmere tank top with a cowl neck and skintight snakeskin leather pants. I looked fantastic from head to toe, and if the guy still thought I looked like a kid, well, maybe that was all the cause I needed for a little pettiness.

As he started passing beer out to my end of the bar, splashing a little in his rush, I hopped off my stool and headed after the sad girl. I like feeding on female humans, because it's easy to get them alone, and because they're smaller and more manageable. Sure, vampires have evolved strength and speed to be able to bring down larger prey, but why work for it if you don't have to?

She had paused in her flight to the bathroom, stopping to talk to a male classmate seated at a table with another group of students. I slowed down, keeping an eye on them. He was talking to the sad girl with a look of compassion on his face, reaching out to touch her arm in a platonic-comfort kind of way. I could have made the effort to listen in if I'd wanted, but I had no interest in whatever "feel better" platitudes the guy was shoving at her.

After a moment I got bored and figured this girl was a loss. I was just about to go back to the bar to see if my free round had earned me any trust from the barflies, but at that moment the girl tilted her head toward the bathrooms and said goodbye. Excellent.

I followed the sad girl as she wound through the tables, keeping an eye on her generous hips with a bit of misguided envy. The poor thing had been born in the wrong era; when I'd been alive, every woman in my town had coveted hips like that, which supposedly made childbirth a breeze. Sure, this girl probably had a hard time buying modern jeans, but at least if she ever decided to have kids they'd pop out like little jack-in-the-boxes.

What do you care, Molly? You'll never have kids.

The thought came out of nowhere, and I almost missed a step. It had been years since I'd had a thought like that. Like sharks and crocodiles, vampire bodies are designed to be perfectly efficient hunting machines, and as such they devote very little energy to functions like hormones and emotional reactions. We're technically *capable* of human emotions, but they no longer come naturally after the end of our human lives. By the time we reach, say, fifty or so years past death, most vampires stop caring about the human world. And then they stop caring about much, period, until finally we just live in a haze of basic needs: blood, a place to pass the daytime hours, money to buy the comforts needed to blend in with humans.

A friend of mine calls this transition the sell-by date. Most of the people you knew from your human life are dead. The world around you has changed, and you can no longer pretend you're living a normal life. If you want to keep in touch with your human feelings you have to work hard at it, and I've never met a vampire who...well, cared enough to keep caring. Personally, I had held onto human feelings for a longer time than most, but I'd eventually reached my sell-by date too, when I'd been dead for ninety years. After that, well, I almost never thought of my previous life as a human, or the opportunities I might have missed by "dying" young.

Shaking off the misplaced sense of loss, I allowed my predator's tunnel vision to take over, focusing in on the sad girl. I followed her down a dimly lit hallway to the women's bathroom, where she bumped open the door with her hip and went in. I counted to ten and followed.

The ladies' restroom was simple and clean, decorated in cautious beiges and rose-pinks, as though using any bright colors might make us chicks explode into spontaneous PMS. There was a long, fake marble counter with two sinks opposite three bathroom stalls, including an especially wide handicapped one at the end. I ducked my head, and saw the sad girl's Doc Martens boots in the middle stall. I pushed in the other two doors just to be sure that there was nobody else in the bathroom. I felt the corners of my lips curl up.

I went to the sink and pulled some mascara out of my handbag. There's only so much you can do with lipstick or blush, but I've discovered that you can pretend to be working on your mascara for *ages* before anyone will think you're stalling. I pulled out the wand and started fussing with my right eyelid, alternately clumping and de-clumping the top lashes at whim, until finally I heard a flush and the sad girl squeezed around the stall door and joined me at the sink. She'd blown her nose and dried her eyes a bit, but she still looked all weepy and gross. Humans.

The girl filled a palm with hand soap and began scrubbing, waving her hands under the automatic sensor on the sink in front of her. Automatic sensors, that's serious cultural progress. I remember when the concept of washing your hands after going to the bathroom was new. "Nice top," I said casually, meeting her eyes in the mirror as I screwed the cap of my mascara back in.

The sad girl glanced automatically down at her shirt, then met my eyes again. "Thanks," she said hesitantly.

I turned sideways to look at her directly, and she automatically copied my body language, facing me. "Hey, have you had the nachos here?" I asked.

She opened her mouth to answer, but I had already opened the connection between us and begun pressing my will into her. "Give me your hand," I commanded. The sad girl immediately stuck out her hand, and I took a very quick glance down to check the veins at her wrist. They were perfect. The whole biting someone's neck thing is a total myth. Why go for an awkward grapple when you can just hold someone's hand and sink your teeth into a great vein? It was easier to press the human if you maintained eye contact too, and the wrist is a much less suspicious place for someone to be injured – people get minor wounds on their hands and wrists all the time.

My eyes went back up to continue the press, and I took a step backward, toward the handicapped stall. And then a shrill clanging erupted from the handbag tucked under my shoulder. What…oh, right. The cell phone.

I sighed. I've had one of these stupid things for nearly a decade, but I never get used to it. There are only a few people with my cell phone number, though, and none of them are what you would call ignorable. "Hold that thought," I told the girl. I dropped her hand and fished the phone out of my bag. The little display window read *Dashiell*. Well, shit. Glancing back up at the sad girl, I made a distinct effort to withdraw my will from her. It was only a second before she shook her head a little, confusion beginning to spread across her face. We were still more or less in front of the mirror, so I asked sweetly, "Did you find that lipstick you were looking for?"

"Huh? Oh, right." Her face relaxed as she bent down to her own handbag. Human brains are so easy. Always thirsty for the simplest explanation.

I stepped back through the bathroom door, into the relative privacy of the dark hallway. "Hello, Dashiell," I said, keeping my tone respectful. There are plenty of vampire lords who still force their underlings to call them "My Lord" or "my Liege" or at least "Sir," but Dashiell's fairly modern, for a dominus. That's the preferred term for his class of vampires, by the way, not like a creepy S&M thing.

"Molly," he said smoothly. "I need you to come to the house. Right away."

"What did I do now?" I blurted, but there was no answer. I checked the phone screen. He'd hung up. Probably just as well.

II.

My car these days is a late-model Mini Cooper, which I'd chosen because it was quick, well-made, and small. Despite my best efforts to learn, I'm a terrible parallel parker. As it turns out, there are some things that vampire reflexes just don't apply to. When I can't find valet or a parking garage I need every advantage my car's size can give me.

Luckily there was a valet booth right outside Roberto's Cabana, and one of the two Hispanic parking attendants brought my Mini around quickly, hopping out and handing me the keys with a pleasant smile. I smiled back, handed him a $10 bill as a tip, and turned to climb behind the wheel. As soon as my back was turned, though, the parking attendant rejoined his friend at the valet booth, and my vampire hearing picked up his sniggered comment in Spanish about useless white children who get fancy cars with Daddy's money. An image of my actual father popped into my mind, and my back stiffened. What was *wrong* with me tonight?

I told myself that I should definitely let this one go. Telling these guys off wasn't worth being late to meet Dashiell.

Or was it?

I wheeled around, glaring at the two valets, who immediately smoothed their faces into polite "How can I help you" smiles. "*Mi padre está muerto, pendejo,*" I told him. "*Yo pagué por mi propio coche . Recuerda eso la próxima vez que estés mamando penes para dinero, canto de maricón.*" Both of their eyes bulged in a very satisfying way. I took one step forward, with my sweetest smile, and plucked the ten dollar bill out of the little shithead's hand. My tires screamed as I peeled away from the bar.

Hey, at least I didn't eat him.

Dashiell and his wife Beatrice live in an absolutely breathtaking Spanish Colonial mansion in Pasadena, located in the kind of old-money neighborhood where someone from Home and Garden is always ringing doorbells and begging to do a cover spread. The house doesn't have a driveway so much as a miniature parking lot — although you don't see many parking lots done in tiny Spanish tiles with a koi fountain in the middle. I parked by the fish and went to the front door, reaching for the bell. I loved this house, particularly the open-air atrium in the middle of the building, but it was way out of even my league. I'm financially very comfortable, even in an expensive, label-obsessed city like LA, but you have to be *stupid* rich to live around here.

The door popped open before my hand got very close, which didn't surprise me. Vampire hearing and all. Dashiell's wife, Beatrice, swung the carved-oak door open with no effort at all, her lips curving up to display teeth that were still stained a faint pink from recent feeding.

"Hello, Molly," Beatrice said coolly. Dashiell's wife and I have never really warmed to each other, mostly because Dashiell had to allow me on his territory under a bit of duress. And also because of every vampire I'd ever met, Beatrice was the most...*emotional.* I despised human emotion in vampires and saw no point in hiding it. "He's on the patio," she told me.

I nodded in reply and strolled through the exquisitely decorated entryway, trying not to get sidetracked. I could stare at the antiques in this house for days, if given the proper opportunity. One thing Beatrice and I do have in common is a love of beautiful things. Instead, though, I managed to go directly to the main sitting room, where a sliding glass door led outside.

And there was the man himself. Vampires tend to gravitate toward an appearance "type" that they can most easily hide behind, and Dashiell looks like a stockbroker right out of Central Casting, with dark brown hair, bland good looks, and expensive suits. Tonight he was sitting in his usual spot at the end of the enormous oval table that takes up most of the atrium, surrounded by stacks of paperwork that were separated into piles and held down with decorative rocks. The rocks had clearly been picked up from the nearby landscaping, but they were doing the trick. Dashiell studied the papers at his right elbow and typed something into a sleek laptop in front of him, ignoring the slight breeze that occasionally ruffled the corners of his stacks.

"Sit down, Molly," he said in a normal speaking voice, which I could hear easily from this distance. "Just give me a moment." His tone was very formal, and he hadn't even looked up. Oh, bollocks, what had I done now?

I didn't want to sit at the far end of the oval table – although we'd be able to hear each other just fine, I wasn't comfortable with the "called onto the carpet" dynamic that positioning implied. Instead, I went and sat at a chair a few feet away from his right elbow, close enough to be a casual conversation but far enough that it didn't look like I was trying to read his documents. Not that he'd be working on anything really juicy in front of me, of course. Vampires have trust issues.

The minutes ticked by while Dashiell continued his reading and typing, and I began to worry in earnest. If I were a human I would have fidgeted, but vampires feel no compulsion to fidget. Instead I thought through my activities for the last week or so, trying to recall what I might have done to piss Dashiell off. Nothing came to mind. I'd been on my best behavior for months now. I *needed* to stay in Dashiell's good graces: if he decided to exile me from his territory I would be well and truly fucked. No other dominus was going to accept my troth - my oath of loyalty - if I couldn't even hack it in *Los Angeles*. But I just couldn't think of any recent transgressions against the few rules Dashiell had. And I certainly hadn't killed any more vampires.

Finally, Dashiell closed the laptop and looked at me, his eyes running over every part of me. It wasn't sexual at all, but rather the look of a surveyor making an assessment of his property. I had hated that look when my first dominus Alonzo used to do it, but after a century I'd finally been desensitized enough not to mind. "How are you, Molly?" Dashiell asked. "How are things with the house?"

I felt a rainbow burst of relief. It couldn't be *that* bad, if he was making small talk first. "The remodel went fine. It took a couple days longer than they first thought, but I moved back in a week ago. "

He nodded. "Any questions about the specifications?"

"Not at all. I told the contractor I suffer from migraines, and needed the room to be completely dark, even through minor earthquakes. Didn't even have to press him. Well," I added with an evil little smile, "not about that, anyway."

Finding a secure daytime hiding place is no easy task, especially in a city where basements are rare. My small North Hollywood house came with a tiny root cellar, but I'd grown sick of spending my daylight hours down there, and had hired a contractor to make a few changes to my bedroom to make it totally sun-proof. I'd even had him remodel the upstairs bathroom at the same time, to make it a little less suspicious. The whole thing had gone pretty well, after I'd "convinced" the guy to treat me respectfully, work as hard and quickly as possible, and accept a reasonable fee. "He had some initial reservations about working for a teenager, but he came around," I summarized.

"Good, good," Dashiell said absently, turning his body to face me. I admired the easy gesture. Human body language doesn't come naturally to us; we have to learn it, which gets a little harder with every year that passes since we were actual humans. "Molly, I have a proposal for you."

I blinked. Vampires still have to blink. "Oh?" I said carefully. I've gotten orders, and I've gotten polite requests that were actually orders. I don't know that any dominus had ever presented a proposal, especially to the black sheep of their territory.

"Have you ever heard of a null?"

He placed a special emphasis on the word, and a little flag went up in my foggy long-term memory. "I've heard the term somewhere," I said slowly, trying to remember. "In the 1920's, I believe. But I can't recall the context."

"They've very rare," he explained. "A null is a person who exists within and without the Old World. He or she is human in every way but one: they negate magic within a certain area around themselves."

"Negate?" I repeated, not understanding. "What does that mean, to negate magic?"

"Just as it sounds," he said patiently. "When someone infused with magic gets near this person, we become as we were, for as long as we remain physically close."

"We become *human* again?" I said distastefully.

"For a short time, yes."

That sounded *terrible*. As a human, you'd have to waste time with all those horrible physical things: eating and drinking and using the bathroom – not to mention dragging around human emotions. I thought of the brief flare of longing I'd had at the bar when I was following the sad girl. Gross. What self-respecting vampire would want to be saddled with human feelings again?

Dashiell was watching my face for a reaction, but I knew better than to show one. "Why would anyone want that?" I asked.

"Molly," Dashiell said softly. "If you spent time around a null, you could age."

Oh. *Oh.* The penny dropped, and my body went absolutely still. "Really?" I whispered.

"Really."

My God. I could actually get older. That was…that was the most exciting thing I'd heard in a hundred years. Spending eternity as a teenager did not work out as nicely as those fucking Twilight books implied. All the logistics of posing as a human were an enormous nuisance for me. My business manager had gone through hell to get me my house, and I was regularly accosted by muggers and cops for running around the city at all hours of the night. And you should see what I had to pay for car insurance in this godforsaken town.

If I could age, though…A dozen questions fought for dominance in my mind. How was this possible? Why hadn't I heard of it before? How many nulls were there? How close did you have to be for it to work?

Finally, I settled on, "And you know such a person?"

"Yes," Dashiell said simply. "Her name is Scarlett Bernard, and she's an employee who's been through some recent troubles. And it just so happens," he continued, "that she needs a place to live."

III.

Twenty hours later, I was pacing back and forth in my living room, listening for the doorbell. Scarlett would be here in a few minutes to meet me and decide if we would be able to work out a roommate arrangement. I'd already cleaned and vacuumed the living room, fluffed all the throw pillows, lit a scented candle – everything you're supposed to do when company comes, at least according to the TV shows I've seen. But I was experiencing several feelings at once, which was as unfamiliar to me as wearing a diaper is to a human adult. I was hopeful, and excited, and actually *nervous*, which was surreal in itself.

The undead do not get nervous.

"Just meet her," Dashiell had said. "See if you two get along." He'd said it so casually, like he was a real estate broker or my own personal Craigslist, but if this actually worked out and I got to *age*, it would change everything for me. I could actually enjoy being a vampire, for once.

Of course, a deal like that didn't come without strings. Dashiell had made a point to warn me that I would have to be very careful around this person. "Don't tell her too much," he'd cautioned. "There's no reason for her to know about our structure, our lives. And if I have a question about her or her activities, I expect you to answer. Do not forget that you have pledged troth to me."

"I won't, sir," I'd told him. The formal address wasn't required, but it came out of my mouth anyway. Vampires have almost no access to magic, outside of the permanent changes to our physiology, but pledges of troth are the one exception to that rule. Once made, they are binding. Since I'd had to pledge troth to Dashiell in order to move here, I now literally had to do whatever he wanted.

I looked around the living room for the thirtieth time, trying to gauge its allure as a potential habitat. Had I over-cleaned? Was it *too* neat now? No, I was being ridiculous. Dashiell had said I wouldn't be able to press her mind, which was an insane concept to someone who's been getting her way with humans for over a century. How was I going to convince this Scarlett to live here? By pretending to be human? I could probably do that; I'd certainly had enough practice. But how does a modern, desirable human roommate behave?

I had no idea. I didn't spend any non-hunting time around humans - hell, I barely spent any time around other vampires. Except for those of us who have found a mate, vampires are solitary hunters, not a book club.

An idea struck me: I could be just like one of the characters on television. What was the show with the young people who all live together and stay the best of friends? Oh, there were probably several shows like that on right now. I just had to act like those characters. I began concocting a new Fun Roommate personality. I would be cheerful, and charming, and funny. I would not demand, but request. Oh, and I should probably fidget when she was here, I decided: tossing my hair, examining my fingernails, jiggling my feet when my legs were crossed. Humans love that shit.

The doorbell rang, and I realized that I had been standing in the middle of my living room, frozen in thought, for nearly five minutes. Jesus, I needed to learn to focus my thoughts better, or this girl would think I was a complete looney. *Be the Fun Roommate*, I told myself.

I zoomed toward the front door, reminding myself to fidget, to be friendly, to act like a TV girlfriend–

I never reached the door. When I was two steps away something crashed into me like an invisible wrecking ball, and I fell to my knees, suddenly ill. No, that couldn't be right, vampires don't get sick. And yet, my whole body felt strangely heavy, and everything had dimmed a little, the colors and sounds fading around me. There was a twinge of pain in my right ankle, the one I'd broken when I was a little girl, slipping on a patch of ice. At the same time I felt naked and vulnerable, like the slightest push would slam me to the ground. I was exhausted — no, no, vampires don't get exhausted either. None of this was right. It…it had sapped me, drained me of my magic. I let out an involuntary sob, my breath coming hard and frenzied. And necessary. It shouldn't be so necessary. I began to gasp, unable to get enough air in my lungs. Was this the null? It was horrible, like a curse.

I hadn't understood, I realized in a panic. Dashiell had tried to explain that I would be human around this girl and I just thought he meant— what? That I would need to shove human food in my mouth? I felt so stupid.

There was a knock on the door. "Come in," I managed to say, my voice sounding weak and muted in my ears. The front door swung open slowly, hesitantly, and then quicker as the girl saw me.

"Oh crap!" she cried, rushing over to kneel in front of me. "Are you okay? Sorry, it hits people kind of hard sometimes…" I shook my head, still breathing rapidly, and she seemed to understand I was having trouble answering. "I could back away, but then you'd just have to go through this again," she told me. "You're hyperventilating, you need to calm your breath. Remember, your body knows what to do. It's not going to stop breathing, I promise." Her voice was low and soothing, and I found myself focusing on her.

She was so *young*, maybe twenty or a few years more, barely older than I'd been when I was taken away to be turned. I noticed her eyes right away: even without vampire eyesight I could tell that they were exquisite, an emerald green you rarely see outside of tinted contact lenses. Her hair was long and tousled, so dark that I thought it was black until she shifted her weight and the light caught the chocolate brown highlights. She was wearing jeans and cheap shoes and a canvas jacket with lots of pockets. She was pretty, too: not enough to get any attention in this town, but enough to have been taken for a new vampire, back when the domini were actively recruiting in the U.K.

But she was too thin, leaning toward scrawny, and there were hollows beneath her eyes that indicated lost sleep and missed meals. And depth. Something was haunting this girl. "She's been through some recent troubles," Dashiell had said. Why hadn't I asked for more details? What was bothering her?

Wait, why would I care?

"See?" the girl said encouragingly. "Your body's breathing for you. You're going to be fine." She sat back on her heels, holding out her hand. "I'm Scarlett, by the way."

"Molly," I managed to say. She was right; while I'd been looking her over I'd forgotten to worry about my lungs working. Already my body had relaxed, remembering what it needed to do to keep itself alive.

I held out my hand and allowed her to shake it it. Her skin was warm and dry. "Do you think you can make it to the couch, Molly? Maybe we could sit and talk for a minute?"

"Oh…right," I said, feeling stupid. I was sitting on my living room carpet with a complete stranger.

We rose at the same time, and Scarlett shut the door behind her. *Be friendly,* I reminded myself as we sat down. Like on TV. Suddenly I felt like most of my vocabulary had been stolen away, leaving me with only a few words to try to make coherent sentences. Small talk. I had to make small talk. "Nice jacket." I managed to blurt.

She looked down at herself. Why do we always do that? "Oh, thanks. It's new."

"Was traffic bad? Did you find the place okay?" I was on a roll now.

She blinked for a second, processing that. "Traffic wasn't too bad, actually," she replied. "I looked up directions before I left, so no problems. Have you lived here long?"

Like a dance, I realized. We were doing a verbal get-to-know-each-other dance, and I just had to remember the steps. I knew how to have a conversation, obviously – it wasn't that different from chatting up my human meals. But now I had to try to communicate through all these bloody *feelings.* They were coursing through my brain so fast it was hard to stop and remember the names for all of them. Anxiety. Nervousness. Grief. Sadness. Sadness? Wait, why was I sad? Where did that feeling even come from? Nothing sad was happening right now. Could…did feelings get left over in your mind, from something that wasn't even going on right now? That was absurd, and I felt indignation.

"I bought the house a few years ago," I said carefully. "I like the location. It has a great old Hollywood history too."

"Oh, were you around back then?" Scarlett asked, well-mannered interest in her voice. Whatever her problems, the girl had obviously been raised well. "I mean, were you in LA during the fifties and sixties, all that Golden Era stuff?"

"No, I was in London then," I said, and memories flooded into my brain. I tried to push them away, focusing on the girl in front of me again.

"Oh, I've always wanted to visit London. When did you come to the US?" Scarlett said politely.

"I…It was…" I faltered. This time I couldn't stop the memories. The decision to return to Wales in the mid-nineties, to finally check on my family after nine decades bouncing around Europe. For ninety years I'd taken comfort in imagining my brothers and sisters growing up, having babies and grand babies, laughing and fighting and marrying and occasionally lighting a candle for poor great aunt Molly who had been taken so young.

That had been the deal, anyway. After he'd taken me Alonzo had promised me that he'd let my family be; that he'd press them to think I'd had an accident and drowned, my body never found. In exchange I had to serve out my training period with him, as his…plaything. For twenty years.

Then I'd finally gone home, figuring it had been long enough; that no one would recognize me. I remembered the excitement and homesickness and longing I had felt as I left London for my home. And then the horrible realization that none of it had happened. Where I thought there were generations of Argalls, a growing, prospering family, there had been nothing, all that time, because Alonzo had ripped out their throats the night he took me. My brothers and sisters, my parents. As I sat on my nice couch in my nice house in North Hollywood, the grief crashed down on me again, and I remembered the realization that I was all that was left, and I was a bloodsucking parasite with about four people in the entire world who knew my first name.

Then I remembered the absolute satisfaction I'd felt when I drove the stake into Alonzo's heart. And then…a light had gone out in me.

As I sat there, remembering all of it, something went wrong with my eyes. They started to prickle and sting, then grow heavy with liquid. I opened my mouth to ask the girl what was happening, but then it came to me. *Crying*, I thought numbly. I was crying. Vampires could produce tears if necessary, but I hadn't…*Argall*. God, when was the last time I'd even thought about my original last name?

And suddenly I *had* to think about my family, had to cling desperately to the memories. I remembered my father's face again, the last time I'd seen him, looking tired and annoyed as he'd gone outside to care for a heifer who was giving birth. My sister Anwen teaching me needlepoint. Baking bread with my ma. I remembered the first time she handed me my baby brother Siors. He was six years younger than me, and so tiny I marveled at it.

After what seemed like hours the tide of memories finally slowed, and I was able to think clearly again. My family had been all I had; but even more importantly, *I* was all they had. I was the only one left to remember any of them, and I'd walked through the last twenty years without giving them a thought. I suddenly realized the weight of that betrayal. How could I have let them be lost for so long?

A hand touched mine. "Molly?" Scarlett's voice was soft, concerned. "Jeez, it's really hitting you hard, huh?"

Without knowing I would, I reached out and grabbed her hand, clutching it with my flimsy human strength. "Is it always like this?" I said, hearing the Welsh accent in my voice for the first time in forever.

I saw understanding flicker in Scarlett Bernard's eyes, and something else. Compassion. She seemed to know that I wasn't talking about my body's reaction to humanity. "Believe it or not," she said gravely, "You get used to it."

"I was so wrong, all this time, I thought I–" I swallowed and shook my head a little. I *couldn't* let this girl leave. I needed her to move in here, to help me learn my way through this. I still wanted to age, but I was also sure I wouldn't be able to remember my family without her. I would be alone again, and they would be lost. I had to make her want to be here.

So I forced my voice to be bright, energetic. Fun Roommate. "I'm so sorry about that," I chirped. "Listen, I bet you'd like a tour of the house." I stood up, letting go of her hand and taking a step toward the hallway. Looking a little bewildered, Scarlett got up and followed me. "There's this great story about the downstairs bathroom…" I began.

Malediction

Prologue

Author's note: this story is set after Hunter's Trail *and* Boundary Crossed, *but before* Boundary Lines.

Samantha Wheaton ran a hand down the center of her cocktail dress, wishing she'd picked something that hid her waistline a little better. The dress that her friend Ruanna had talked her into buying was short and emerald green, with a tiny fringe on the bottom that made Sam feel rather pleasantly like a flapper from 1926. But it was snug in the middle, and Sam felt uncharacteristically self-conscious. She'd lost most of the baby weight by now, but there was a little pouchy area on her lower abdomen that she feared would persist forever. In Colorado she would have just laughed it off and said it was a monument to her breeding capabilities. Everything was different in LA, though, and now and then she felt that superficial attitude creep into how she looked at herself in the mirror.

Fuck it. Sam dropped her hand to her side, squared her shoulders, and looked around. The fundraiser was being held in a venue hall near Silver Lake; a medium-sized building with white walls, wooden rafters, and a few wooden posts that were as beautiful as they were structurally necessary. Sam liked the decor, and liked being able to put her back against a post as she surveyed the room. *That's probably*

Allie rubbing off on me, she thought with a smile. She'd called her twin sister in the afternoon to wish her a happy New Year, and they'd chatted for a few minutes about Sam's daughter, Charlie, and Allie's plans for New Year's Eve. Sam had hoped her sister would have a date, or at least be going to a party with friends, but no, of course not. Instead, Allie was babysitting for their cousins. Sam supposed she should be grateful that Allie was at least going to have some human contact.

"Sam, there you are!" Ruanna rushed over, looking chagrined. "I am *so* sorry. I was talking to the funding director and I totally lost track of time. You okay?"

Sam smiled inwardly. Her friend had made a big deal about it being her first night out since the baby, and now she was obsessed with making sure Sam enjoyed herself. "I'm fine, Rue," she assured the other woman. "I'm just people-watching."

"But you shouldn't have to stand here by yourself!" Ruanna insisted. "Bad friend, Rue!" she berated herself.

Sam laughed. "Not at all. I was just thinking how nice it is to be wearing makeup and hairspray and a spit-up free dress."

Ruanna relaxed a little and patted her chignon, which was leaking black curls. "And how many times have you called John to check on the kid?"

"None," Sam replied with great dignity, but she couldn't help but break out in a grin. "Of course, we've been texting like crazy." She held up her cell phone, which hadn't left her hand since they'd climbed out of the car.

Rue rolled her eyes and thrust out a hand. "That's it. Give me the phone."

"No way!"

"Samantha Wheaton," Rue lectured, hands on her hips, trying to suppress a smile. "We are here for human social interaction and to beg money for the program. With our faces. You know you're better at charming donors than I am."

This was true—Ruanna had a huge heart and endless energy and enthusiasm, but she had a tendency to get overexcited and stop paying attention to the potential benefactors. Sam was better at reading their reactions and adjusting her pitch to suit their particular personalities.

Ruanna waggled the fingers on her outstretched hand, and Sam wrinkled her nose in mock annoyance. "You can have it back at the end of the school day," her friend insisted.

Sam considered refusing in a playful way, but Charlie was asleep in bed by now, and besides, her friend was right—why come out tonight if she was just going to stand in a corner texting her husband? She sent off a final quick message to John: *Rue is confiscating the phone. Home in a few hours. Love you!*

When Rue had stuffed the phone into her clutch, Sam said, "Okay, where do you want me?"

They worked the room a little, with Ruanna handling introductions and Sam smoothly guiding the conversation to where they wanted it: the app. Ruanna and Sam both volunteered with Forever Homes, a group that went into the high-kill LA County shelters and took photos of dogs that were scheduled to be put down. They posted the photos on a number of websites where people routinely looked for pets, with the special notation that the animal's life was at risk. If people were looking for a pet anyway, the theory went, why not direct them to the ones who needed homes the most?

The organization also coordinated some foster and adoption events, but Sam's area of specialty was the photos. It was going well— she was a decent amateur photographer—but what the organization really wanted was enough money to hire a team to create and market an app. Then prospective pet owners could just open the app on their smart phones and immediately see the pictures and bios for adoptable dogs in the county. The finishing touch was that even if someone didn't want to adopt the dog in question, they could donate a little money toward the animal's care with the touch of a finger.

"You are, without a doubt, the best closer I've ever seen," Ruanna whispered a half hour later, as they moved away from a group of Hollywood producers. Each had promised a grand to the fund. "Thank God you're using your powers for good."

Sam smiled. "It's an easy sell," she demurred, covertly checking her watch, the silver Rolex her father had gotten her for college graduation. It was only a little after ten, but she was starting to miss her bed. And her breasts ached with the need to feed the baby. Sam was beginning to doubt that she would actually manage to ring in the New Year.

Just ahead she saw a very slim woman in her mid-thirties with dark hair cascading down her back in perfect loose curls. "Oh, hey, there's Lizzy," she said. She didn't know Lizzy Thompkins all that well—they'd met through Ruanna—but the three of them had carpooled from the Long Beach area. Lizzy was another volunteer photographer, although she preferred working with cats, whereas Sam liked the dogs best. All smooth curves and tawny skin, Lizzy reminded Sam of one of those really beautiful muscle cars. Tonight she was wearing a bronze-colored cocktail dress with one strap and heels that were taller than Charlie.

"Finally," Ruanna said, sounding a little relieved. She could be a mother hen about her friends. "I've barely seen her all night."

Spotting them, Lizzy took the arm of the man beside her and guided him over to Sam and Ruanna. The guy was a little scrawny, but he was decent-looking in a "nerd cleans up good" kind of way. Sam chided herself for thinking in superficial LA terms again.

"Hey, you two," Lizzy said cheerfully. "This is my new friend, Henry. He does educational programs at some of the LA schools, and we're both members of Protect America's Wolves."

With a wide smile, the man extended his hand to Sam. "Henry Remus. It's so nice to meet you." His voice was unnaturally high, like he was doing an impression of a ditzy woman. She took the proffered hand, just barely managing not to wince at the limp, damp grip that set off an immediate pang of dislike. That smile was *too* wide, and his eyes were a little too eager. *Crazy eyes*, Sam thought, then immediately felt guilty. *So what if the guy was a little socially awkward*, she told herself. His money would spend the same as anyone else's.

"Lizzy here tells me you guys are starting up an app," Remus said in his high voice. "I just love animals. Canines especially." He smiled again, and this time there was a glimmer of self-satisfaction to it, like he'd told a private joke. Remus added, "You know, I have a few connections in game design. Why don't I buy you ladies a round of drinks, and we can head out to the patio and discuss it?"

He stepped toward them, and was it just her imagination or had his whole demeanor gotten more aggressive? Almost … violent. Sam took an instinctive step backward, feeling strangely creeped-out by this guy, who hadn't actually done anything improper. Still, she decided to let Ruanna handle this pitch on her own. She opened her mouth to excuse herself, but before she could speak Ruanna looped her arm through Sam's and stepped forward.

"We'd love to," Ruanna said firmly. Samantha Wheaton found herself being propelled toward the bar.

Later, during a few fleeting moments of groggy consciousness, Sam would remember this moment and curse herself for not trusting her instincts about this man. Of course, he wasn't a man, not really.

He was the thing that killed her.

1. Lex

Ask Jesse Cruz how I died.

I had to hand it to my sister—in life she had always known how to make an entrance, and after her death, she could sure as hell clear a room. I meant that literally: the moment after she said those words, the room we were sitting in abruptly vanished, and I woke up covered in a film of cooling sweat.

I sat up in bed, breathing hard, displacing several annoyed-looking rescue pets that had crowded into the bed with me. Raja, the biggest cat, yawned at me and stretched, kneading his claws into the blanket still tossed over my legs. The claws punched straight through the fabric and into my skin, making me yelp. Revenge accomplished, he stalked off the bed and out of the bedroom.

I scrubbed my hand over my face, trying to slow down my breathing. It's important to note here that the conversation with Sam, my dead twin sister, was *not* a dream. Lots of people dream about their deceased loved ones—hell, I dreamed about the soldiers who'd died under my watch on a regular basis. But I'd recently discovered that I was a boundary witch, one who could control magics that crossed the line between the living and the dead. Shortly thereafter, I found out that I could do a lot more than *dream* about Sam. I could call her actual soul to mine, have a conversation with her in a safe place that my mind created for that purpose, and then send her back to wherever she was the rest of the time.

It was a neat trick, but I was still learning how it worked and how to control it. One thing I'd discovered very quickly, however, was that there were strict limits to what Sam was allowed to tell me. She couldn't say anything about her current ... situation, or whatever you want to call the afterlife. I was fairly certain that she hadn't done anything to land herself in some iteration of Hell, but I wasn't sure if she was in Heaven, Limbo, a spiritual holding dimension, or, hey, waiting in a long line for reincarnation. But if she tried to tell me anything that was off-limits, she would be abruptly blinked away from me, which is exactly what happened after her cryptic message about Jesse Cruz.

I did, at least, know who he was: Cruz was the former LAPD detective who had investigated my sister's murder. I'd visited him after Sam's disappearance ten months earlier. He was the one who'd explained why they didn't expect to find my sister's body.

When I spoke to him that day, I'd also run into an associate of his, a young woman who suggested I was more than human. I'd shrugged it off at the time, but months later, after I found out about my connections to magic and the Old World, I started to wonder if Cruz was tied up in it too. I had actually tried to contact the detective again, only to find out that he no longer worked for the LAPD.

My life had gotten really chaotic after that—a group of vampires had been intent on kidnapping Sam's daughter Charlie—and I'd never followed up. Now Sam herself was pointing me back toward Cruz. Why?

I swung my legs over the side of the bed and looked at the clock. Ten in the morning. I'd been asleep for all of three hours. Great. I went over to the small desk in my bedroom to look for Cruz's LAPD business card. He wasn't a cop anymore, but he'd handwritten his cell phone number on the back.

I shuffled papers and books around for twenty minutes, and even went through the trash can next to the desk, but I couldn't find it. I cursed loudly enough to wake several of the dogs. I spun around and glared at them. "Which one of you ate the business card I need?"

Like a choreographed move, the dogs swiveled around to look at each other before turning back toward me and tilting their heads with cluelessness. I sighed. "Okay, you're right. It *does* sound like more of a cat offense."

I turned on my old laptop and brought up the automatic reply message I'd received back when I'd tried to email Cruz at the LAPD. The wording was just as opaque as I remembered: "The employee you've contacted is no longer with the Los Angeles Police Department" and then some boilerplate language about different LAPD divisions and services that might help me instead.

I grabbed my cell phone off the nightstand and called the specific station where Cruz had worked. I was transferred around a few times, but I gritted my teeth and hung in there, identifying myself and repeating my request to every new person. After nearly thirty minutes, I finally got on the line with an actual captain named Miranda Williams, who said she was sorry for my loss and hoped I was doing well.

The solicitation threw me a little. I never expect good manners out of Los Angeles. "Um, thank you," I said awkwardly. "I'm actually calling because I'm trying to get a hold of Jesse Cruz. I tried emailing him, but I got a bounce-back message saying he no longer works for the LAPD."

"Yes, I'm afraid Jesse has left us for greener pastures," Williams confirmed, and there was real regret in her voice. "But as I'm sure you know, we have positively identified your sister's killer, so the case is considered closed."

"Because Henry Remus is dead," I said flatly. Remus was the serial killer who'd murdered Sam.

"Yes, ma'am. And *his* killer is now serving her time at the California Institution for Women, here in Corona. I'm sure Jesse told you that as well."

I blinked, trying to remember the details from my last visit to LA. The news had flown around so quickly: Sam was missing, Sam was dead; they found the killer, the killer was dead. It was hard to process much after that, and I'd never given much thought to the question of what had become of Remus's killer. I remembered thinking I should drive over to the jail and shake her hand, but not much else.

"Was there a trial?" I asked. "For the woman who killed Remus, I mean." I would have been happy to testify that she'd done the human race a serious favor.

There was a long pause and a shuffle of papers as Williams looked for the information. "Petra Corbett. No, there was no trial. She claimed it was self-defense, that Remus came after her the way he did your sister and the others."

"And she still went to prison?" I asked.

"For fifteen years, yes. We only had her word about the self-defense, and she did try to cover up Remus's death by desecrating the body to make it look like a canine attack." She cleared her throat, indicating that the matter was closed. "At any rate, is there something *I* can help you with, Miss Luther?"

Her voice was kind, and I found myself liking her. "I would still really like to speak to Jesse Cruz," I pressed on. "I understand why you wouldn't want to give out his number, but is there any way that you could call him and ask him to get in touch?"

I was all ready to argue or plead, but Williams readily agreed to call Jesse. I hung up the phone feeling as if I'd accomplished something.

There was no chance of going back to sleep, so while I waited for Cruz to call me back, I went online and looked up newspaper articles about the case. Ten months earlier, after Petra Corbett was arrested and the papers went nuts, I had gone on a self-imposed media blackout, which was easier than it sounds given that I live in Boulder and the murders were in LA. At the time, I figured that obsessing over the details wouldn't bring Sam back, and, more importantly, I hated seeing my sister's name in print, always attached to the word "victim." That wasn't how I wanted to think of her, or how I thought she should be remembered.

I had some distance now, though, and I managed to force myself through most of the articles, which turned out to be a *lot* of material. Since the bodies were never found and Petra Corbett had accepted a plea deal rather than going through a big public trial, I hadn't expected to find many articles. But the *LA Times* had run a whole series on the case, complete with an editorial speculating on what Remus might have done with the bodies—I was happy to ignore that one—and a long profile of Jesse Cruz, hero cop.

I skimmed the profile, which revealed that my sister's murder wasn't the only high-profile case Jesse had caught. The year before, he'd been involved in catching the guy who'd killed those people at La Brea Park, a major case that Sam and I had actually discussed on the phone a couple of times. Was that why Cruz had left the force? Because he'd seen too many awful murders? At the same time, the LAPD was enormous. Wasn't it kind of strange that one cop solved both those cases?

Unless it was an Old World connection? Sam's suggestion that Cruz knew more than he was letting on seemed to support that, but if there *was* a connection, what could it be? He wasn't a vampire; I'd seen him during the day. Male witches were rare, but possible. Or I supposed he could be a werewolf, though I knew very little about them.

All of a sudden I felt silly. A werewolf cop? That sounded ridiculous. Maybe I was completely wrong about Cruz being part of the Old World. What evidence did I even have, aside from an offhand comment his friend made about me and Sam's cryptic message?

As if on cue, my phone rang. I didn't know the number, but it had a Los Angeles area code. "This is Lex."

"Hi, Ms. Luther. It's Jesse Cruz." He sounded guarded. I couldn't really blame him. "I understand you were looking for me."

I sat back in the chair, suddenly unsure of where to start. Humans were not allowed to know about the supernatural, so if Cruz *wasn't* part of the Old World, I would be putting him at risk if I revealed anything about it. But how the hell was I supposed to get a straight answer if I couldn't explain my reason for asking the question? "Hi, Detective," I said, intentionally using his old honorific. "Please call me Lex. And thanks for calling me back."

"I'm not a detective anymore, actually. But you knew that."

"I was kind of surprised to hear the news. Would you mind if I asked what you're doing instead?"

There was a long pause, and I suspected he was trying to think of a nice way to blow me off. Instead, he just asked, "Is there something I can do for you, Lex?"

Oh, fuck it. Frontal assault. "You could tell me how my sister really died."

2. Jesse

Jesse Cruz was already having a crappy day.

The studio was shooting overnight in Vancouver and they kept calling him with the most inane little questions. Would a punk kid still hold a weapon sideways like a 90s gangster, or was that trend over now? What about an older gangster, one who might have been raising hell in the 90s? What kind of automatic weapon would a retired cop on a pension have on hand to combat a home invasion?

And so on. Jesse had to come up with an answer for every single inquiry. He'd gotten smarter about that, though: during his first month as a police consultant, he'd given careful consideration to every request, asking any number of follow-up questions. Does the weapon have to be automatic? Is he right-handed or left-handed? Does he have access to illegal stuff? Does it have to be American-made? But that tactic seemed to just confuse and irritate the producers, and by the second month, Jesse had finally realized that they didn't actually care if the answer was *right*, or even all that plausible. They just wanted to be able to say, "Oh, we asked the consultant, and this is what he approved." Then if the fan message boards complained about authenticity, some PA could go on and write, "The hero cop of Los Angeles signed off on this, so pipe down and go back to jacking off in your mom's basement. Oh, and please keep watching the show!"

Now he just gave them his best guess, and they ran with it like it was scripture.

Jesse arrived at the studio at 9:30 feeling tired and irritable, not to mention frustrated by the way his cell phone wouldn't stop ringing. If it wasn't the producers on the Vancouver team, it was yet another junior agent asking for a lunch meeting. Right after the Henry Remus case, Jesse had gotten calls from all the heavy-hitters, wanting to buy the rights to the life story of the young cop who'd caught two serial killers in less than two years. The big fish finally petered off after six months of *no's*, but the baby agents were still circling him like hyperactive puppies. He'd changed his cell phone number twice, but somehow they kept finding it.

When he'd seen Miranda's name on the caller ID, Jesse had been relieved: here at last was someone he enjoyed talking to, and who wouldn't want anything from him. Except as it turned out, she *did* sort of want something from him, and now all of Jesse's best efforts to avoid talking about the Henry Remus case were blowing up in his face.

Tell me how my sister really died. If Allison Luther only knew how impossible that was. While he groped for an answer, Jesse closed his eyes, trying to picture her face: youthful, sort of innocent-looking, but with a hardness born of experience. She could play an angel in a movie, if not for her nose, which had been broken at least once. The nose, along with her broad shoulders and tightly muscled limbs, gave the impression of serious strength. He'd only met her briefly, but her features were seared into his memory: the cleft chin, the little widow's peak on her forehead. Those bright blue eyes. He had nightmares about those eyes, only in the dreams they were open and staring, covered in a white film. Lex wasn't an exact copy of her fraternal twin sister—the woman whose body Jesse had disposed of—but their eyes were the same.

The images unnerved him, and he opened his own eyes and said carefully, "Ma'am—sorry, Lex—do you have some reason to believe there's new information about your sister's murder?"

"Yes, I do."

"May I ask what that is?"

There was a brief pause. "Let's call it an anonymous tip."

Her voice was certain, confident, and it puzzled Jesse. What the hell could that mean? Someone had called her and told her there was more to Samantha Wheaton's death? Jesse quickly ran through the short list of the people who knew about the cover up. He trusted his brother, of course, and Scarlett. Dashiell and Will would sooner kill the entire LAPD than release secrets about Old World crimes. Who else was there? Lizzy Thompkins? Last time he'd talked to Scarlett, she'd said Lizzy was guarded by other werewolves around the clock, but maybe it was possible.

Still, it wasn't like he could talk about it. "I'm sorry, Lex, but I can assure you that we got the right man. And the right woman."

"Maybe you did," she said, her voice cooling. "But I didn't get the full story. And I think I deserve it."

Did she? He thought of all his nightmares, and decided that even if he had been allowed to say anything about the Old World, it was better for Lex's mental health not to hear it. "I don't know what to tell you," he said finally.

"Why don't you start by telling me about your friend? The one who knew I wasn't human."

Who knew I wasn't human. Jesse considered that for a second. "Back up. Let's say for the sake of argument that I believe you're not human. That you are, in fact, a witch."

"Okay, let's." She sounded unsurprised.

"*I'm* still human. If you are what I think you are, you'll understand why I can't just jump in and answer all your questions."

"If you can't answer them," she said slowly, "that means my sister's death *was* supernatural."

Oh, goddammit. He'd walked right into that. "Look," he tried, "I've told you everything I can about Samantha's murder. I'm sorry."

"Okay, fine." It sounded like her teeth were gritted with irritation. "If you won't give me answers, I'll come out there and find someone who will." The line went dead.

Jesse looked at his phone with alarm. "Well, fuck."

He glanced around the production office, but no one was trying to get his attention at the moment, so he dialed his sometimes partner Scarlett Bernard. They hadn't seen much of each other over the last ten months. *Which is pretty much what happens,* Jesse thought wryly, *when you get dumped for some other guy.* Scarlett had a new life now. She was getting more respect in the Old World, starting to call some of her own shots, plus she had her boyfriend Eli and her teenage assistant Corry. Jesse, on the other hand, wasn't even a cop anymore. She had no reason to contact him.

And it was probably better that way. He'd gotten any number of invitations to lunch or coffee from actresses and assistants since starting this job, but he'd turned them all down. He wasn't ready—not just because of Scarlett, but because of ... well, everything. The Remus case. The things he'd done to try to stop the killer were nearly as bad as the murders themselves. At least Remus had an excuse for his insane behavior.

Scarlett answered on the second ring. "Bernard."

Right, she didn't have his new phone number. Stupid of him to forget to give it to her. "Hey, it's me," he said.

There was a pause, and for a second Jesse thought she didn't recognize his voice. *That* would hurt. But then she said, "Hey, Jesse. Long time no see. What's going on?"

"This is sort of an official call," he said. "I need you and your colleagues to know about a possible ... situation."

"Let's talk in person," she said immediately. "My colleagues still get kind of touchy about having these conversations over the phone."

They arranged to meet at Hair of the Dog when Jesse got off work. It wasn't his favorite place to hang out, since Scarlett's boyfriend was the head bartender, But he didn't *really* have anything against Eli, who was a decent guy once you got past the whole werewolf thing, and the bar was more or less halfway between Jesse's new place in Studio City and Scarlett's apartment in Santa Monica.

Besides, Jesse could use a drink. He leaned against the wall for a moment, thinking about Allison Luther again. When they'd met in person back in January, Lex had struck him as a decent person and a good sister. All she'd wanted was to get her family some answers, and it had broken his heart a little to know he was one of the reasons she'd never get them. Jesse thought of Lex's sister Samantha, and the horrible injuries that she'd suffered. He hadn't personally tossed her body into the furnace, but he might as well have.

His thoughts were interrupted by the approach of a frantic PA. The PAs, Jesse had discovered, were always frantic. "Cruz! They need you in the writer's room!"

Jesse sighed and went back to work.

3. Jesse

It was after seven by the time the writers wrapped for the day and he could start the drive down to the West Side. Hair of the Dog was on a nondescript block of Pico, a hole-in-the-wall place with great beer and surprisingly tasty nachos. The majority of the city's werewolves were there nearly every night, driven by their need to be with the pack, and although the general public were always welcome guests, most of them tended to avoid the place. There was something a little too "clubby" about the regulars.

He took a parking spot a couple of streets east of the bar, once again missing his police parking privileges. As he approached the place, he noticed that Will, the pack alpha and bar owner, had installed a new door for the main entrance. The old one had been heavy glass, but this one was thick, solid wood on cast-iron hinges, tough to pull open and a hell of a lot tougher to break down. Jesse approved.

Inside, there was a square bar in the center of the room, surrounded by a smattering of tables. A hallway in the back led to the owner's office and a back room with pool tables. The walls were covered floor to ceiling in pictures of canines, but Jesse barely noticed them anymore. And then he saw her.

Scarlett sat at the bar, perched easily on a stool with a soda in front of her. Her long fingers swirled the straw in lazy circles as she chatted with the bartender. To his relief, it wasn't Eli but a short female werewolf he'd met once or twice—Esmé, he thought. Scarlett threw her head back and laughed at something the other woman had said, and Jesse felt a rush of ... something. Wistfulness, maybe. It wasn't even romantic, exactly, he just ... missed her.

Esmé looked over at him, as did a couple of the other werewolves scattered around the room, and Scarlett followed her gaze.

"Hey, Jesse," she called out, grinning. Her bright green eyes sparkled with good humor, and she was wearing her dark hair down, which was rare. She'd gotten it cut, Jesse noticed, so it hung just past her shoulders and had some layering. "How's tricks?"

"Hi." Jesse propelled himself over to her. He was two feet away before he caught the slightest hint of movement in the darkness near her feet. "Oh," he said in surprise. "Hey, Shadow." He squatted down to pet Scarlett's "dog", which was not a dog at all, but a bargest—an ink-black monster of legend that was spell-made to hunt and kill werewolves. Shadow had been a dog once, though: 180 pounds of the ugliest dog Jesse had ever seen in his life. She was some kind of mixed breed that included Peruvian hairless, pit bull, and maybe some wolf. Or, he thought, squinting at her, maybe some jaguar. After giving him a quick, threat-assessment once-over, she thumped her club tail and didn't bother getting up. He scratched first her furry ear, then her hairless one.

"I didn't know you were bringing her," he said to Scarlett.

"Corry's my usual dog-sitter, but it's a school night for her. I *could* have left her with Eli," Scarlett said wryly, "but he's terrified of being left alone with her, not that he'd ever admit it. I don't think she'd hurt him without the command, but we're still working on, um … rehabilitation."

Jesse bent closer to the bargest so Scarlett wouldn't see his smirk. Eli was a werewolf, and Shadow had been bred to kill his kind. The year before, a killer witch had brought Shadow to LA with the intention of wiping out all the werewolves in the area. That witch, Petra Corbett, was now in prison for Remus's murder, but the bargest was too rare and valuable to give away, not to mention nearly impossible to kill. Scarlett's bosses—*partners*, Jesse corrected himself—had asked her to adopt it.

"And Will doesn't mind you having her in the bar?"

She snorted. "I think he likes it, actually. She never leaves my side, obviously, but the werewolves are all scared of her. It keeps them on their best behavior when we're around."

He scratched the bargest's mostly hairless back until she craned her head around to give his hand one regal lick of thanks. Finally, he straightened up. "I like the haircut," he said to Scarlett.

"Oh." She touched it, a little self-conscious. "Thank you. Will said we can talk in his office where it's quieter. Do you want a drink first?"

Jesse ordered a beer, then followed Scarlett as she and Shadow threaded through the tables to the back office. Scarlett closed the door behind him and sat down in Will's office chair. The bargest settled at her feet.

"Your knee's better, I see," he commented. She looked good.

"Yeah. Physical therapy was a bitch, but it was worth it. I even started running again last month." She gestured for him to pull up the visitor chair. Jesse sat. "So what's up?"

He took a gulp of the beer, set it down on the desk, and said, "Remember that woman who came to see me at the LAPD last year, after the Remus case?"

The smile faded off Scarlett's face. "Uhhhh…no?"

"Right after we stopped Remus, you came to my office to see me about Lizzy, and one of the victim's relatives was with me," he reminded her. "You said something felt weird about her, and she obviously had no idea what you were talking about. I had to pull you out into the hall."

Scarlett nodded, her eyes going distant as she considered it. "Yeah, I remember now. She felt Old World. A little like a witch, but not quite right, and not quite anything else, either. And her magic was, like"—she waved a hand in the air, looking for a word—"*suppressed*, I guess would be the best way to put it. And dark." Scarlett shuddered. "I don't know. She was only in my radius for like, ten seconds."

"Well, you might get another chance at her," he said grimly. He told her about Lex's phone call and her declaration that she would find the answers on her own. "When we met last year, she didn't seem like she knew anything about the Old World, but she sure as hell does now. And she sort of suggested she's a witch."

"Well, fuck," Scarlett said promptly, and he couldn't help but grin.

"That's what I said."

"Who was the anonymous tip?"

"I can't figure it out. My best guess is Lizzy."

Scarlett shook her head emphatically. "Trust me, it's not possible. Lizzy is … having problems. She's being watched very carefully." She took another drink of her soda and thought it over. "If she knows about the Old World, it's really weird that she went to you."

"Because I'm not supernatural?"

"Well, duh, but also because if she really is a witch she should have gone through the proper channels: had her clan contact Kirsten and clear everything through her. Although I'm still not convinced she is a witch."

"Well, what else could she be?" he asked.

"I don't know." Scarlett was frowning, like she was searching her memory for something. Finally she shrugged. "Witch magic is hereditary. Maybe she's just got like a drop of witchblood, and she's unaffiliated with a clan. That means she's just some random with no pull." She shrugged, like she was waving off a housefly.

"Yeah." Jesse drank some more beer. He didn't really disagree with anything Scarlett was saying, but at the same time, he hated the thought of Lex still not knowing what had happened to her sister. "Couldn't we just tell her what she wants to know? If she really is a witch, I mean."

Scarlett shook her head. "I'll talk to the others, but I have a feeling they'll say no."

He understood that "the others" meant Will, Dashiell, and Kirsten, the leaders of the respective supernatural groups in Los Angeles. "Why?"

"They're really big on 'need to know basis,' remember?" She shrugged. "It's just how they think: the Old World gets pretty territorial, and if they believe this woman poses any kind of threat to how we do things ..." She trailed off and let Jesse fill in the blanks. "Besides, it's just not a great policy to spill secrets to every random who stumbles into town looking for them."

Jesse, who had seen Lex's angst over her missing sister up close and personal, thought that was unfair, but this was something they'd been through before: Scarlett wouldn't let other people's pain over her job keep her from doing it. He suddenly felt exhausted. "Well, what do you want me to do if she tracks me down?"

"Exactly what you did. She can't prove anything. I'll mention it to the others, but for now, we gotta stick with information embargo."

"Okay, fine." Jesse stood up and drained the beer. Scarlett gave him a hopeful look.

"Do you want to stick around for a game of pool or something?" she offered. "I haven't seen you in a while. I'd love to hear about the new job. That actor who plays the FBI agent, does he really—"

"Thanks," Jesse interrupted, "but I should probably get going."

He left her sitting there in the office, and somehow managed to not look back.

As he drove north back to Studio City, Jesse couldn't help but feel like there was some aspect of the cover-up he was forgetting. Will, Kiersten, Dashiell, Dashiell's vampire wife, Scarlett, Noah …. He shook his head, not getting it.

It nagged at him.

4. Lex

I was ready to leave for LA immediately, but I had a few hoops to jump through first.

If Jesse Cruz wouldn't talk to me, I knew I'd have to get answers from someone else, and I figured my best chance was Petra Corbett. I wasn't sure she even knew any details about Sam's death, but I was betting she knew *something*. Her whole story about self-defense and a fake animal attack was just too weird. If there was something fishy about Sam's death, the answer was probably with the woman who had the even fishier story. Hopefully she could give me something that I could use as leverage with Cruz.

Of course, there was a voice in the back of my mind that kept asking why I needed to do this: what did it matter? Sam was dead, and nothing would change that. In my dream, Sam had said that I "deserved to know" what really happened, but did I *want* to know? What if I found out that Remus wasn't really the killer? The evidence against him was overwhelming, and I was absolutely certain that he'd killed most of the other women he'd been accused of murdering, but was it possible that Sam wasn't among them? What if the real killer had gotten away after blaming the friendly neighborhood serial killer? What if it was someone I knew?

What if it was someone who could get to Charlie?

And that thought was what convinced me that even if I wasn't sure I *wanted* to know the truth, I definitely *had* to seek it out. If there was any chance that Charlie would be at risk because of information I didn't have … I couldn't allow that.

But it turned out that the process for visiting a prisoner at the California Institution for Women was pretty complicated. I had to get Petra's permission before I could visit her, and there were forms to be passed back and forth to the prison. While I was waiting to hear back from Corbett, I prepared for the trip. I had to arrange for my cousins to look after my animals, and for time off from both of my jobs—my new position assisting Colorado's head vampire, Maven, and my part-time gig at a local convenience store, which was sort of my cover job. I was expecting a little resistance from Maven, particularly given how new our situation was, but to my surprise, she readily agreed to give me a couple of days off to "get my things in order," as she put it. I wasn't about to look the gift horse in the mouth, so I just thanked her.

I didn't tell my family or even Quinn, the vampire I was sort of planning on dating at some point, where I was going; I just said I'd be visiting some friends in the Los Angeles area for a couple of days. I think all of them assumed that meant I was going to see some army buddies, and I let them. It was a lot easier than saying that I had to go learn more about my sister's murder.

Finally, I received word Petra Corbett had agreed to see me, for whatever reason—maybe just out of boredom—and a little over a week after my conversation with Sam, I had all my ducks in a row. I wasn't sure my wheezy Subaru could make the fifteen-hour drive, so I booked a plane ticket and a rental car instead, and found a cheap hotel in the Valley. I gritted my teeth at the expense, which was nearly half my checking account, but it wasn't like I could put a price on the information.

I landed in Los Angeles on the Saturday afternoon before my appointment to see Corbett. The most obvious use of my extra time was to talk to Lizzy Thompkins, the survivor who'd been with Sam the night she died. We'd never met—she and Sam weren't close, as I understood it, and she hadn't come to the memorials, but she would be the person who knew the most about my sister's last hours.

Unfortunately, when I tried to look her up from Boulder, I

couldn't find any sign of her. Lizzy seemed to have disappeared, at least from the Internet. I'd expanded my search range, messing around for hours on both Facebook and the web page for the organization where Sam, Ruanna, and Lizzy had all volunteered—but no dice. She'd just sort of vanished.

With Lizzy ruled out, I considered visiting the actual site of the killings before deciding against it. The police had probably spent weeks picking over every last square inch of that location, so I was unlikely to learn anything new. It would stay on my list of last-resort options in case I couldn't find answers elsewhere, though. For now, I headed down to Long Beach to visit Ruanna Martinez's husband and kids.

I'd met them before, in better times. On a previous trip to LA, Sam and I had picked up Ruanna for a girls' night out. Then I'd talked to Ernesto briefly when I came to town to try and find Sam. And, of course, I'd seen him and the kids at Ruanna's memorial service. Her youngest daughter, Gabby, had taken a brief shine to me that day, and I'd walked the toddler around and around the church courtyard in circles until it was time for her nap.

I called ahead, and Ruanna's husband Ernesto opened the front door before I even got out of the rental car. He was a short, barrel-shaped man with sad eyes and a look of exhaustion etched into his leathery face, but he still put on a welcoming smile as I headed up the sidewalk. "Allison," he said, reaching out to embrace me. I've never liked being called Allison, but Ernesto didn't know that, and if I said anything now he'd feel bad.

"Hello, Ernesto," I said, returning the hug. I'm not a hugger, either, but I have a big family, and I recognized the gesture for what it was: a sign that my presence was not just welcome—it was appreciated. Inside the little one-story house, I said hello to the three Martinez kids: Antone, Angelica, and Gabriella, who hid behind her father for a moment, darted out to throw her arms around my waist, and then raced back into the house. Ernesto and I laughed, and I noticed that his laugh sounded creaky, like he hadn't used it in a while.

Like in many homes, the kitchen was clearly the center of the Martinez family's personal universe. We sat down at the big wooden table in the middle of the room, and I pretended not to notice the stacks of clutter on every surface, dirty dishes in the sink, and toys on the floor. The house was a mess, but it wasn't that much worse than some of my cousins' homes back in Boulder. Ernesto made coffee, and we chatted about Los Angeles weather and my flight. I gave them an update on Charlie, who was saying a lot of words now, though not always very well. After a few minutes of this, Antone and Angelica wandered off to the living room to watch TV with Gabby.

Ernesto set a mug of coffee in front of me and sat down. I took a sip, letting him get settled, and finally asked the question I'd been holding back—whether the police had given him any further information about the case.

His face sank, seeming to age an extra ten years. "Not in months. I know you're probably anxious for answers about Sam, but I'm not sure I can tell you anything you don't already know."

I thought it over. "What about the night of the fundraiser? When I came here to look for her, we mostly talked about the logistics. But how did they seem that night? Happy? Worried?"

"Happy, for sure. Sam was a little nervous about leaving Charlie for the first time, you could tell, but she seemed excited. They were all dressed up, you know. I took pictures." Abruptly, he hauled himself off his chair and went to a stack of papers near the microwave. He fished out one of those white envelopes that holds developed photos and handed it to me. "I had 'em printed a couple of months ago. I was afraid something might happen to the computer."

I opened the envelope. Inside was a glossy color shot of Ruanna and Sam, posed just a few feet away in the Martinez living room. Sam looked so beautiful, with her short curled hair in soft ringlets and her face made up. I flipped through a few other shots. There was one of Ruanna and Ernesto, which Sam had probably taken, and at the back, one of just Sam. I pulled it out and examined it. I'd bet money that Ruanna had taken it while Sam wasn't paying attention. The angle was short, just like Rue had been, and she'd caught Sam in a moment of contemplation. My sister was leaning against the wall, patting the purse that hung from her shoulder on a thin chain. She was staring into space with a tiny smile on her face: part anticipation, part sadness. Her cell phone would have been in that front pocket. Her connection to John and Charlie. My eyes stung with sudden tears. I looked up at Ernesto, who handed me a paper towel before sitting down across from me again. "Can I keep this photo?" I said, wiping my eyes.

"Of course you can. I should have sent you a copy ages ago; we've just been so busy ..." he trailed off, glancing around the kitchen as if noticing the mess for the first time.

"No problem. I set the photo on the table in front of me, thinking I should make a copy for John too. "I wish I knew how it happened," I said softly.

"Maybe it's better we don't," Ernesto replied. "You probably heard that they found the ... you know, the place where he did it," he said, waving his hand. He was dancing around the newspapers' favorite term, which I appreciated.

"Yeah. Did you go there?"

He nodded. "I ... I had to .... The police had it cordoned off, but even from a distance, whenever they opened the door to go in you could see the red walls. All that blood ..." He seemed to choke on the words. "Maybe it's better we don't know," he repeated.

I suddenly felt like a monster. Why was I putting this man

through hell a second time? I patted his hands where they sat folded on the table. "It's okay, Ernesto. I shouldn't have asked. I'm so sorry."

"No, no. It's all right." He flipped his hand over and took mine, his fingers dark with oil stains that would never wash out. Ernesto was a mechanic at one of those really expensive car dealerships—Lexus or Rolls Royce or something. He gripped my hand, seeking comfort. I didn't think I had any to give, but I didn't pull away, either. "It was good of you to come see me and the kids. And you deserve answers."

That's exactly what Sam had said. "We all deserve answers," I said in a low voice. Trying to change the subject to something lighter, I said, "How are the kids doing?"

He shrugged. "Antone is adjusting okay. Angelica has her ups and downs. But Gabby … It's been ten months, nearly a third of her life, but she still thinks Mommy's gonna walk back through the door." He pulled his hands back, rubbing his face. "I don't know, I keep thinking maybe if there had been a body; if she could have said goodbye … I don't know. She doesn't even have a grave we can visit." He hung his head, a man beaten down by exhaustion and grief.

Before I left, I asked him if he'd ever heard from Lizzy Thompkins. He told me she'd left town as soon as the police had finished interviewing her.

"Where did she go?"

"Beats me. Someplace where she can start fresh, I'm guessing." For a moment he looked wistful. "Can you blame her?"

5. Lex

When I went to bed in my crappy hotel room, I half-expected to see Sam again. I was here, following her instructions, wasn't I? Surely she'd want to check in on my progress? But I just had regular dreams filled with tangled snatches of images: sunshine and graves and a green dress with fringe.

By eight a.m. I was driving south toward Chino. Traffic was light this early on a Sunday morning, but I still had to pay close attention to freeway signs. I could drive the route from the airport to Sam's neighborhood in Long Beach from memory, but I didn't know East LA very well. It appeared to be an industrial area, filled with plenty of factories, concrete, and patches of scrubby bare land, but very few private homes. Compared to the rest of the city, this part of town seemed barren.

The California Institute for Women was surprisingly enormous, bigger than many college campuses. I'd arrived plenty early, but it still took ages to park, go through security, and wait my turn for visitation. The other people in line were mostly families: fathers and grandparents toting small children, many of whom were dressed up, either to see their mothers or maybe for church afterwards. We were divided into groups while our inmates were summoned, and then at last it was my turn to go into the visiting room and meet Petra Corbett.

The prison's exterior may not have been what I was expecting, but the visiting room was: a giant, shabby space with big picnic-style tables bolted into the floor. It looked exactly like a middle-school cafeteria, with a prisoner sitting at each table. I scanned them until I found Petra Corbett, which was easier than I'd thought because most of the prisoners were Latina or black. I'd seen pictures of Petra in the paper and knew she looked like a Hitchcock blonde—slender and cold. In person, in a prison, Petra looked even more dangerous, like she was smugly hiding a weapon, secrets, or both. Probably both.

When I arrived at the table, I reached out to shake her hand, which was allowed. I introduced myself and said, "Thanks for agreeing to see me."

She blinked for a second, as though she needed to run my words through a mental translation filter. Then she nodded. "I do not get many visitors," she said slowly, in a French accent thick enough to put Pepé Le Pew to shame. "I have no family here and zee man in charge has made sure his people stay away from me."

"The man in charge?"

She gave me a critical look. "You are not from here either, I take it."

"No."

"What are you?"

The question was so direct, so matter-of-fact, that I had to sort of admire it. Here I'd been struggling through verbal gymnastics to get Old World creatures to reveal themselves, and she came out with a simple "what are you?" Had I been a normal human, I would probably find the phrasing a little odd, but I would have just answered with the name of my profession.

Revealing yourself to humans is usually anathema, but I was a witch, and Simon had told me that we get a little more leeway on the whole revealing-ourselves thing. Humans just assume we're Wiccan or delusional. "Witch," I said quietly.

Her eyes brightened. "As am I." A witch. Interesting, but I wasn't sure how it connected to anything else. "But I still do not understand why you wanted to see me," she added.

"I'm looking for information about my sister, Samantha

Wheaton."

Her brow furrowed as if she were trying to place the name, then her face cleared. "She was his victim, yes? Remus?"

"Yes," I said, hope blooming in my chest. I showed her a small portrait photo of Sam, one she'd sent me while I was overseas. "Did you meet her?"

She glanced at the photo for a second and shrugged. "No. I do not know zis woman. I only heard zee name because of my lawyer and zee newspapers."

I tapped my fingers on the table, disappointed. "Okay … what about Henry Remus? What can you tell me about him?"

Her blue eyes narrowed and crackled at the edges, and she said a few sentences very quickly in French. I didn't know the language, but from the tone I was pretty sure she'd said some colorful things about old Henry. "He was loup-garou. It eez …" She snapped her fingers rapidly, trying to think of a word. I glanced at the guard, but if Petra's arm waving bothered her, she didn't show it. Frustrated, Petra raised her chin and silently made a howling motion.

"Werewolf," I said, suddenly understanding. "He was a *werewolf*?"

"Well, yes." She gave me a strange look, like I was a complete idiot.

I stared at her for a long moment, while all around us people cried and laughed and said things in low meaningful tones. It was like being in the eye of a hurricane of feelings. I was too busy trying to incorporate the new information into what I already knew about werewolves, which was basically nothing. Years ago, when I was just a kid and knew nothing of magic, there had been a war in Colorado between the witches and the werewolves. Maven had helped remove the wolves from the state, and to this day they weren't allowed in

Colorado. I had no experience with them, which meant I had no context for this situation.

But I also had no reason to think Petra was lying to me—there would be nothing for her to gain from it. "Okay, he was a werewolf. Did he really kill those women?"

Petra shrugged, as if the deaths of four women were such an afterthought to her that she'd never gotten around to considering it. "I zink so. Somebody did."

"Did Remus really attack *you*? Try to kill you, like he did my sister?"

She spat. Well, she didn't really spit, but she mimed it, and the guard shot her a warning look. Petra didn't even notice. "No! I am more than a match for one werewolf, with or without my Belle. But I never put my eyes on Remus. I was framed for his murder."

"You were … framed." I felt as stupid as I sounded, but what the hell was going on? "Who framed you?"

"The same people who stole my Belle. That disgusting little wetback and his harlot."

I winced at the vitriol in her tone. Not only did she look like a Nazi dominatrix, she had the racism to go with it. But who could she … oh. Of course. "Cruz," I said with new understanding.

"Yeas," she hissed, pointing a bony finger at me. "Him. He and his whore assaulted me, took my Belle, used her to kill zis Remus, and blamed the whole thing on me." Her fists clenched with rage, and her eyes blazed with fury. At the same moment, several nearby families who had been talking peacefully suddenly began to argue, getting louder and louder.

I glanced from them to Petra. Could she be causing that with her magic? No, that was crazy, I decided. It had to be a weird coincidence.

Hurriedly, I said, "What is this bell you keep talking about? Like a metal bell?" I mimed swinging a handbell back and forth.

She shook her head, beginning to calm. "No, no. Belle is my ... mmm ... my pet. *Ma petit tueur.*" She smiled, but it was cruel and cold. "She is trained to kill zee loup-garou."

I still wasn't really getting this. "Like ... a dog?"

Petra shrugged. "If you like."

Like a dog, but not a dog? "Okay," I said very slowly. "Let me see if I understand. You don't know if Henry Remus really killed those women, but you do know that Cruz and his friend assaulted you, stole your dog, and killed Remus. Then they blamed his death on you."

With great satisfaction, she leaned back in her chair and crossed her arms across her chest, nodding.

"Did you tell anyone that you were framed?"

She gave me an impatient look. "Of course not. This is not a human matter."

"We're in a human prison," I pointed out.

She sniffed. "My lawyer did not think the sentence would be so tough. He thought perhaps two years. But zee judge was a negro, and did not favor me."

Um ... right. Moving on. "Why would Cruz do this?" I asked. "Why go through all the trouble of stealing Belle and framing you?" Was that why he'd refused to talk to me? Afraid I'd poke holes in his cover story?

Her eyes flickered away for a moment, and then she gave me a disdainful little shrug, like she couldn't be bothered to figure out why scum like Jesse would do anything. Another thought occurred to me. "Wait, why were you in the US with a werewolf-hunting dog in the first place?"

Again, her eyes slid away from me, but I saw her lips curl. I let the silence build between us, hoping she might give something away. "He is working with zem, you know," she said finally, her voice barely more than a growl. "He helps zee filthy curs, plays slave to their tempers and their ... what is zhis word"—she snapped her fingers again—"*perversions.*"

"What does—" I began, but I was interrupted by a loudspeaker, which warned us that the morning visiting hours would end in two minutes. Shit. I'd barely begun to understand what had happened to Sam. I tried to formulate a really good question, one that would clear up this whole mess, but Petra spoke first.

"Zhey will know you were here," she warned. "Zhere are people watching zee prison, people who are ... ahh ... in his pocket."

"Whose pocket?"

She waved a hand, frustrated with my incompetence. "Dashiell. Zee man in charge." Glancing around warily, she crooked two fingers and held them against her teeth. *Vampire.* "He is going to be unhappy with you."

I thought of Jesse's not-so-warm reception on the phone and everything Petra had just accused him of doing. "Yeah, well, Dashiell might have to get in line."

I drove all the way back to the hotel in a daze, trying to figure out what the hell had just happened. I had this weird feeling of displacement. It seemed like I should be pleased with the interview, since I'd apparently caught Jesse Cruz in a massive lie, not to mention a hell of a lot of criminal behavior. And if Petra was telling the truth, I'd also discovered a pretty huge miscarriage of justice. She was, after all, in prison for a crime she didn't commit. That should have galvanized me, but instead I just felt … confused. Even if every word Petra had said was true, hell, even if you discounted the weird gaps in her explanation, there was something *off* about the woman, and it wasn't just her rampant racism. Whenever she talked about werewolves, her eyes had smoldered with fevered hatred. Were they really the abominations she seemed to think they were? And how did any of this connect to Sam's death? I felt like I'd gone one step forward and about five steps backward. Or maybe sideways.

In the hotel parking lot, I turned the engine off and just sat there, staring ahead. What was I supposed to do now? Confront Jesse? He'd obviously done something shady, but he seemed pretty determined not to tell me the truth, and there wasn't a lot I could do to force his hand. It wasn't like I could take this to the police, and given how involved this Dashiell was supposed to be, he probably already knew the whole story. Hell, maybe he was the one who'd issued the orders. If that were the case, trying to find him would only lead to—

A sharp knock hit my car window, about four inches from my face. I jumped, adrenaline exploding into my bloodstream, my hands reaching for weapons that I hadn't brought. Beside the car, I saw a pretty girl in her early twenties with unnatural bright green eyes. I remembered those eyes. This was the woman who'd told Cruz I wasn't human. She'd found *me*.

She made a little rolling motion with one finger, and I buzzed down the window. "Hi, I'm Scarlett," she said with a professional smile. "And I think we should probably talk."

6. Lex

I'm not proud of what happened next.

I opened the car door hard enough to knock the girl backwards. She stumbled a few feet and then tripped over a curb, landing on her ass. "We need to *talk*?" I asked in indignation. "You think? Who the *fuck* are you?" I got out of the car. Fear replaced the glib smile on her face, and I couldn't help but feel kinda pleased with that. "*What* the fuck are you? Another witch?" I stalked forward, closing the distance between us. My fists were clenched at my sides, and I squeezed them even harder so I wouldn't hit her. Somewhere behind me, a dog began barking furiously.

"Stop," she said in a low voice. There was a tiny spot of blood on her lip. She'd bitten it when she tripped. "Think about it. You know what I am."

That did bring me up short. I glared at her, confused, but Simon's training finally kicked in. I breathed out, closed my eyes, and tried to drop into the mindset that allowed me to see the magical spectrum. It worked sort of like looking in thermal imaging goggles, only instead of body heat I could see peoples' life sparks. I opened my eyes to look at this girl—but nothing had changed. My vision was the same. At the same time, I felt a little … calmer. Lighter.

The same way I always felt around Charlie.

"You're a …" *Oh.* Subconsciously, I reached out a hand to steady myself on a nearby car. A null. Like Charlie. An adult null. I didn't know much about them, but I knew they were rare. That's what made Charlie a commodity. I hadn't expected I'd ever meet another one.

"Yeah. Can I stand up now?"

Still in shock, I reached down and helped her up, feeling a little chagrined. I hadn't actually meant to knock her down. The dog stopped barking and I realized the timing wasn't coincidental. "Yeah, that's, um, my dog," Scarlett said, dusting off the back of her jeans. "She's in the van, and she's a bit protective."

"How did you know where to find me?" I asked.

"Dashiell—he's more or less in charge of Los Angeles—has people at the prison. They called his daytime security team, who called me. Then we tracked your phone," she said unapologetically. Seeing my expression, she added, "Look, try to see it from our perspective. The Old World is very territorial, and you came sauntering into town—"

"Because Cruz wouldn't answer my questions!" My voice had come out in a whine, which I hated. I squared my shoulders and glared at her.

She wasn't exactly intimidated. "He couldn't," she countered. "Cruz is human, and on the periphery at best." There was a note in her voice that gave me pause. Regret? Sadness? "I asked him not to tell you anything, so he didn't." She looked around. No one was listening to us, but a couple of shady-looking guys were just exiting the hotel. "Look, can we take this conversation somewhere *other* than the parking lot of your seedy hotel?"

I glanced at the building beside us, but her assessment was kind of fair. "Fine. But first, I want to know who you are."

Her eyebrows furrowed. "I told you—"

"Yeah, yeah, you're Scarlett Bernard, and you're a null." I waved a hand. "But who the hell *are* you? Why are you the one who came here to see me?"

"My job is keeping the Old World under wraps. I make sure we're discreet. And walking into a prison to see Petra Corbett was *not* discreet."

"What else was I supposed to do, if Cruz wouldn't talk to me?"

"You were supposed to give up and go home," she said, not unkindly. "The humans don't know anything, and we figured that if you didn't have any way of tapping into the Old World here in town, you'd give up." She shrugged. "It didn't occur to me that you'd go through the official channels to set up a visit with Corbett. Stupid of me, but I suppose I have a tendency to forget about the world outside of … us."

"Aren't I part of that *us*?" I countered. "Don't I have an Old World membership card, just like you?" For a moment I considered dropping Maven's name, but no, that was a terrible idea. If I claimed to be here as her representative, I would be bound to politics I didn't fully understand. Besides, my position was way too new for me to start milking it.

She sighed. "Look, I don't know what things are like in … Wyoming?"

"Colorado."

"Sure. I don't know what things are like in Colorado, but in LA the three Old World factions share fairly equal power. It's rare for all three groups to get along in one city. It makes us very wary of people who come into our territory and start asking questions." She tilted her head, assessing me. "That's what I thought you were up until now, just some relative with a little witchblood who thought there was something off about the official story. But you're more than that, aren't you? You're a *hell* of a lot stronger than you were last winter."

I was surprised that she could tell, but then again, what did I really know about nulls? I had a thousand questions for her, except I couldn't even think of one just then. I said numbly, "Boundary witch. I'm a boundary witch."

Her eyes went round and the color drained from her face. She let out a shaky laugh, trying to cover the reaction. "Of course you are. *Fuck*. I gotta think a second." She turned and paced a couple of feet away, but I could hear her still cursing under her breath, though I didn't understand why. Finally, she paced back to me. "That changes things. Look, there's a Coffee Bean down the street, let's—"

She paused as we both heard the buzzing from the pocket of her canvas jacket. "Hang on," she said, frowning. "That's probably work."

"What do you do?"

"I clean up after the rest of them," she said in a clipped voice. Before I could ask anything else she put the phone to her ear. "This is Bernard."

As she listened, her face clouded over with something like irritation. She had to be a terrible poker player. "Again? Who was supposed to be watching her? … Okay, fine. I'll be right there."

Stuffing the phone back into her jacket pocket, she looked at me. "I have to go, unfortunately. It should only take an hour or two, and we can pick this up later."

I planted my feet. I wasn't about to let another null—one who seemed to know about what I could do—out of my sight. "I'm coming with you," I said firmly.

"Um, no. I have a job."

Fuck this. I'd had enough of being shut out. I crossed my arms over my chest. "I could just follow you, you know."

She stared at me, and I let the hardness seep into my eyes. I could win a staring contest with a petulant twenty-something, no problem. Finally she sighed, held up a finger and walked a few feet away, toward a nearby street lamp, to make another phone call. I let her go, but I watched carefully in case she tried to run off.

This call lasted a little longer, and when it started to get heated, I stepped closer to hear. Scarlett didn't seem to notice.

"You *know* why I can't," she was saying. She listened a moment, then began, "Jesse, you don't understand, she doesn't—argh!"

So she was talking to Cruz. To my surprise, she actually banged her head against the light pole in frustration. Her voice got low again, and I missed the rest of the call.

She came rushing back toward me a few moments later. "Look, Lex, we need to cut a deal."

I crossed my arms over my chest again. "I'm listening."

"You can ride with me and I will tell you everything you want to know about your sister. In exchange, you need to get out of LA by sundown."

I suddenly felt like we were in an old Western. I wasn't offended, exactly, but I was definitely confused. "Why sundown?"

"Because," she explained impatiently, "the prison called Dashiell's daytime security team and they're the ones who called me. When the sun sets, Dashiell's guys will fill him in and he'll call me for a status update. I'll have to tell him you're a witch and you're poking into the Remus thing—that much I can't keep from him—but if anyone in my Old World actually meets you and finds out what you *really* are"— she gestured helplessly—"they're gonna be pissed, Lex. Boundary witches can fuck with people, and they won't like that. They'll think you're a threat." She smiled wryly. "You're a lot like nulls that way."

I actually opened my mouth to explain that I worked for Maven in Boulder and was therefore not a threat, but I snapped it shut almost immediately. For all I knew, she and Dashiell might have some sort of rivalry. He could consider my presence an insult. Or a message of some kind. It was too risky. Scarlett led me toward a white van where the world's ugliest dog was pressing its nose out a cracked window, snuffling at the glass. It was enormous.

I told myself to focus. "How do I know you'll tell me everything?"

"My story will be corroborated." She looked sad, which confused me. Why would she look sad?

"By who?

"Lizzy Thompkins."

7. Jesse

Jesse was in his third meeting of the day when his phone screen lit up with Scarlett's number.

The consulting firm that employed him usually lent him out to the same specific show, but they were on hiatus this week, so he'd been asked to attend meetings with producers for the upcoming pilot season. At his request, Jesse's assistant had scheduled them back-to-back on the studio lot. Getting them all over with at once had seemed like a great idea at the time, but after the third time one of the producers asked what it felt like to shoot someone, Jesse was about ready to flip a table and storm out of there. And he had another two meetings to go.

He ignored Scarlett's call, but a moment later she texted him. *9-1-1*. He tried to suppress the little rush of excitement, but when she called again a moment later, he couldn't resist excusing himself to step out into the hall.

"What the hell is going on?" Jesse asked, instead of "hello".

"Remember your new friend Lex?" she said, her voice too sweet. "Well, she's here, and she's been to see Petra Corbett—"

Jesse interrupted her to curse in Spanish. "I knew I was missing someone! I forgot they put her here in So Cal."

"I think Dashiell arranged it so he could keep an eye on her, but that's the least of our problems. Lex is extremely dangerous, and if I tell my bosses what she is and that she's poking around, I think they might kill her. Oh, and Lizzy escaped again. I need to go make sure she doesn't hurt anyone, so I gotta ditch Lex, but she says she'll *follow* me—"

"Whoa, whoa. Slow down." He rubbed his face, suddenly

remembering why he was better off far away from the Old World. "Why is she dangerous? Does she have some kind of evidence?"

"Noooooo," she drawled. "But as it turns out, she's a boundary witch." She paused with great significance, like that was supposed to mean something to him.

"What's a boundary witch, Scarlett?"

Pause. "Shit, sorry. I forgot you didn't know. Olivia told me about them ages ago. You know how some witches specialize? Her specialty is death magic. And Jesse, she is powerful as shit. Way more than she was last winter."

He tried to process all that. Death magic was exactly what it sounded like—spells that involved someone being killed or brought back to life. Often both. The only good thing about death magic was that it was extremely difficult for regular trades witches to perform. Scarlett had told him stories about witches who'd been killed while messing around with death magic. If she had ever told him that witches could specialize in it, Jesse had forgotten. Or, more likely, his mind had blocked it out to save him the mortal terror.

He tried to focus on the problem at hand and the cop part of his brain kicked in. "Do you have some indication that she's planning to practice death magic here in LA?"

She pushed out a breath. "I'm sorry. I'm flustered, and worried about Lizzy, and I'm not explaining this well at all. If Olivia was right—and granted, it's Olivia the psycho hose-beast we're talking about—boundary witches are dangerous, but not just because of the obvious. They can press vampires, Jesse. Having them around is like playing with uranium. If Kirsten or Dashiell find out she's in town, they're gonna flip. And Will's gonna be just as upset if he finds out she's been nosing around about Henry Remus. I could see any one of them wanting to make her *go away*."

Her voice was matter-of-fact, but he knew even Scarlett wouldn't agree to killing an innocent woman, regardless of whether she had the potential to cause havoc. Scarlett might live in a grayer world than Jesse did, but she had her limits too, and that was why he kept falling in love with her. But it also meant that she would dig her heels in and possibly put *herself* in danger.

The solution seemed obvious to Jesse, but then again, he didn't actually answer to these people. "So don't tell them, Scar. Tell Lex what she wants to know and get her the hell out of town."

Given how frantic she'd just sounded, the pause on the line seemed to last a long, long time. "I can't do that," she finally said, sounding shocked that he'd even suggest it.

"Why not? I thought you were a partner now. Make an executive decision."

"You *know* why I can't," she protested.

"Because of Lizzy? She'll back up your story."

"You don't understand, she doesn't—argh! I don't have time for this!" Her voice got quieter. "Look, I have to get to Lizzy before she hurts someone. Will you come?"

Her tone was pleading, and Jesse had to remind himself that this was how he'd gotten in over his head in the first place—trying to fix things for her, trying to control her, save her. On the other hand, she was asking for his help this time.

But why him?

As if she could read his mind, Scarlett added, "If I'm gonna do this, I can't tell anyone else. Not even Eli; he'd have to keep it from Will. *Please*, Jesse. I need your help."

The magic words. Jesse couldn't resist them—although, he

thought, with a glance at the meeting room door over his shoulder, it wasn't like he even wanted to. Helping Scarlett could actually make a difference, and it would save him from the absurdity that was his day. "Tell me where."

She told him, and he grimaced. Of course. They had to go back to where this whole mess had begun:

Henry Remus's personal torture chamber.

Millard Fillmore Elementary School was in La Crescenta, bumping right into the back of Deukmejian Wilderness Park and the San Gabriel Mountains. It was an average LA public school: a number of overcrowded, loosely grouped buildings that generally looked stuffed to the gills with the trappings of education. Extra chairs and desks were propped against the walls near the doors, and there were two portable trailers parked on school grounds to handle the classroom overflow.

Despite the desperate need for more space, however, there was an old, half-rotted garden shed at the very back of the property that was almost never used. During the Remus investigation, Jesse had learned that the school's janitorial team thought the small building was owned by the park, while the park staff thought, rightly, that it belonged to the school.

At any rate, although the shed was right in the heart of the city, both the park staff and the school emptied out by 5:30 p.m., and there were no houses nearby, certainly none close enough for anyone to hear screaming. This was where Henry Remus had brought his victims to be slaughtered. He'd killed four women and a number of animals there, drenching the walls and dirt floors with their blood. The press, with its addiction to obvious puns, had naturally dubbed this building the Blood Shed.

It still stood there, a monument to a very twisted mind. It had been months since Remus's death, but the school couldn't decide what to do with the shed. The immediate suggestion, of course, was to tear it down and more or less salt the earth where it had stood, but there were objections from the DA's office and the press. The wooden shed was a huge piece of evidence and there were still several wrongful death lawsuits pending. In addition, there was so much blood inside that even with the help of local FBI labs, they were still trying to process samples for DNA. What if they found more victims?

Eventually the school board had just thrown a few padlocks on it and tried to forget about the whole thing. For a while they had to pay security guards to keep the press away, but ten months after Remus's killing spree even the hungriest LA journalists had finally given up or lost interest.

In the days after Remus's death, Jesse had spent a lot of time in that horrible little room, watching LAPD criminologists collect used hypodermic needles and tatters of clothing. He still had nightmares about the Blood Shed, and would have been happy to personally toss a lit match into the ghastly place.

Jesse was a lot closer to the shed than Lex's hotel was, but he had to make his excuses and go on a quick run to his old precinct. By the time he pulled into the deserted school parking lot Scarlett was already there, leaning against her enormous van, the White Whale. Lex was standing a few feet away, her body language more deferential than Jesse had seen it, like something had taken precedence over her own quest. There was another woman with them: about thirty-five, cropped blonde hair, tan, and a frown that looked permanently etched onto her face. She was standing close enough to Scarlett to be human, but she had the lean, excessively healthy look of a werewolf. Her arms were crossed defensively across her chest, and Jesse suspected this was the person who'd been responsible for Lizzy Thompkins that afternoon. Behind the three of them, he could just see the shed door hanging open a few inches, with darkness seeping out from inside. He parked one space away from the van and got out.

"Sorry I'm late," he said to the three of them. "Have you been waiting long?"

"We just got here," Scarlett assured him.

"What's going on?" There was a sense of expectation in the air, like they'd been waiting for him before they could act.

"She's holed up in there, in human form," Scarlett explained. "We're not sure how to get her out."

"Wasn't the shed locked?" Jesse asked. The werewolf he didn't know gave him a withering look, which made him realize the stupidity of his question. Of course it had been locked, but human padlocks were no challenge for werewolf strength. "Sorry, I withdraw the question. And we haven't met."

"Sorry, this is Astrid," Scarlett said. "She was supposed to be responsible for Lizzy today."

Astrid stepped forward to shake hands, but her face was stormy. "I just went for a fifteen-minute run," she snapped, her eyes still on Scarlett. "She was taking a nap, and—"

Scarlett cut her off. "Yeah, but the full moon's in two days. She's agitated."

"You think I don't know that? It's October, the fucking Blood Moon, and I'm agitated too, by the way, which is why I needed to take the edge off! Jesus, you think that just because you're sleeping with a werewolf you know the first thing—"

"Enough!" Jesse held up his hands to stop her tirade. Lex was watching the exchange with an eyebrow cocked, as if she were mentally storing all the information for later. "It's not important now. What do we do?"

Astrid turned to face Scarlett, demonstrating in spite of her attitude that she considered the null the leader in this situation. "I told you, I can just go in there and drag her out by force."

"And I told *you*," Scarlett countered, "it's too risky. Aside from the fact that the shed is both rickety and police evidence, you'd probably have to hurt her, and she's been hurt enough." The compassion in Scarlett's voice surprised Jesse a little, although it probably shouldn't have. They had both been there when Remus was killed. He'd seen the way Lizzy had limped toward Scarlett—terrified, bleeding, and cringing.

For a second the werewolf seemed as if she would snap back a retort, but instead her tightly bunched shoulders slumped and she nodded her agreement. She mumbled something about a walk and stalked away, moving toward the edge of the parking lot. As she left, Jesse caught sight of her expression. She looked ... haunted.

Confused, Jesse glanced at Lex, but her face was soldier-blank. He returned his focus to Scarlett, because somewhere in his heart he still considered her his partner. "I don't get it," he said quietly. "Lizzy seemed okay when we left her with Will. What's going on?"

"She's been losing it, bit by bit," Scarlett said, sounding tired. "Will thinks it's because the alpha magic hasn't adjusted. She still sees Remus as her alpha, and her alpha is dead. At the same time, Remus attacked and violated her, and the human part of her can't forget that. Will is kind to her, of course, but the trauma ...." She spread her hands helplessly. "Sometimes she makes progress and seems almost normal, for a werewolf, but then she backslides. And she keeps coming back here, like it's a homing beacon."

"What do you usually do?"

"Normally I just stand here and make sure she doesn't hurt

anyone until Will can get here and talk her out," she replied. "But he's up in Napa today talking to wine distributors."

"Can't you just go in and get her?" Scarlett was a null. If she got close enough to Lizzy, the werewolf would become human again.

She winced. "As a last resort, yes. But we tried that before, the third time she got away, and it wrecked her. She came out, but they had to pull her away from me. By force." It always seemed to come back to force with the werewolves. "If we wait long enough, she might just tire herself out, but we're running out of time. I checked the school's schedule, and there's a PTA meeting here in"—she checked her watch—"ninety minutes. They'll start setting up soon."

"So what's the plan?"

"Do you think you could try talking to her?" Scarlett asked hopefully. "She usually doesn't like men, but you were there when we ... found her. She might trust you."

He glanced at Lex, who had been listening to the whole exchange with that same guarded, impassive expression. She met his eyes but didn't comment. "All right," he said. "I'll try."

Scarlett nodded. "I'll be close. Remember, she may look human, but if she tries to scratch or bite you, get the hell out of there. Are you armed?"

Jesse shook his head. His guns were locked up back home.

"Okay," she said. "Well, if you think she's gonna bite you, scream. You'd make a terrible werewolf."

It was only then that he realized the risk he was taking. When they'd worked the Remus case, Scarlett had explained that in theory, a single bite or scratch from a werewolf could change a human. It almost always took a serious mauling, though, and everything he knew about Lizzy Thompkins suggested that she was too passive for an attack.

He'd risk it.

Lex, who had been quiet for this whole exchange, abruptly stepped forward. "I'm coming with you," she declared.

Jesse raised an eyebrow. "No, you're not."

"Yes, I am."

He looked at Scarlett, but she just shrugged. "How much did Scarlett tell you on the way here?" he asked Lex.

"About Remus being a nova wolf, and the Luparii, and that her dog is not a dog," she said. "That's as far as we got. I still want to talk to Lizzy." Her gaze slid off him, and he shot a questioning look at Scarlett.

"She wants to make sure I'm telling her the truth," Scarlett said, shaking her head.

Jesse glared at the witch. "And you want to use a traumatized woman as a lie detector test?"

"No. If she's that far gone, it can wait. But I know trauma and PTSD. I might be able to help."

Jesse wavered. He wanted to trust that Lex would put Lizzy's welfare above her own questions, but he just didn't know her that well.

Seeing his indecision, Lex added, "Plus, I'm female. It might make her more comfortable with you."

He sighed. "Fine. Let's go."

8. Lex

As we approached the squat, one-room utility shed, which was a little smaller than a two-car garage, I ordered myself to calm the fuck down. Scarlett's explanation that the nova wolf wanted to change more werewolves had been straightforward and matter-of-fact, which I appreciated more than she could know. But I was still roiling with anger and hatred, not to mention desperate for the rest of the story, and I had a feeling that my rage was only going to get worse once I saw the evidence of his crimes. But I couldn't go in there agitated. Werewolves were supposed to be pretty perceptive, and I wasn't going to be much good to Lizzy if I went in there looking like I was ready to start smacking heads together. I took deep breaths, using the tricks we'd been taught in the army for slowing your heart rate. It helped a little.

I wasn't sure what to expect in the shed—the press had made a big deal about how much blood had coated the inside walls, but I'd assumed it was a salacious exaggeration. As we got closer to the open door, however, I could already smell it: old blood and feces and urine. They must have cleaned it up at least a little, which meant this was just the smell of what they couldn't wash away. It stank even to me, and I wondered how it would affect a werewolf. Didn't they have an enhanced sense of smell? This had to be torture for Lizzy. Why would she keep coming back here of all places?

When we reached the door Cruz automatically stepped forward, motioning for me to flank him. Cop instincts. I didn't like being in the "protectee" position, but Lizzy knew him, not me, and if she was as freaked out as everyone thought, a familiar face was probably the best bet.

It was dark inside the windowless shed, but a tiny bit of LA sunlight leaked in through cracks in the old wood. Cruz and I instinctively paused and let our eyes adjust to the dim interior. In that brief moment I heard the sound of whimpering. It shot straight into my heart. If I hadn't known better, I would have sworn it was coming from an injured dog.

I stepped forward into the shed, ignoring Jesse's arm as it rose to caution me. I felt dirt under my feet, saw shadows on the walls. No, not shadows, I realized—bloodstains. On every wall, like someone had done a sloppy job with a paint roller.

Sam's blood.

I ignored it and focused on the small form huddled in the corner. This had to be Lizzy Thompkins, squatting or laying down, but I couldn't see more than a shape, with another, darker shape next to her. I considered using the flashlight app on my phone, but decided it might spook her. "Lizzy?" I asked softly.

Movement. She lifted her head and snarled, *"I said go away!"* There was something dark streaked down her chin, and I took an automatic step backward. The sobbing resumed.

Cruz moved up so we were more or less side by side. "Lizzy, it's Jesse Cruz. Do you remember me?"

The sobbing stopped for a moment. "Jesse?"

"Yeah, honey, it's me," he said gently. Out of the corner of my eye I could see him crouch down, and I did the same. "What's the matter?"

A choked, sobbing laugh, like Lizzy couldn't even begin to answer that question. I could relate. "I killed a cat," she said mournfully. The words chilled me. "I didn't mean to, but I was so upset and it jumped at me ..."

"Never liked cats much," Jesse said, sounding calmer than I felt.

She sniffled and her head turned sharply to face me. "Who are you? You smell … I know your smell …"

"I'm Lex," I said. "Sam Wheaton's sister. I've been hoping to meet you."

There was a moment of silence, and when she spoke again it was in a terrible whisper. "Will you bleed for me?"

Cruz and I looked at each other. "Maybe you should go—" he began, but somehow I understood what she wanted. What she was asking.

"Do you have a knife?" I asked him.

"Lex, I really don't think—"

"Just give it to me."

He sighed and squirmed for a moment, and then I was handed a small Swiss Army knife. At that same moment the breeze picked up a little and the shed door drifted inward, letting in a bit more light. I fumbled open a blade and pierced the tip of my right middle finger, then held it out to Lizzy.

She darted forward to grab my hand, and for the first time I realized that she was naked, her clothes in a pile beside her. She took a great deep sniff, let out another one of those desperate giggles, and took another sniff. "*Yes,* yes, you smell like her! Your blood's just like her blood, but it smells like something else too." Sniff, sniff. "What does it smell like?"

"Death," I said. "There's death magic in my blood."

She only paused a moment before asking hopefully, "Will you kill me?"

My eyes filled with tears, but I made sure my voice was strong before I answered, "No, honey. I won't kill you." But I was giving serious thought to bringing Remus back from the dead just so I could kill him again. "If there's another way to help you, though, I will."

Lizzy made a snuffling noise and crawled forward. She was about my age, but she was painfully thin, small enough to curl herself up against my body; just like a hurt animal seeking comfort. I put my arms around her and glanced at Cruz over the top of her head. His eyes were full, too. I tried not to look at the cat.

After I'd held her for a moment, Lizzy said abruptly, "Sam died so hard."

I struggled to suppress my flinch. "Do you want to tell me about it?" I shot a questioning look to Cruz. Scarlett had said Remus was trying to change more werewolves, add to his own little pack, but she hadn't gotten to Sam's part of the story yet.

"He was experimenting on the women," Jesse said softly. "Trying to find the best way to change a female into a...um..." He squirmed, looking uncomfortable.

"A mate," Lizzy sobbed. "I was supposed to be his mate. Lucky me." Her voice was bitter. "Sam he ate."

I couldn't keep the shock off my face. Cruz looked away from me. "He ... *ate* her?"

"Well, most of her. Bite by bite," she said into my stomach. "I miss him so much."

Revulsion flooded me, and it was all I could do not to throw Lizzy Thompkins away from me and run out of there. Scarlett had said something about alphas and pack structure—this woman's werewolf instincts were revolting against her human judgment. Against *all* human judgment.

Lizzy sat up and sidled away from me. "I can smell the change in you," she said mournfully. "You're disgusted, and I don't blame you.

I'm disgusted too. But my body ... my body keeps telling me to come back here, to this place where I can smell my friends' death all around me ...because that's where he was." After a moment she laid her head down on the ground, and her whole body went slack.

There were other things I could ask her about Sam's last moments, but I couldn't bear it. Tears were already spilling down my cheeks and I had to focus to control my breathing. Jesse looked like he wanted to say something, or maybe touch me, but I shook my head. I'd asked, hadn't I? I'd wanted to know. No, I'd *demanded* to know. Now I had to live with the knowledge.

After a few more minutes, Lizzy's breathing slowed. I didn't think she was sleeping, just ... spent. Nearly catatonic. I nodded at Jesse, who went over and picked her up like she was a child. She settled her head against on his shoulder and mumbled something.

"We're going to take you home," he told her. He tilted his head so I would follow him out. I didn't need to be told—I couldn't get away from here fast enough.

"Don't have a home anymore," Lizzy muttered. "Just different cages." I winced.

When we left the shed, Scarlett immediately backed away. True to her word, she'd stayed close in case we needed her. Now, she hovered about twenty feet away, clearly worried about Lizzy but unable to do much more than wring her hands. Part of me wanted her to run over and give Lizzy some respite from her emotional agony—her sickness. But maybe it was crueler to give her relief that wouldn't last.

There were only three cars in the lot: Scarlett's van, Jesse's sedan, and a nondescript Toyota. Astrid was leaning against the side of the car, having returned from her walk. She glared at each of us in turn as if daring us to remark on her absence. No one did. She opened the back door of the Toyota, then watched with her arms folded defiantly across her chest as Cruz laid Lizzy across the backseat.

When she was settled Astrid went to the trunk and pulled out a rough blanket, passing it to Jesse so he could drape it over the woman's nude form. "Nice, huh?" Astrid asked, watching him. "Did you get the whole show?"

"As much as we could stomach," Cruz said with a glance my way.

"Why is she like this?" I asked the other werewolf.

She gave me a look, like I was being thick on purpose and she didn't like it. "Um, because she's a werewolf? There's a reason why they call it a curse."

"But *you're* a werewolf," I said disbelievingly. "She's, like ... damaged."

A bitter smile quirked up one side of her mouth. "Don't be fooled, lady. We're all damaged. That's what werewolf magic does to you. Some of us just wear it better than others."

I shuddered. Back home, Quinn talked about werewolf magic like it was just another branch of the Old World, but this ... this was *repulsive*. Henry Remus was a monster, and he'd turned what was left of this poor woman into a monster too.

"What will happen to her?" I asked.

She shrugged. "My shift with her ends tonight. Tomorrow she's some other pack member's problem." Astrid stomped over to the driver's door, practically snarling. She seemed so upset, but I didn't get the sense that it was with us, or even with Lizzy. With herself? Remus? I didn't know, but I was done asking questions.

When the two werewolves pulled away, Scarlett came up to stand beside Cruz and me. I felt the little loosening again, the sense of decreased pressure I always felt around my niece. It was beginning to annoy me, coming from her. "I'm sorry, Lex," Cruz said, still watching the Toyota's taillights disappear. "About Sam."

I shook my head. Be careful what you wish for. Sam had said I deserved to know the truth, that a werewolf was responsible for her murder. But I hadn't stopped there. I'd wanted the *whole* truth, and now I couldn't stop seeing images of my sister's body, her beautiful, perfect body, which had been home not just to her soul, but to Charlie's, being mauled. *Bite by bite.* My fists clenched. I turned to face the others.

"The bodies weren't lost, were they?" I asked. "You had them all along."

Scarlett and Cruz exchanged a fleeting look that managed to communicate something very complicated. Then Scarlett nodded at me. "I couldn't risk the LAPD finding evidence of werewolves," she explained. "That's my job."

"I understand," I said quietly. "I get why you had to do it. But I want my sister. I want to take her home and bury her."

"That's impossible," Scarlett said.

"I know, you don't want the cops to run tests, but I'll find a way around that. I can claim religion, maybe." Hell, I would get Quinn out here to press the coroner if I had to. "Remus is dead, so it's not like they'll be in a hurry to double-check her for more evidence."

"I'm sorry," Scarlett said in a clear, professional voice, the kind that doctors use to break bad news to the thousandth patient of the day. "That's not possible. I incinerated the body."

My jaw dropped open. I looked at Cruz, but he was staring abashedly at the ground in front of his toes. "You ... incinerated ... my sister."

Scarlett didn't look away. "In a furnace," she said simply. "It's what I do."

I punched her in her stupid face.

9. Jesse

Jesse saw the blow coming and tried to get in between the two women, but he only managed to sort of awkwardly bump into Lex, forcing her to stagger a little so that the punch lost some of its force. It wasn't enough: Scarlett was knocked onto her ass. Blood trickled from her lip. Before any of them could react, Jesse heard a pounding from behind them: frantic, rhythmic, like something being thrown up against a wall. He turned just in time to see Shadow explode through the shattered safety window in Scarlett's van.

"Now you've done it," Scarlett said. She just sounded weary.

A furious bargest in action was a sight to behold. Shadow had been created to kill, and as she shot across the small parking lot, she looked like a black wave of unstoppable, inevitable, instant death. Jesse took one step forward, but he spared a second to glance at Scarlett, who seemed unruffled. She trusted Shadow not to actually hurt anyone, so he did too.

The bargest's rage seemed to soften as soon as she hit Scarlett's radius, though she continued on her course toward Lex. To her credit, the witch didn't run or even move. She put her hands in her pockets and gazed downward, and Jesse realized she had some experience with unstable dogs. Shadow planted her feet a few feet away from Lex, and what little fur she had stood up in anger as she growled and snapped. "No, Shadow," Scarlett said soothingly. "I kind of deserved that. Don't eat her. Lex, could you please sit down near me?"

Calmly, but with an astonished look on her face, Lex went over to Scarlett and lowered herself onto the grass next to the null, trying to look nonthreatening. The two of them sat there for a moment while Shadow's head whipped between them, and Jesse almost laughed. They looked so much like two chagrined students in detention, with Shadow as the mean teacher in charge. He folded his arms across his chest, watching.

"I can't believe you just disposed of my sister," Lex muttered to Scarlett, with one eye on the angry bargest. "Like she was nothing. Like she was garbage." Her voice was wavering, and Jesse realized she was trying not to cry.

"I told you," Scarlett said stubbornly, "it's my job."

"Some job you've got," Lex snapped, and the bargest snarled at her, advancing. Lex pulled her knees to her chest and hugged them— she had no way of knowing it, but this was one of Scarlett's gestures, and the bargest backed off again. "And everyone thinks *I'm* a monster," Lex mumbled.

Jesse didn't actually expect a reaction from Scarlett, but to his surprise she went still. A tear ran down her cheek before she swiped it away. Sensing her mistress's mood, the bargest settled onto the ground in front of Scarlett and shoved her head under Scarlett's hand.

When the null spoke, she sounded as young and lost as Jesse had ever heard her. "If I don't, who will?" Scarlett whispered. "If I don't do these horrible things, they'll force them on Corry or Eli, or some other innocent. It's not too late for them."

Jesse blinked then, wanting to go to her, knowing he couldn't.

Realizing what she'd just implied, Scarlett's face hardened. "I'm sorry that Remus killed your sister before we could stop him. I'm sorry for your loss," she said to Lex. "But if you're waiting for me to apologize for what I did, it's not gonna happen."

Lex stood, easing herself to her feet so the bargest wouldn't be alarmed. "I'll keep my end of the bargain," she said stiffly. "I'll be gone by sunset. If somebody can take care of my rental car, I'll go straight to the airport from here."

Scarlett nodded. "I'll get someone from Dashiell's team to handle it."

Lex tilted her head in acknowledgment. She looked up at the sky for a moment, eyes squinting to take in the top of the palm trees that speckled the school's landscaping. "And I hope I never come back," she added, mostly to herself. And with that, she started toward the parking lot, already pulling out her phone.

Jesse heard himself say, "I'll give you a ride." Lex paused, looking surprised, then nodded her thanks. She went and got her duffel bag out of Scarlett's car and walked over to Jesse's. He beeped the remote to unlock it so she could climb in. Before he followed, Jesse squatted in front of Scarlett. "You okay?" he asked, resting a hand on her shoulder.

She nodded, her eyes cast down, lost in thought. He wondered if she was seeing bodies going into a furnace. He certainly was. Jesse started to pull back, but she reached up and squeezed his hand where it lay. "She's not wrong, is she?" Scarlett asked conversationally.

"No, she's not," he said. "But neither are you. And punishing yourself for what happened won't solve anything."

Her bright green eyes lifted to him in surprise, then narrowed. "You're one to talk. How's the new job, Jesse?"

He flinched. Stood up to leave. "See you around."

"Yeah?" Scarlett said, hope in her voice.

Jesse paused, considered it. Shrugged. "Maybe. Yeah."

The drive to the airport was silent and heady, like a black cloud had squeezed into the car with them. Jesse pulled over at the Frontier terminal and put the car in park. "Are you all right?" he asked Lex.

Her face was impassive. The soldier again. "I will be." Without another word, she got out of the car, hoisted her duffel bag, and began walking toward the airport entrance. Jesse almost put the car back in drive, but he remembered himself just in time. "Lex, wait!" he yelled through the open window. She paused and turned back, a question on her face. He grabbed the bag from the glove compartment and followed her onto the sidewalk.

"I have something for you," he rushed to say. "Almost forgot." He thrust the little evidence bag toward her, and Lex accepted it with a frown before turning it over and opening the seal. She reached in and pulled out a shiny silver Rolex. Lex turned it over in her hands, exposing an inscription on the back. *Congratulations, college graduate! We love you—Mom and Dad.*

"This was Sam's," she murmured, then looked up at him. "How did you get this?"

"She left it for us," he said gently. "Remus drugged her so she wouldn't fight back, but she still had the sense to take it off and drop it outside the shed, so we'd know she'd been there. Your sister was smart. If Remus had been a normal man the LAPD could've arrested, this evidence alone would have helped us convict him."

She nodded, her eyes brimming with tears. "But how did *you* get it?"

"Called in an old favor. The case is very closed, so they'll eventually return all the evidence to the proper owners. But they're backlogged. I just thought … while you were in town …" he drifted off, feeling suddenly embarrassed. To his surprise, she stepped forward and threw her arms around him, hugging him close. Her shampoo smelled like evergreen trees and she was surprisingly solid with muscle. Jesse returned the hug, and for just a second he had that feeling again, like he'd helped someone. Done something good.

Lex stepped back, smiling with embarrassment. "Err … sorry.

And thank you." She clutched the watch to her chest. "I'll get this to Charlie." She hesitated for a moment, then added, "Would you tell Scarlett I'm sorry for hitting her?"

"Of course. And ... try not to judge her too harshly, okay?" Jesse said tentatively. "I know what we did was awful, but I swear, we were respectful to Sam. And the others."

She nodded. "What I do for the Old World isn't all that different, it was just ... easier to be upset with her than with Lizzy." She shuddered. "Thank God we don't have werewolves in Boulder."

As he drove out of the LAX traffic juggernaut, Jesse felt exhausted—and he couldn't shake the feeling that he'd made a mistake with Lex. He should have corrected her, made her see that not all werewolves were evil any more than all professional football players were womanizers. There was something a little ominous about her attitude, and he had a feeling the next werewolf who crossed her path might pay for it. Then again, he thought, werewolf PR wasn't his job.

Of course, that thought only reminded him of his actual job. Jesse sighed, and headed back to work.

Boundary Blood

Author's Note

Midnight Curse was a turning point in the Old World books for any number of reasons. I knew I wanted to jump-start Scarlett Bernard's story, and begin a new self-contained three-book arc for her that would set itself apart from the *Dead Spots-Trail of Dead-Hunter's Trail* trilogy. I wanted to try visiting the well-traveled Dracula playground, and I also thought it'd be really interesting to have a boundary witch as a main villain. I'd spent three Lex novels talking about all the chaos and evil boundary witches could afflict on a city; I figured it was time to make good on that. At the same time, I had been planning a story about the Vampire Trials for ages, *and* at the same time, I wanted to write a story that had real-world implications.

One my favorite things about urban fantasy—and something I talk about frequently at conventions—is its potential to sneak in allegories about the real world. After six books of what I fondly refer to as "vampire kablooie," I wanted to talk about toxic masculinity, and how men abuse women. Digging deeper into Molly's story seemed like the perfect opportunity to combine all of those objectives.

Midnight Curse is the culmination of all those efforts, and I'm really proud of how much complexity and development is woven into the story. Because it was such an ambitious project, however, the novel created two new story offshoots that I've been eager to to revisit: Lex's aunt Katia, and the four new vampires that Dashiell sent up to San Francisco. Because I was writing a Scarlett trilogy at the time, however, I couldn't really have more than a few mentions of what was going on in other parts of the Old World. This compilation gave me a chance to finally remedy that.

Chapter 1

One hundred and eighty-eight miles. That's how long my new aunt and I had been riding in silence, as I drove us north along the spine of California.

I've never considered myself a particularly talkative person—in fact, on more than one occasion my friends and family back in Colorado have complained that I am too withdrawn, especially in the years since I was discharged from the Army. But Katia ("just Katia; I do not use a surname") made me look downright chatty.

We hadn't talked much during the whole last week—at least, not to each other. Eight days earlier, Katia had testified at the Vampire Trials about working for Oskar, an abusive vampire pimp. Like me, Katia was a boundary witch, able to press the minds of vampires. Oskar had forced her to subdue the female vampires whose bodies he sold. Sometimes Katia's job was to make them forget about beatings. Sometimes the johns did a lot worse.

Testifying about all that seemed grueling in itself, but Katia was also recovering from an actual *bullet to the heart*, an injury that would have killed any human or witch without boundary blood. Aside from the trip to the Trials, she mostly stayed in bed at the safe house Dashiell, the cardinal vampire of LA, had loaned us. During the day Katia took painkillers so she could sleep, but every night she forced herself to stay awake and on the phone, making arrangements for the stable of female vampires that had been abandoned in Reno. Now that

Oskar was dead, they all needed somewhere to go, with vampires who wouldn't abuse them again. Katia had made placing them her personal mission.

When I listened to her on the phone, Katia was persistent to the point of ferocity, her voice strong and determined despite her wound. If she wasn't calling potential sponsors, she was talking to the abused vampires themselves, and I made a point to give her privacy for these moments. She could barely walk to the bathroom without help; I wasn't exactly worried about her escaping through a window.

By the time dawn arrived she would be weak and pale, meekly asking me for another Vicodin. I gave her the pills, she went to sleep, and then we started the cycle again. It didn't take a genius to figure out that she was doing some kind of penance.

During that whole time, I had nothing much to do except wait, pace, and keep an eye on Katia's wound…and the doors and windows. Although she'd been operating under Oskar's orders, Katia had made a lot of people in Los Angeles *very* unhappy. My friend Jesse had loaned me a Glock, and I had a handful of the shredder stakes that had come on the plane with me, in my checked bag, but I wasn't taking chances. Also, I was very bored. I checked in on the phone with my boyfriend and my niece every day, and Jesse brought us groceries a couple of times and stayed for a game of cards, but for the first four days that was the extent of my human interaction.

Then, on the fifth day, Scarlett Bernard dropped by at two in the afternoon, while Katia was sleeping. When I opened the door she was holding a manila envelope the size of a folded sheet of paper. "Hi," she said, thrusting it toward my midsection. "For you and Katia."

I didn't touch the envelope. "What is it?" I asked, keeping my voice low.

"Money. We found it with Oskar when Molly…um. When he died."

Scarlett's friend Molly was the one who had killed Oskar. I'd seen her at the Trials, though we hadn't talked much. "I don't think Katia will accept it," I said, looking at the envelope. "You should give it to those other four women, Oskar's new victims."

"This is about a tenth of what we found," Scarlett told me, waggling the envelope a couple of times. "Molly is going to make sure the lost girls get set up, probably in the Bay Area."

"The lost girls?"

"Yeah, you know, the USC students? Lost girls? Get it?" She bounced on the balls of her feet a few times, grinning.

"No. I don't."

Her smile faded. "There's a movie…never mind; it doesn't matter. If she wants, Katia can give whatever's left to the women in Reno, but you guys are going to need some traveling money."

I gave her a look, but I couldn't argue with the logic. I accepted the cash. And that was the end of the day's entertainment.

After eight days, Matthias, the doctor treating Katia, had declared that she was ready to travel with me back to Colorado, with a stop at the brothel in Reno to collect her belongings and make sure the vampires had gotten to safe locations.

I rented us a late-model Subaru for the trip, hoping the smooth suspension would be easiest on Katia's wound. We couldn't exactly fly without getting a lot of questions about Katia's injury—plus I wanted to have weapons during the stopover. If Oskar had enemies in LA, I figured he probably had even more back in Reno.

From the moment Katia climbed into the car, though, she rode with her body wedged into the corner of the seat and the door, one hand always an inch away from the handle like she might duck and roll out of there at any moment. Or, I realized eventually, like she was trying to stay as far away as possible from a threat. I tried not to take it personally.

I offered her one of the books Jesse had brought me, but Katia just shook her head and sat there staring out the windshield. Eventually even I got uncomfortable with the silence.

Unfortunately, I reflexively reverted back to my Luther impulses and kept trying to ask her what she needed. Should we stop for food?

Bathroom? Did she want more water? Painkillers? Was she carsick? Would it help if she stretched out across the backseat instead? She kept shaking her head, tight-lipped, and finally I heard my dead twin sister's voice in my head—one of the weird perks of having boundary witchblood.

Babe. I think you're making it worse.

I sighed, but Sam was right, as usual, and I shut up.

I sort of expected Katia to fall asleep after that, but instead we began a hundred and eighty-eight miles of increasingly oppressive silence.

We stopped for a bathroom and gas break in Visalia, CA, and I was painfully relieved when Katia climbed out of the car and began shuffling inside. I followed her just far enough to give the attendant some cash from the envelope, and then I went back out to fill the gas tank. I started the pump, leaning against the Subaru and closing my eyes, soaking in some of the afternoon sunshine.

What the hell was I doing?

As if in answer, my phone buzzed, and I pushed off the car so I could dig it out of my pocket. I smiled when I saw the name on the caller ID. Lily Pellar was a strong trades witch in Boulder, and my best friend. I took the call. "Hey, Lily."

"Hey. Can you talk?"

"Sure." I turned toward the gas station. Through the massive front windows, I could see Katia moving through the aisles, probably looking for a snack. "What's up?"

"I just wanted to check in," Lily said. "Quinn told Simon you two were leaving today."

Simon was Lily's brother, another friend. He was tight with my boyfriend Quinn, although both of them would insist otherwise. "Word travels fast. We left this morning."

"How is your aunt doing?"

I returned the gas nozzle to the machine, not sure how to answer that. "Honestly? I have no idea. She barely talks."

"Well, she did get shot in the *heart*."

"Yeah, but...I don't know. She's not asking me any questions about Boulder or my life or anything. She seems...shut down."

Lily laughed hard enough to hurt my ear a little. "What?" I asked with irritation.

"Nothing, nothing. It just sounds like you're describing yourself."

"Hey!" I protested. "I'm not shut down. I'm...politely reserved."

"Uh-huh."

I screwed the cap back on the Subaru's gas tank and closed the cover. "I guess I just thought she'd be...happier? More relieved? I mean, she was being used by a psychotic vampire pimp, half of LA wants her dead, and we managed to get her out of there unscathed. But she seems..." I had to search for the right word. "Grim. Like she's waiting for me to change my mind and shoot her." I scanned the gas station's windows again. Katia was just shuffling her way to the cash register.

"If you do," Lily advised, "aim for the head. I heard boundary witches are *super* hard to kill."

I made a face, which she couldn't see. "That's not funny."

"It's a little funny," Lily said. Then, in a careful voice, "Are you treating her like a hostage?"

"What? No!" At least, I didn't think I was. "I guess the problem is that I don't know *how* to treat her. I mean, she's related to me...but she's also a witch who's done bad things. It's weird."

This time Lily's laugh was wry and a little bitter. "Welcome to my world."

I winced, thinking of Lily's older sister Morgan, who had been responsible for a number of deaths a couple of years earlier. "Sorry, Lil."

"It's okay. Just..." Lily sounded uncharacteristically cautious all of sudden. "Have you thought about what you're going to do with her when you get back here?"

I glanced up and saw Katia making her way through the exit door

94

with a bottle of water cradled in one elbow. I wished I'd thought to pull up to the door so she didn't have to walk so far. "She can barely walk. I don't think we're going to go rock-climbing."

"Yeah, but eventually she's going to get better," Lily pointed out. "Then what's she going to do?"

"I don't know. Whatever she wants, I guess."

Lily sighed into the phone. "Lex. You must know by now that it's more complicated than that. Colorado has a cardinal vampire. Who is also your boss."

Katia reached the vehicle, finally. She looked pale and exhausted, but a little triumphant—it was the farthest she'd walked by herself without help.

"I'm aware," I said to Lily. My voice came out chillier than I'd intended.

Over the hood, Katia gave me a questioning look. I waved a hand to say that everything was fine. "Listen, I have to go. We need to get back on the road."

"Call me when you get home, okay?" Lily sounded a little worried, and I regretted how sharp I'd been.

"I will. Promise."

After I'd hung up, I opened the driver's door long enough to tell Katia I was going to go use the bathroom, too, and I went into the gas station on autopilot.

Lily was right, of course. Over the last week, I had pictured moving Katia's things into my spare bedroom, helping her get settled, introducing her to my various rescue animals. I'd envisioned all the steps required to get her from injured in LA to healthy in Boulder. But…then what? What was I supposed to do with her?

I bought water and some pretzels on my way out, and climbed back into the silent vehicle. Katia was already wedged in her safety position against the door. I opened my mouth to ask if she needed anything, but shut it again. I was only making a pest of myself. So I started the car and got us back on the road.

Chapter 2

When you're an adopted child, there's a tiny little window in your mind that you can't help but leave open for long-lost family. Sam and I'd had a very happy childhood, and we'd always known that our birth mother, Valerya, had died in labor. But as kids we did sometimes talk about what it would be like to meet our father, or find a long-lost brother or cousin. Our Luther family was huge and loving and satisfying in every way. But there was always that tiny little window of *what if*. What if someone came for us?

And then, a year and a half after Sam's death, someone did: our half-brother Emil, and our birth father Lysander, who was a monster— literally. And hey, I killed him too, and spent two months scattering his remains across the globe and killing the people who'd helped him. Long story. Also very satisfying.

Anyway, after that, I had figured that was it for biological family, and the little window in my mind had finally closed. I moved on with my life, my real family, and my relationship with a vampire named Quinn. If anything, I tried *not* to think about my evil bloodlines.

Valerya isn't evil, babe, came Sam's voice again. She had some sort of communication with our birth mother, though she wasn't allowed to explain much to me. *She's not like Lysander, or even Sophia.*

Usually I spoke out loud to answer Sam, but I couldn't exactly have this conversation in front of Katia. *Yeah,* I thought back, *but what about her sister?*

No answer. Typical. Sam and I may have had a link, but she had a lot of limitations in what she was allowed to tell me. Although I wasn't sure when she was being quiet because of restrictions, and when she was just enjoying being dramatic. With Sam, I could see it going either way.

Four interminable hours after we left Visalia, we reached the outskirts of Sacramento. The sun was beginning to sink, and I finally broke the silence. "What do you think about stopping at a hotel for the night?" I asked.

Katia turned her head and looked at me with surprise. It was only five p.m., and just three more hours to Reno. "Are you tired?" she asked.

"No...."

"Then why don't you want to drive on?"

Her frankness was a little disconcerting, but at least I could tell her the truth. "Uh...driving at night is kind of hard for me," I admitted.

"Ah." Katia gave me a knowing look. "You see the remnants, yes?"

That got my attention. I wasn't used to people understanding boundary magic. I glanced over at her. "Yes. I can drive if I have to, but it's really distracting. I worry about crashing." I hesitated for a second—should I leave it there?—but then added, "Don't you? See them, I mean?"

She gave a little shrug. "I see...mmm...something shining in the air, like dust moving through sunshine. But I would have to do a special ritual to view them properly, and I choose to ignore them."

"Huh."

Katia paused for a moment, as if hesitant to give up a closely guarded prize. Then she added, "Valerya saw them."

"My...mother." I found myself testing out the phrase. I *had* a mother, a wonderful, living mother who had called me the night before to find out if I could come to dinner on Sunday. Discussing Valerya felt like a betrayal. At the same time...I was curious. I knew so little about our birth mother. I had one picture of her, and I'd briefly heard her voice two times, when there was an emergency and she'd managed to speak to me the same way Sam did. But it wasn't nearly enough.

"Yes." Katia gently touched the bandage under her shirt. "I could probably use some rest in a real bed," she conceded, not looking at me.

"Thanks." The next words were out of my mouth before I could consider them. "What was Valerya like?" I knew hardly anything about her.

Katia stared straight out the windshield again, but I could see her putting together what she wanted to say. "She was…cautious. Reserved." She gave me a sidelong glance. "You know how we must become boundary witches, I assume."

I nodded. "We have to die. When we're teenagers."

"Which is partly why there are so few of us. Most parents refuse to intentionally put their children through that." Her voice was matter-of-fact, although she pronounced "intentionally" very carefully. English hadn't been Katia's first language, although I couldn't detect an accent. She must have worked to lose it.

"But your parents…?" I prompted.

"Did not refuse." She still sounded businesslike, but there was an edge of bitterness to her words. "I was only four when they killed Valerya— I didn't even realize at the time what was happening, just that afterward, there was a new distance between them and her. I put it together later, after...my turn."

I knew that part of the story, because Katia had told Scarlett, who had told me. Oskar had found Katia as a young teen and arranged for her to be killed. Then he allowed her to believe he had saved her life, and she owed him service.

Eager to change the subject, for Katia's sake, I asked, "Was Valerya reserved with you, too?"

A rare smile lit her face. "No. With me she was…fun. Not silly or chatty, but she would draw and make daisy chains and turn cartwheels. She told me once she wanted to be a teacher."

That was the most Katia had ever said to me in one conversation. Her voice had softened as she spoke, and when I glanced over at her there was a tiny, private smile on her face.

Then her head swiveled to stare out the window again, and I knew the conversation was over.

I called ahead and got us a reservation at the newest hotel in town, a Best Western. Hotels often had their own resident ghosts, and I'd learned to always stay at the most recently built one I could find. When we parked in the hotel lot—I already had my hand on the door handle to climb out—Katia spoke again, still staring through the windshield.

"Lex…"

I went still, surprised by the softness in her voice. "Yeah?"

"What will happen to me, in Colorado?"

My empty stomach churned with nerves. "Um, what do you mean?"

She turned to look at me, and in the light from the parking lot lamps I could see worry etched on her face. "Your boss, this vampire, she made a deal for my life. But what does she plan to do with it?"

"I don't think she has any particular plans for you," I said truthfully. "None of us really expected…" I waved a hand between us. "This. You're an outclan witch, so you'll have to swear an oath of loyalty to Maven, but you don't have to work for her. We can find you a job somewhere else." That might actually be the easiest part— between my human family, my old convenience store job, and Maven's coffee shop, I wasn't too worried about finding Katia work when she was physically up to it.

My aunt shifted uncomfortably in her seat, but made no move toward the door. I longed to go inside the brightly lit hotel and stretch my legs after the long drive, but I also didn't want to break the spell of Katia actually speaking to me. "What is this oath?" she asked warily.

"Well, vampires swear troth, an oath of loyalty, to their superiors. Everyone in Colorado has either sworn loyalty to Maven, or is loyal to someone else who's loyal to Maven. Like a…" Again, I struggled for the right words. "A family tree of allegiance, I guess. It's required because it keeps Maven safe, and that keeps us all safe."

There was a long silence. The parking lot lights were dim, and

Katia already had the greatest poker face of any non-vampire I'd ever met, so I couldn't gauge her reaction. "Thank you for explaining," she said finally. Her face closed down again, and I knew there was no point pushing her to discuss it further. She would just shake her head at me.

I went in and got our room key, and then came back out to grab the duffel bag and help Katia walk in. I'd asked for a room on the first floor, and Katia managed to shuffle the whole way there by holding onto the luggage cart I pulled along. We probably made a strange processional, but nobody gave us a second look. That's another reason why I like to stay in big chain hotels—people treasure their anonymity.

When we reached the room, Katia immediately collapsed onto the queen bed closest to the door. I opened my mouth to ask her to trade, so I would be closer to the door if there was an attack, but stopped myself. Lily's question—*are you treating her like a prisoner?*—was still echoing in my thoughts. Asking her to move would sound like I didn't trust Katia not to run away in the night. Besides, I thought as she limply scooted herself onto the pillow, she didn't look like she could make it another four feet to the other bed. She was very pale from the long walk, and even panting a little.

"Do you want the Vicodin?" I asked her, trying not to sound anxious.

Katia shook her head. "Just…some ibuprofen, please."

I got the pills and a bottle of water out of the duffel bag, and helped Katia get comfortable and medicated. By the time she was settled, her eyelids were sagging. I stood over her for a moment, trying not to loom threateningly. "I'm sorry to keep asking this, but is there anything else I can get you?"

"Right now…I will rest." Her eyes were closed, and in less than a minute her breathing was slow and heavy.

I worried at my lower lip for a minute, thinking, but I didn't see how anyone could attack us. The room was paid for with a dummy credit card from Maven, and I'd picked a hotel at the last minute. Besides, I was dying to get some exercise.

I was already wearing workout-friendly clothes, so I went over to the generic hotel desk and scribbled on a piece of paper. *Gone to the exercise room, will bring back some food.* I left the note on bedside table right next to Katia, along with the remote control, a bottle of water, and the burner phone she had been using to make her calls.

I dumped out my backpack and threw in my own cell phone, wallet, room key, and the Glock Jesse Cruz had lent me, just in case. I pulled the straps over my shoulders and made my escape.

Chapter 3

The hotel's exercise room was small, but deserted. I ran on the treadmill for a full hour, enjoying the chance to finally stretch out and *move*. I'd done some push-ups and planks in the living room of the safe house—out of desperation, I'd even resorted to a few of Lily's yoga moves—but this was the first time in a week I'd gotten any real physical activity. I pushed myself harder than I normally would, and was panting and red-faced by the time I hopped off the machine and headed for the weight bench. I would have loved to do a full-body workout, but I didn't want to be away from Katia for that long. I did a few quick compound lifts and left the room sweaty—and feeling more like myself than I had since I'd left Boulder.

There was a sandwich place on the same block as the hotel, so I walked over and bought a couple of subs for Katia and myself. On the way back I noticed a remnant in the middle of the street: an old man clutching at his heart. I could have laid him to rest, but instead I averted my gaze. He was very faint, and I figured he'd be fading away on his own before too long.

As I reached the hotel room, shifting the bag of sandwiches to my right hand so I could dig the room key out of my pocket, I heard Katia's voice coming through the door. This wasn't surprising—she'd been on the phone every night since we'd met—but her tone gave me pause. I couldn't make out the exact words, but she was practically snarling.

For one terrible moment, I thought she might be under attack.

Quietly, I set down the bag of sandwiches and took one arm out of the backpack strap, swinging it around to reach for my sidearm. I kept my hand on it but didn't draw it out—the hotel had security cameras in the halls. Then I pressed my ear against the door.

"—picking up where he left off!" There was a pause, and then: "Yeah, well, you know where to find me, you parasitic harpy *bitch*."

The room went silent. Not an attack, then—she was on the phone. I'd only known Katia for just over a week, but I'd never heard her use that tone...or any curse words at all.

I stood there for a long moment, frozen with indecision. Should I confront her about it? It could have been a conversation about placing one of the female vampires that had just gone wrong—maybe Katia was just upset because someone said no?

But why would she say "You know where to find me?"

"Sammy?" I muttered under my breath. "Any suggestions here?"

But there was no advice from my sister. Of course. Not for the first time, I wished the psychic dead twin thing was something I could control, even a little bit.

Re-zipping the backpack, I picked up the bag of sandwiches and tapped the key card against the door lock, pushing it open.

Katia was sitting propped up in the bed, turning the burner phone over in her hands. "You're awake," I said mildly.

Her dull eyes rose to look at me. "Yes. I was making calls again." Her voice was weary.

I hovered in the doorway, undecided. If she had been pretending to sleep as I walked in, I would have confronted her, but as I stood there holding the food the only thing I could think of was how thin she looked. Thin, and just...lifeless. She still had the poker expression, but her reddish-brown hair hung on her shoulders in greasy chunks—she could take a bath alone, but washing her hair would require someone else to help, and she didn't want me to do that.

Most of all, she just didn't look like someone I needed to be afraid of. I made my decision. "I got you a sandwich," I said, taking off the backpack and stepping forward into the room.

After we ate, I took a shower and turned on the television, flipping channels while I looked for something that was equally entertaining and inoffensive. I settled on a PG-rated movie about an underdog sports team that manages to win it all with the help of an inspirational new coach. I had no idea what Katia thought of it, but she stayed awake for the entire thing, and she waited until a commercial break to use the bathroom, so I figured that was a good sign.

When the movie ended at ten, I turned the television off and rolled on my side so I could look at her. "Do you need to make more calls tonight?" I asked.

Katia shook her head. "I have done as much as I could," she said wearily. "I think I would like my pain pill now."

That surprised me—Katia had never gone to sleep before four a.m. or so—but she *had* stayed awake most of the day. I retrieved the Vicodin from the duffel bag, along with a bottle of water. Katia took the pills and settled into her bed, closing her eyes.

I wasn't tired enough to sleep yet, so I turned on my bedside lamp and opened one of the books Jesse had brought me. I read until I got tired, a little after midnight. I made one more trip to the bathroom, checking on Katia's even breathing, and then headed for bed myself.

When I'm lucky, I have the sort of tangled, subconscious-in-a-blender dreams that seem standard for most people—or I have magical visits with my dead twin sister in the bedroom we shared in high school. Boundary witchblood is weird.

The rest of the time, though, I have recurring nightmares about my time in the Army—specifically the last day I remember clearly, when my Humvee was blown up by an IED. And I usually wake up screaming.

That night, the nightmare began where it always did: with us getting our orders to patrol the supply route in advance of a shipment. It was only mid-morning, but we were already sweating through our uniforms, and the oppressive sunshine made it difficult to see without squinting. The air was heavy with familiar smells: body odor, sand, fuel, and the faint stink of rot, which came off the nearby ditches. One of the sewers was spilling into the ditch water, and we could often hear buzzing flies underneath the voices of soldiers and the rumble of heavy machinery.

I knew, as I always did, that I was back in the dream, but despite my sickening dread, I was unable to open my mouth and warn the others. It was almost like being a remnant, but in reverse: I was conscious, while the scene around me was on repeat. I was aware of exactly what was going to happen: we would climb into the Humvee and drive about fifteen miles down the road, where we would hit the IED. I would be hit by shrapnel in my upper back and legs. Cisco would die in the first explosion. Meyers and Randolph were able to crawl out before they were shot in the head.

Then the bad guys would come for me.

As the others climbed into the truck, laughing and joking, I wanted more than anything to scream my warning at them, but as usual, I was a prisoner in my body, inside this memory. All I could do was open my door and shift my weight to climb into the Humvee, as I had in real life.

This time, though, something different happened.

Suddenly I found that I could move my body autonomously, and my foot fell back down to the ground, sending a shock into my ankle. "What the hell?" I muttered, then stood there for a second blinking in surprise, because I'd spoken out loud. I wasn't supposed to be able to do that.

I ducked my head and looked inside the Humvee. Cisco, Meyers, and Randolph were all frozen in mid-conversation. I jerked myself back out and looked around, turning in a slow circle. The entire scene, the whole 360 degree memory, had abruptly gone still and silent. Even the flies.

"*Allie!*" a familiar voice yelled.

I had to step away from the Humvee to locate the source: Sam, standing right in front of my truck, squinting against the sun. My sister didn't look much like me: she had a smaller frame, a brunette pixie cut, and resembled Valerya more than I did. But it was still Sam, with her feet planted inside my nightmare.

"Sammy?" I trotted around the corner of the vehicle, quickly closing the distance between us. "What's going on? You've never—"

"There's no time," she said breathlessly. "You've got to wake up."

The horizon seemed to lurch. "Charlie?"

"No. Katia."

I relaxed. "She's fine; I just saw her—"

"No!" Sam was starting to look frantic. "She's gone on to Reno to die. You have to stop her!"

"*What*—"

And I came awake in the dark hotel room.

Chapter 4

When I opened my eyes, the first thing I saw was the digital clock: 1:30 a.m. Throwing off the covers, I felt around for the switch and flicked on my bedside lamp, half-convinced that Sam was full of shit— or that she hadn't actually been in my dream, but was my subconscious finding an exciting new way to fuck with my head.

But Katia's bed was empty.

Still not fully awake, I jolted unsteadily to the bathroom, which was empty too.

My next thought was the Glock. I do not keep a gun under my pillow, because people who get PTSD nightmares should not be armed. So I hurried toward my backpack, which I'd left on the desk. When I unzipped the main compartment, nearly pinching my fingers in my haste, I found the sidearm and the handful of shredders, right where I'd left them.

Katia had known I was armed, and had chosen not to take them. I moved the weapons aside and checked the money in the envelope: nearly fifteen hundred dollars. She had taken a single hundred-dollar bill, probably for gas.

By then I knew she was gone, but I still went through the motions of going over to her bed and yanking back the covers, just in case there was a note, like maybe she'd gone to the lobby for coffee. I even picked up her pillow—and found two tiny white pills with pink speckles. The Vicodin.

"Fuck!" I said out loud. Katia had palmed the painkillers, which meant that whatever she was doing, she'd been planning it since 10 p.m. She had played me.

She's gone on to Reno to die.

I believed Sam, but I still didn't understand. Driving three more hours to commit suicide made no sense—why go so far? Hell, there was a gun *right here*, and even a boundary witch couldn't survive the right bullet wound. For that matter, why would she decide to kill herself now, after going through eight days of painful healing?

I tried to think of the last words we'd spoken. She'd asked me for her pills, she'd talked to someone on the phone, sounding pissy, and before that...

Maven. I'd told her she would have to swear an oath of loyalty to Maven.

"Lex, you oblivious fucking idiot," I said out loud.

I grabbed my cell phone where it was charging on the desk and dialed the number for the burner phone, which I'd thankfully remembered to program in before we'd left LA. It rang for awhile, and then I got a "the user has not set up a voice mailbox" message.

I had to go after her. I grabbed my jacket off the back of the chair and swung it on, but the familiar weight was missing from the left pocket. I stuck my hand in the pocket anyway, and came out with a receipt from the sandwich shop and nothing else. No keys.

She'd taken the car.

Cursing some more, I threw the few belongings I'd removed back into the duffel bag and tossed the receipt in the trash on my way to the door—but then I skidded to a stop. Dropping the duffel, I backtracked to the garbage can and picked it up. There was a a shiny black object inside: Katia's burner phone, with the battery and SIM card removed. It didn't have a protective case, and it looked like she'd bent it until the screen spiderwebbed.

Shit. I felt a wave of real fear. More than anything, it scared me that she'd left it right there in the trash, making no effort to cover her tracks. She didn't care if I knew what she'd done.

Scooping up the duffel bag and backpack, I yanked open the hotel room door, practically flying down the hall to the front desk—but no one was there. "Hello?" I called toward the open door behind the desk. "Anybody there?" I rang the obnoxiously loud metal bell on the counter.

"What? Yeah, sorry." A young woman in her early twenties came through the doorway with bleary eyes and just a little stumble. Her name tag said June.

"Did you see a woman come by here?" I demanded.

"Uh…"

"About my size, same hair color, long-sleeved shirt and yoga pants?"

"Um, I'm not sure. I was working in the back."

"Working or sleeping?"

She flinched, which gave me my answer. "Ma'am, is there some kind of problem?"

"Yes!" I heard how harsh that sounded and tried to force myself to calm down. "My aunt sleepwalks, and she's not in the room. Did you see her go by here recently?"

"I didn't see her, no."

"Can you check the security cameras?"

June looked uncomfortable. "We'd have to stop recording to check the current memory card, and I'm not authorized without a manager present."

"Where's the manager?"

She checked her watch. "He comes on at four."

"Fuck!" I turned and walked away from the counter before I started screaming at the dumb kid. I counted to ten, trying to calm my breathing. In a low voice, I muttered, "Sammy? You there?"

Silence. It might have been my imagination, but when I concentrated and sort of extended my senses, it felt…empty.

Sam talked to me in my head nearly every day since she'd died, but for the first time, I wondered if she burned through energy to do it, the same way I burned through energy using boundary magic. Was it possible that interrupting my Iraq dream had cost her too much juice? Did she have to rest and regain her strength now, like living witches did after using magic?

It seemed possible, but it wasn't really going to impact my current situation. I was on my own—and need a ride, *now*. Which was a problem. I had plenty of resources in Colorado and Los Angeles, and a few human friends scattered around the country, but I didn't know a soul in Sacramento.

I turned around and looked across the lobby at the desk, sizing up the young woman on duty. June was probably in her early twenties, with green streaks in her hair and a discreet stud in her nose. And she was about the only option I had at the moment.

I went back to the desk and tried for a contrite smile. Judging by June's recoil, I didn't pull it off. "I'm sorry I was short before, June," I said, careful to speak slowly. "I'm just worried about my aunt."

"I can't access the video feed," June said nervously. "I mean I literally can't; I don't have the code."

I held up a hand. "That's okay. But what I really need right now is a ride."

June perked up at the mention of something within her expertise. "Do you want me to call a taxi for you?"

"Nope." I stepped closer to the counter and leaned forward, lowering my voice. "I want to know if you have any friends who would like to make some money."

June swallowed hard. "Ex- excuse me?"

"I need a ride to Reno, right now, to catch up with her. I've got a thousand dollars for anyone who can take me there." I met her eyes directly, so she'd know I was serious.

The young woman looked at me for a long moment, and I wondered if I'd made a mistake. Then she tilted her head to the right, toward where the counter ended, and began walking along the counter parallel to me. She came out from it, crossing the hallway to a particular spot against the wall. I glanced around and realized it was a blind spot with the security cameras.

"Are you serious?" June intoned, crossing her arms over her chest. "A thousand dollars for a ride to Reno?"

In answer, I shifted my backpack around and fished out the envelope. Holding it so June wouldn't see its contents, I counted out five hundred-dollar bills and held them up, stuffing the rest of the money in the bag again. "Five hundred now, five hundred when we get there. It's a real offer."

I extended the hand with the money, and June looked at it for a long moment with something like hunger. She knew my sleepwalking story was bullshit, but I was hoping it wouldn't matter. I lived in a college town; I knew how badly twenty-year-olds were in need of cash.

Then her eyes finally returned to mine. "Let me make a call."

Chapter 5

Twenty-two minutes later, I was tossing my duffel bag, backpack, and jacket into the backseat of a 2010 PT Cruiser and climbing in after them. A hasty effort had been made to clear off the space, but crumbs and fragments of french fries were still embedded in the woven blanket over the seat, and there was a powerful smell of cannabis and pizza. I couldn't have cared less.

The driver was a white kid with bloodshot eyes and greasy brown hair, who drummed his fingers on the steering wheel. He was around June's age, early twenties, and when I got in he half-turned in his seat and introduced himself as Stevie. "Need to get to Reno in a hurry, huh?" he said cheerfully.

"Let me stop you right there," I said as I buckled my seatbelt. On the floor behind the driver's seat I saw a discarded trucker-style hat with the name of a nearby pizza chain, which explained at least half of the smell. "If you want the money, I need discretion—and peace. No questions, no small talk, no bragging about this later. It's just going to be another weird thing you did one night, no biggie. Got it?"

He thought about that for a second. "No offense, but how do you know I won't, like, leave you in the middle of the desert somewhere?"

"Because you won't get the other $500. More importantly, if you try, I'll use that steering wheel to knock your teeth into your stomach."

Okay, that was a little crude. I was really tired, okay?

Stevie turned in the seat to look at me, his eyes widening. We regarded each other for a moment, and I saw him glance down at the muscles in my arms and shoulders.

"Yes, ma'am." He turned around to face forward, put on his blinker, and pulled onto the street. "No chitchat."

"In fact," I said, "do you have headphones?"

"Yeah, but it's illegal to wear 'em while you drive."

I held an extra hundred-dollar bill between the two bucket seats. "How committed are you to that particular law, Stevie?"

He took the money.

I told him I didn't have an exact address yet, but I would before we got anywhere near Reno, and after that Stevie put in his earbuds and started listening to something that was probably supposed to be music but sounded like it had been made exclusively by computers. Even through the earbuds, it was loud enough to carry into the backseat, which was all I cared about.

I waited until we were on a major highway, heading east, and then I dug my phone out of my pocket.

The problem was, I had no idea who to call. If Katia was going all the way back to Reno to kill herself, there could only be one place she was going: the brothel. But I didn't know the location, and I didn't know how to reach anyone who would. She had smashed up the burner phone with all the phone numbers of the people she'd been contacting that week, so I couldn't call one of Oskar's vampire victims. As far as I knew, Maven didn't have any contacts in Nevada, and even if she did, I didn't want to use her name or make her ask for favors for me. Maven was already a little nervous about bringing a second boundary witch into Colorado; if I started throwing her name around, it was possible she would decide Katia was too much trouble and cut her loose.

I idly scrolled through my contacts, trying to think. Then, feeling like a complete idiot, I realized that *I* had a contact in Nevada: my friend Sashi, who was a healing witch in Las Vegas. I checked my watch: two a.m. She'd be working, but she usually answered if she could. I hit the phone icon.

It rang four times, and then connected. "Hello?" Sashi yelled. In the background I could hear the kaleidoscopic ringing and jingling of slot machines. "Lex?"

"Hey, I need a favor. Can you talk?"

"Let me call you back in…eight minutes."

The line went quiet as she disconnected, and I spent a few anxious moments jiggling my knee up and down while I looked out the window. I could feel Stevie giving me the occasional glance in the rearview mirror, but he didn't comment. He was smarter than I'd thought.

Sashi called back ten minutes later. "All right, I'm back in the car," she said breathlessly. "I was just finishing up with a client."

"Hangover?" I knew they made up the majority of her work.

She snorted. "*Four* hangovers. Him, his girlfriend, and their bodyguards. What's the favor?"

"I know you're outclan," I began, "but do you know much about the witches in power in Nevada?"

There was a long silence, and I winced. Sashi tried to stay the hell away from Old World politics, and I was basically asking her to dive back in. "I know," I added preemptively, "and I wouldn't ask if it wasn't an emergency. My information is that Reno is a witch town; I'm trying to find the clan leader."

Oskar, Katia had testified, moved around every decade or so with his stable of lost girls, and he usually set up shop in cities that had weak leadership—which often meant witch leadership. As long as Oskar left them alone, most witch clans would ignore a single vampire business in their town, rather than start a fight that other vampires might come along and finish. He had been in Reno for nine years, which meant the locals had to at least be aware of him. It was the only way I could think of to find the brothel quickly, and without using vampire channels. If I pulled one of those threads, it would inevitably get back to Maven.

Sashi sighed. "I don't know offhand, no. The witches here in Vegas hate me, but I do know a couple of them. I can make some calls."

"What's it going to cost you?" I asked.

"Oh, probably just some posturing and drama. Possibly a favor in the future. They might hate me, but most of them have human friends and family."

"Can you get me a name and a number?" I heard the slight begging sound in my voice—and so did Sashi.

"Can you give me an hour?"

I checked my watch. It was still only a little after two, which probably wasn't going to endear Sashi to any of the witches. "Yes, but I'm afraid not much more than that."

"Right. Call you back."

While I waited to hear back from Sashi, I debated whether or not I should call Quinn and tell him what was going on. Part of me desperately wanted to talk to him—because that's kind of what you do with the person you love, when there's a crisis.

But if this escalated in any way, Quinn would probably need to tell Maven. Even if it didn't escalate, he would have to tell her if she asked him a question about Katia…which brought me right back to Maven not liking me bringing Katia into her state.

I tried calling Lily instead, figuring she could give me advice on dealing with the Reno witch clan, but she didn't answer. It was the middle of the night, and she had been seeing a schoolteacher from Lafayette for the last few weeks.

Feeling a little guilty about waking him, I called Simon.

Simon Pellar was the fixer for his witch clan, which meant he always answered the phone. He picked up on the third ring. "Lex?" His voice was thick with sleep. "What's going on?"

"You don't happen to know what witch clan is in charge of Reno, do you?" I asked.

To Simon's credit, he only took about five seconds to respond. "No, sorry. What's going on?"

"Worth a shot. Um, listen, it would probably be better if I don't fill you in on what's going on, but if you don't hear from me by the morning, call Sashi, okay?"

There was a long pause. Lily or Quinn would have demanded to know what was going on—Quinn out of worry, Lily out of eager curiosity—but Simon and I had a different relationship. "I'm gonna write that down on this post-it note by my bed," Simon said finally. "So I don't wake up and think this was a dream."

"Thanks, Si. Talk to you soon."

Chapter 6

Sashi called back forty minutes later with a report. "Reno and surrounding is the territory of Clan Reine," she said, without any preamble. "Sara Reine is the current clan leader. She's apparently a bit…eccentric."

I had to raise an eyebrow at that. I knew a lot of witches, and it was hard to imagine what might qualify as eccentric for one of them. "How so?"

"She's quite young for a clan leader, and according to my *very* disapproving source, her interests include bladed weapons, medicinal cannabis, and therapeutic massage," Sashi said, sounding a little amused. "The general complaint is that she's unpredictable."

"Hmm. Do you have contact information?"

"I have a phone number and a link to her Facebook page."

"Her…Facebook page?"

"Yes, for her business: she's a freelance photographer. I'll text you."

"Thanks, Sashi," I said, trying to sound as sincere as I felt. "Really. I can't tell you how much this helps."

"Will you call me tomorrow and let me know what's going on?"

I promised to do so, and we hung up. Sashi's text came through a second later. I clicked on the Facebook link first and studied the photo at the top. Sara Reine was indeed young, maybe in her mid- to late twenties, with a cheerful grin, fashionable glasses, and magenta hair.

She wore a black tank top and cutoffs, and had an actual black cat draped over one shoulder.

I wasn't sure what to make of that, so I just called the phone number, readying my apology for waking her.

"Hello?" The voice was wide awake, speaking a little loudly to be heard over what sounded like the Moulin Rouge soundtrack.

"Sara Reine?"

"Yes, who's this?"

I blew out a breath, wishing I'd prepared something beyond "sorry for waking you."

"My name is Lex. I'm calling about a man named Oskar who used to work out of Reno."

There was a short pause. The music was turned off, and there was some rustling. When she came back on the line, Reine's voice was wary. "My understanding was that Oskar is no longer among the un-living."

"He's dead, yes. But my aunt was one of the women working for him. I'm trying to find her, and I need the location of the…business. I was hoping you could help."

"Your *aunt* is one of Oskar's…workers?" she said skeptically, and I realized my mistake. She thought I meant that Katia was a vampire, and vampires were always cut off from their families.

At the same time, if I explained that Katia was a boundary witch, Reine might hang up on me—or head to the brothel to shoot Katia herself. In my experience, trades witches hated boundary witches. To be fair, boundary witches had historically been responsible for some pretty despicable things.

But I didn't have a lot of options here, and it seemed like Sara Reine was known for having a unique perspective. So I took a chance. "Her name is Katia," I said simply. "She's a witch."

"Huh." There was another pause, probably Reine thinking it through. While I waited, I checked to make sure I could still hear Stevie's "music." It was coming through loud and clear.

"I met Katia a couple of times," Sara Reine said finally. "She was okay. Kind of shut off, but it seemed like she wanted to be there about as much as any of the other girls."

"That's about right."

"But my people were just out at the site yesterday," she went on, "making sure nobody was sticking around to keep the business going. It's totally deserted."

"This is all happening tonight, right now," I explained. "Look, I can't get into it on the phone, but Katia's in trouble, and I think she went back there. I need to find her before she gets hurt."

"Who would hurt her?" Now Reine sounded suspicious, like maybe I'd planned a secret war in her territory. Shit. Why was I so bad at subterfuge?

Fuck it. "Herself."

"Ah. You know, normally this is where I'd call around and get your credentials, figure out if you are who you say you are—"

"We can do that, if you want. It's just that I don't have much time."

"But," Reine went on, as though I hadn't interrupted, "I s'pose I don't really care who knows the location of an abandoned brothel, you know what I mean?"

I slumped against the seat. "Yes. Thank you."

"This your cell phone?"

"Yes."

"I'll text you the GPS coordinates, that'll be easiest. Then I'd appreciate it if you'd lose this number…unless you need something through the official channels."

"Understood."

According to my phone, Reno bumped up against a national forest, Humboldt-Toiyabe. The GPS coordinates Sara had given me were located right on the edge of the forest, at the mouth of a canyon—or maybe a gorge; I could never remember the difference. At any rate, there was a lot of flat, rocky ground that eventually elevated into mountains, and the brothel was tucked in a sort of depression at the bottom of them.

Following Sara's instructions, I guided a nervous Stevie along a dirt road surrounded by a whole lot of dark nothing. Finally, a couple hundred yards before we reached the GPS coordinates, I spotted some bright streetlights up ahead, almost like a community park, and realized it was our destination—they'd probably rigged up lights so the johns could see. I told Stevie to stop the car there, and thrust the rest of the money between the seats.

"You sure?" he asked, looking at the oasis of light with some trepidation. "I can take you the whole way."

"This is fine." I didn't really care if he knew the location of an abandoned brothel, but I had no idea what kind of shape Katia was in. It seemed pretty good odds that someone was going to use magic, and I didn't have any vampires around to erase memories. "Take care, Stevie."

I grabbed my duffel bag and backpack and took off at a sprint, not bothering to watch the kid drive away. The duffel bag bounced uncomfortably against my thigh as I tried to run, so I abandoned it near the road. It contained only clothes and toiletries; I could come back for it later.

The nearly-full moon peeked out from behind the clouds just then, lighting my path, but I still stayed on the asphalt, having no idea what kind of wildlife lived in this part of Nevada. The last thing I needed was to be bitten by a snake on top of everything else. I fell into an even rhythm, my breath fogging as I ran. It was colder than I'd expected, in the upper thirties maybe, and I was sort of glad to be running.

As I got closer, I could see that the brothel complex—because that's what it was, an improvised complex—was on a patch of rocky land surrounded by a ten-foot-high chain-link fence with razor wire at the top. Inside the fence, laid out on the flat desert sand, there was a main building the size and shape of a modest single-family house, with my rental car parked in front of it. Behind the building, eight smaller buildings were set out in a semi-circle—probably where the johns had gone with the girls. As I got closer, I figured the little structures had probably been the more expensive variety of those pre-made sheds you saw at big box stores, but it was hard to tell now.

Because every single one of them was on fire.

"Katia!" I screamed as I finally reached the main building. I raced around the side to the back—and found her sitting on a massive decorative boulder, next to a bunch of empty gas containers, watching the flames.

I guessed she *had* used that hundred dollars for gas.

Her legs were splayed out in front of her, arms braced against the rock so she wouldn't fall off it. I could see her panting from exertion, and I felt an overwhelming surge of relief. She was alive.

"Katia!" I yelled again, and she whipped her head around with a look of panic. I could see that her breath was coming in shallow pants, and she looked as pale and weak as she had when I'd first arrived in Los Angeles.

As I ran to her, she started to stand up, but couldn't do it. "You can't be here," she said, her eyes huge. "You have to go, now. Please."

"Are you fucking *kidding* me?!"

"Please, Lex, you must go," Katia begged, and I realized there were tears in her eyes. The smoke? "Just leave me here, and run." She did stand, then, giving me a weak little push. "It's fine, everything is fine, just go."

The shed that was closest to us let out a loud crack as the fire finished chewing through something big. I'd never thought of fires as being loud, but there were eight of them, and the snapping and popping, plus the groans of warping metal, was noisy in surround-sound. "I'm not going anywhere without you," I told my aunt. "Look, if you want to burn down this last building, fine, I'm in. But then we need to get you to a bed." Katia swayed a little on her feet, and I added, "Or maybe a hospital."

She was shaking her head. "You go. Take the car. You can come back for me in the morning."

Do not *leave her there.*

"Yeah, thanks, Sammy, I got it," I muttered, planting my feet. Apparently Sam had regained enough juice to state the completely obvious.

To Katia, I said, "You're not listening! I'm not going anywhere unless you're coming, too. And you are weak as shit. Please don't make me pick you up. It will embarrass us both."

Katia's face crumpled, but her voice was strong as she yelled back, "*You're* not listening! You have to go, *right now*, before you get hurt!"

I glanced toward the fires. They were loud and hot—it was not even forty degrees out and I was sweating in my mid-weight jacket. But each one was isolated, and the ground all around them was basically dirt. Already, the flames were beginning to die down on the far right shed, where Katia had probably started.

Turning back to her, I crossed my arms over my chest. "Those fires aren't going to hurt me, Katia."

"No," called a voice over my shoulder. "But we will."

Chapter 7

I spun around, using the turn to pull one arm out of my backpack strap so the main compartment would swing down toward my body.

Four women wearing mirrored sunglasses stood at the corner of the main building, the firelight dancing over them. They were all beautiful, dressed in expensive clothing, with a certain look of haughty, detached power that I recognized immediately. Vampires. That, or supermodels, but I was playing the odds here.

"Who are you?" I called to the one who had spoken, a redhead with Slavic cheekbones.

She stalked toward me slowly, like a predator, and I used my left hand to fumble at the backpack's zipper. "Natasha," she snarled.

"What's with the shades?"

I couldn't see her eyes through the sunglasses, but her head turned toward Katia, ignoring me. "Hello, den mother. So nice of you to call."

I didn't want to turn my back on them, but I swiveled my head just enough to look at my aunt. "You called them?"

A moment ago she'd been pale and swaying, but now she stood tall, obviously putting all her energy into looking unhurt. "Yes. These are Oskar's *old* whores, from the last batch."

She had never used the word "whores" before, ever, and I stared at her in confusion until I realized that behind Natasha, the other three women were spreading out, starting to flank us. Shit. I backed a step closer to Katia.

"Apparently," Natasha said, "Katia here has decided to pick up where Alonzo and Oskar left off. She had the gall to call me and offer to make me an *investor*."

I couldn't help it—I let out a short, snorting laugh. "No, she didn't."

"Yes, I did," Katia said, stepping up beside me. She flicked her fingers at me, her expression suddenly bored. "This woman knows nothing. She simply gave me a ride out here when my own car broke down."

I stared at her for a moment with my mouth open. *She's gone on to Reno to die.* Katia wasn't going to kill *herself.* She was going to let these

124

women do it.

And there was no way in hell I could take four vampires alone. Even *two* was unlikely.

"Katia—" I started, but my aunt cut me off.

Her eyes bored into mine as she said with slow, exacting pronunciation, "You can walk away now. This is not your problem." Then she looked away, as if my gaze had burned hers. I could practically hear her unspoken words: "*I* am not your problem."

"But—"

Natasha interrupted me with a wave of her hand, indicating for the woman on her right to step forward. "Alice, take the Good Samaritan around the building, press her, and send her on her way." Natasha's lips pulled back in a shark grin. "Then we can focus on our dear Katia."

"You think those sunglasses can stop me?" Katia said, lifting her chin. "I'm a boundary witch. None of you will remember any of this tomorrow." She gave them a contemptuous smile. "Just like old times, right?"

Oh, for God's sake.

"We're aware of your abilities," Natasha scoffed. "We're prepared to be thorough." The woman on Natasha's left actually snarled, and three of them began crowding around Katia, way too close.

Shit shit *shit*. Everything was happening too fast. I needed to slow this down—which meant I needed to get their attention off Katia.

I could have allowed Alice to take me around the corner and pressed her—but I had no idea what kind of damage the others could do to Katia in that time. Instead, when Alice started to grab my arm, I blocked her hand, crouched, and swept her legs out from under her.

I wasn't anywhere near as fast as a vampire, but Alice wasn't expecting it, or maybe she just wasn't a fighter. Either way, she landed *hard* on her back, letting out a grunt of pain. I bounced upright again, the backpack strap dropping down to my wrist.

The three standing vampires stared at me in surprise, while Alice flipped herself sideways and sprang to her feet. I took those few seconds to sidestep so I was lined up directly in front of Katia. Over my shoulder, I said fiercely, "Yes. It *is* my problem."

Turning to the vampires, I yelled, "*Stop this!* Katia is lying to you. She doesn't want to restart the brothel; she wants to die. She's trying to give you her life to make up for what she took from you. What *Oskar* took from you," I corrected. "But nobody else is going to die because of that piece of shit."

There was a moment of silence, broken only by the groaning of a particularly big piece of metal in one of the fires. Then there was movement behind me, and Katia dropped backward onto the boulder.

I thought about it for two seconds and made the decision: turning my back to the furious, confused vampires, I crouched down in front of Katia, looking her over.

The bravado that had kept her upright had finally failed, and her hands were shaking in her lap. When I took one of them, it was freezing. "See?" I said. "This is why you should just take the pain pills."

Katia let out a choked laugh that was probably half sob. "Please, Lex. Just go."

"You know I can't do that."

Natasha was suddenly at my side, looming over me. "What is going on?" she asked, frowning down at Katia. "What's wrong with her?"

"She was shot in the heart last week," I replied. I thought about tugging down the collar of Katia's shirt, but I wasn't going to violate her personal space like that.

"She does look like shit," Natasha observed.

"She could be worse." The woman who had been at Natasha's left, the one who had snarled at Katia, appeared at my other side. Vampire-fast, she lifted her arm and backhanded Katia hard enough to send my aunt sprawling off the boulder.

"No!" I reached out to grab at her shirt, but I was too slow. Katia collapsed on the ground, her body limp. She looked dazed.

"Libby!" Natasha sounded shocked.

"I don't care!" the vampire—Libby—shouted. "I don't care whether or not she is really restarting what he did. She helped him hurt us, and she wants death. I say we give it to her."

"Lex," Katia groaned. I bent over her so I could hear her. "Don't hurt them."

Libby scoffed. "Like she could."

I helped Katia scoot so she was more or less propped up against the boulder, but I thought Libby had a point. I couldn't take on four of them alone, and definitely not when they were crowding me like this. Alice and Natasha were on one side, maybe two feet away, and they still looked more confused than anything else. The fourth vampire had sidled near Libby.

"Who are you?" Natasha demanded, looking at me.

"I'm Lex. Katia is my responsibility."

"This is boring," came a voice from the back. It was the vampire standing next to Libby, and although I couldn't see her eyes past the sunglasses, her body language did indeed look bored. She was tall, and in life people had probably called her gangly, but becoming a vampire had erased that coltish awkwardness and replaced it with predator grace, which she used to shoulder her way past Libby, until she was looming over us. "Katia is a black witch. She's a threat to vampires. Let's just kill her, and we can get on with our night."

Katia bowed her head, accepting the suggestion.

"No," I said firmly, standing up so I was nose to nose with the fourth vampire. I was trying to ease one hand into the backpack, but I needed to work the zipper open, and it was hard with vampires so close. "I won't let you do that."

She leaned in without touching me and sniffed, that long, dragging in of air thing I'd seen Quinn do when he was tracking someone. Then she straightened up, her mouth curled with disgust. "She's just a witch. Not a very powerful one, if she hasn't even tried to back us off."

They couldn't smell my blood, so they couldn't tell what I was. And if they found out, I had a feeling I wouldn't last very long.

Natasha looked me up and down. "Are you connected or something?" she asked.

It was a smart question. This was right about when any sane person would start dropping names, beginning with Maven's. She might have been hundreds of miles away, but my boss was powerful enough to be notorious.

Unfortunately, that was a two-way street, in terms of my actions. "No," I said.

Natasha nodded to herself, making her decision. "Okay. We have no problem with you," she said to me. The fourth vampire made a little grunt of dissent but didn't comment. "But we have business with Katia. This is your last chance to walk away."

In my peripheral vision, I could see the fourth vampire beginning to circle. She and Libby were the real threats. The other two weren't committed.

"I have a counter offer," I said, finally getting my hand into the gap I'd made in the backpack zipper.

"Lex, don't," Katia said weakly.

The vampires weren't idiots—they could see me reaching into the backpack. But they thought I was going for something to trade for Katia. "What, money?" Libby said scornfully. "We don't need—"

Without pulling my hand out, I shot her in the chest.

Chapter 8

Vampires can survive pretty much any single gunshot wound—which is partly why they never really expect anyone to shoot them. When the firearm went off, they all jumped, and I used the opportunity to yank the gun out of the bag and shoot Libby again, in the stomach. Then I turned to the vampire whose name I didn't know, and put two rounds in her before Natasha slapped the gun out of my hand. So much for the element of surprise.

The two wounded vampires automatically stepped away, examining the bullet holes with pained interest. Natasha, thinking I was disarmed, turned her head to look at them. "You okay?"

I still had the newly ventilated backpack in my right hand, though, and I used the moment of distraction to reach in and pull out my four shredders. Alice was the first to see the motion, and she started to say, "Tash, she's got something—" when I plunged the shredder into Natasha's abdomen.

I genuinely felt kind of bad about doing that. Normal wooden stakes weren't any more lethal for vampires than they would be for anyone else, but the shredders were spelled to more or less create a tiny explosion in whatever organic material they were touching when they came to rest. Stab a vampire in the heart, the heart bursts, no more vampire. But I didn't want to kill these women, if for no other reason than it would make my suicidal aunt feel even worse.

But having your stomach—or liver, or whatever I'd hit—literally blow up was probably excruciating. Natasha dropped to the ground, her hands clutching her midsection. Alice snarled at me. "What did you do to our sister?" she demanded. The other two injured vampires held their distance. All of them were eyeing me with hostile interest, feeling the need to recalculate my threat level.

"Katia, go to the car," I muttered, holding a shredder stake in each hand. While everyone was distracted I'd tucked a third in my belt, but that was all I had for weapons. The shredder that I'd used on Natasha was spent, and no more useful now than any other pointy stick. I had lost sight of the Glock in the darkness.

"Lex—"

"*Do it!*" I barked at her. My aunt rolled onto her stomach and began crawling toward the car. Her progress was agonizingly slow. I shuffled along behind her, keeping the stakes pointed at the women, but in what felt like seconds, three of the four vampires were up and prowling toward us, leaving only Natasha still healing.

Alice was coming up the middle, and the other two were starting to flank me, limping along. They obviously weren't going to attack until they were healed, but that was going to happen long before we made it around the building. Fuck. I scrambled to think of a new plan.

"Nothing she can't heal from," I told them, trying to keep backing up without looking away from them—or stepping on Katia. "Hurts like a son of a bitch, though. You might want to get her out of here."

The fourth vampire, now working her way to my left, bared her teeth at me. "But see, now we *do* have a problem with you."

"I didn't get your name," I said conversationally.

Her lips pursed, and I figured she was probably glaring at me behind the sunglasses, but she spat out, "Maude."

Maude? Really? "I don't suppose you'd want to just wait here while Katia and I drive off?"

Maude snorted at me. "You shot me. You hurt my sister. You'll die with Katia."

I sighed. "I was afraid you'd say that."

Katia kept crawling, but I stopped and lowered my hands to my sides, staring at Maude. She still had one hand pressed to her stomach, and a trail of blood running down her clothes, but she was the biggest threat.

I had never tried to press a vampire wearing sunglasses before, but I didn't know what else to do. So I looked straight into the center of the lenses and envisioned a tunnel, opening up a connection between us. I wasn't sure how much power to use, but I wasn't going to get extra chances at this, so I put everything I had into it.

And connected.

Maude stopped moving, which made Alice and Libby stop out of uncertainty. "You want to go back and help your friend," I told Maude, choosing my words carefully. "You want to let us go."

Then I held my breath, and the moment seemed to balance on the edge of a knife. I kept pressing my will into where I thought Maude's eyes would be—and after a heartbeat, she turned around and mechanically made her way back to Natasha.

"She's a black witch too!" Libby shrieked. Alice froze up, looking scared, but Libby dove at me.

I was as ready for it as I could be, but she still knocked me over, so I dropped down on top of Katia, who cried out with pain.

As I fell I lost my grip on the shredder in my right hand, but I was able to get the point of the other one up, aiming low, away from Libby's heart.

It pierced her lower abdomen, and she began to scream—which is when Alice leapt at me.

I scrambled to get the extra shredder out of my belt loop, but I was too tangled up with Katia, and there was no time to tug it free and get it pointed before Alice was on top of me. She grabbed the shredder and threw it away, into the darkness beyond the fires. Then she wrapped a hand around my throat and began to lift me, standing up at the same time.

I couldn't breathe. I kicked and beat against Alice, managing to claw the sunglasses off her face, but she kept her head turned away from me so I couldn't press her. She snagged one of my wrists and lifted it toward her mouth, pulling back her lips to display sharp canines.

"I will drain you for that," she hissed, and sank her teeth into my wrist.

Chapter 9

Vampires usually press their victims not to feel pain, but even if Alice had been inclined to take pity on me, boundary witches can't be pressed. Sharp, screaming pain lanced through my wrist so badly that for a moment it felt like she'd pierced all the way through the bone. I wanted to cry out, but I didn't have the air.

Spots started to appear in front of my eyes. Katia was yelling something, but I didn't understand it. I realized, in a dazed, unconcerned sort of way, that I was about to die. I thought of Charlie, and felt a great swell of grief that I wouldn't see her grow up.

And then something hit Alice's shoulder with a meaty *chunk* sound.

Alice yelped, dropping me. I collapsed in a heap on the ground, and before I could move there was another *chunk* sound—and a fucking *arrow* buried itself in the center of Alice's throat.

Coughing, I got to my knees, holding my bleeding wrist with my free hand, and raised my head. In the overhead light I could see a small woman in jeans and a beige macrame sweater, pushing her glasses up on her face as she calmly loaded another arrow into what looked like an actual crossbow. Had I ever even *seen* a crossbow in real life?

Sara Reine raised the weapon and shot Natasha, who had recovered enough to advance on us. Then she flicked a hand carelessly, and both Natasha and Alice screamed out with pain.

It was a second before I realized that the tail of the arrow in Alice's throat now pointed at the sky. Reine had bent the arrows while they were still in the vampires.

That was one way around the "witch magic doesn't work on vampires" problem I'd never considered. "Ladies," she said pleasantly. "I'm Sara Reine. Reno and its surrounding area belong to Clan Reine. I can't have you attacking witches in my territory."

"These are black witches!" Maude yelled, pointing at Katia and me. "And the one on the ground is responsible for years of pain—"

"Oh, I don't actually care," Reine assured her, pulling another arrow out of what looked like a leather quiver strapped to her back. "The moment she steps out of my territory, you can rip out her ribcage and wear it as a hat, for all I care. But you *cannot attack witches in my territory.*"

She'd been loading the crossbow as she spoke, and now she raised it at Maude. "Move against them, or against me, and my clan will consider it an open challenge for territory. Is that what you want?"

Maude seethed. Through teeth clenched with pain, Natasha said, "No. We live in Lake Tahoe, on the California side. We have no interest in this place." She said the last two words with disgust.

"Then I suggest you get the fuck out of Reno." Reine had advanced so she was right next to Katia and me, and now she turned the crossbow so she could look down the sights at Natasha. "Now."

Muttering and cursing under her breath, the vampire motioned to the others to follow her. "This isn't over," she warned Katia as she passed us. Her hands were fussing with the arrow still bent inside her, and I figured it was hard to snap off the tip of an aluminum arrow that was slippery with blood. "We won't forget what you did."

"Neither will I," Katia said softly.

The four of them limped and stomped away in the direction of the road, disappearing into the darkness.

I looked at Sara Reine. "How do we know—"

She held up a hand. I had thought she was squinting after the vampires, but now I realized her face was twisted in concentration. "Hang on."

I waited, helping Katia get in a comfortable seated position. After a minute Reine said, "They just tripped the perimeter spell I put on their vehicle. Hold on…yeah." She nodded to herself. "And that's the one I left on the road. They're leaving."

She lifted the strap of the quiver over her head, stretching out her neck muscles, and plopped down on the ground next to us. "Whew. That was tense."

"Uh, yeah. Pretty sure you saved our lives just now, Ms. Reine."

She snorted, and waved a hand. "Call me Sara. Ms. Reine is my tortoiseshell."

"Your what?" Katia looked confused.

"Cat," I told her.

"And I didn't do it for you," Sara continued.

"Then why?" I asked her, rubbing at my throat. I was going to have a bruise.

Katia answered before Sara did. "Territory."

Sara nodded. "That fucking Oskar has been a bee in my bonnet for years. Except I like bees. Anyway, I'd been making plans to get rid of him, but I'll be honest, I was pretty relieved when the folks in LA took care of him for me. The last thing I want now is any other vampires thinking they can fuck around on my patch."

"You could have let them kill us before you ran them off," I pointed out.

Sara grinned. "I suppose I could have. All right, you got me. I'm a sucker for an underdog story, and you were putting up a hell of a fight." She looked at me appreciatively. "Damn, woman. Where the hell did you get stakes like that?"

I smiled, climbing to my feet and reaching down to help Katia. "Text me your address, and I'll send you a box of them."

"I might take you up on that," she replied, looking thoughtful. "I bet I could configure them for this crossbow."

"Now that could get *really* tense."

I put one of Katia's arms over my shoulder, and after slinging the crossbow's strap over her free shoulder, Sara Reine did the same. We helped Katia walk around the side of the main building and back to the car, where she pulled away and leaned against the hood.

Katia was tight-lipped and just as pale as she'd been earlier, if not more so, but I could see tears leaking from the corners of her eyes. I followed her line of vision to the main building, which seemed *more* threatening somehow, now that the little sheds were gone. I wasn't exactly expecting Disneyland, but it just *looked* like a place where terrible things had happened.

With a sigh, I looked at Sara Reine. "Would you be terribly offended," I asked, "if I were to set this one last building on fire?"

She brightened. "Hell, no. I was just thinking I'd come back and do that tomorrow anyway. You can save me a trip."

Chapter 10

I helped Katia collapse in the passenger seat of the Subaru, and then the local clan leader and I went back for the cans of gas.

While we were checking to see which ones still had any liquid left, Sara remarked, "She's pretty fucked up about working for Oskar, huh?"

It wasn't the kind of question I would ordinarily answer, but Sara Reine had saved our lives—I figured she deserved a little trust. I glanced over my shoulder, but of course my aunt hadn't followed us. "Yes," I said. "She wanted those vampires to kill her, but I wouldn't let them. That's how the fight started."

Sara let out a low whistle. "Fuck. That's...complicated."

"Yes."

"You gonna help her?"

"Yes," I said, knowing it was true.

"Good."

We carried the fuel around the sides of the building, splashing it on the edges of the wood frame. I knew the smarter move would have been to actually leave accelerant inside the building, but I didn't think I could stand to go in there and see more signs of Oskar's abuse. I just didn't have it in me, not tonight.

I sort of expected Katia to have passed out in the car, but when Sara and I met at the front of the building, I could see her sitting like a wide-eyed statue, still staring at the complex, though her head leaned against the window.

I got in without comment and backed up the Subaru to keep it away from the fire. Through the windshield, I saw Sara hold up a book of matches with her eyebrows raised. I nodded for her to go ahead. I felt no compulsion to light the match myself, and Katia was too weak to move.

The gasoline caught immediately, and Sara paced a few steps away, hands on her hips as she admired her handiwork. I heard a sob, and turned to see that Katia was crying openly, her shoulders shaking.

"Oh, hey…" I looked helplessly around the car for a moment and then managed to produce a wad of napkins. I reached over and pressed it into Katia's hand, but she didn't move. She just kept crying as the building in front of us began to blacken. Behind it, I realized, the sky was beginning to lighten. How was it almost dawn?

Katia choked on another sob as Sara Reine trotted over to us, grinning like a kid. I started the car and rolled down my window.

"I've never burned down a building before," Sara exclaimed. "It's kind of cool!" She leaned in my open window for a second, her arms folded on the sill. "I'll be in touch about those stakes. Might want to stay in the city limits until full dawn. Just to be safe."

I nodded. "Will do. You want a ride to your car?"

"Nah. It's just on the road, and I like the walk." Ducking her head, Sara looked over at the crying Katia. "It wasn't your fault, sweetheart, not all of it," she said softly. "Be careful not to take more blame than you deserve."

Katia just looked away, out her window. With a little shrug, Sara straightened up and turned away. I let her get near the back of the Subaru before I craned my neck out of the window and called, "Hey, Sara?"

She looked over her shoulder. "Yeah?"

"'Rip out her ribcage and wear it as a hat?'"

She gave me a toothy smile. "It's from *Buffy*. You don't watch *Buffy*?" Then she gave me a little curtsy, turned, and skipped back toward her car.

I watched Sara in my rearview mirror until she disappeared, thinking that if I hadn't seen a wedding ring on her left hand, I would have loved to fix her up with Lily.

When I looked over at my aunt, Katia was still crying, but she was using the napkins to wipe her nose. I didn't say anything, figuring she probably needed to get it all out.

Some time passed, and finally Katia's tears subsided. In a quavering voice that had, for the first time, a hint of an Eastern European accent, she said, "I feel terrible about what we did to them."

"What *I* did, you mean." Katia hadn't actually hurt anyone.

She didn't answer, and I sighed. "Yeah, well, I feel kind of bad about it, too," I admitted. "But not as bad as I did before they tried to kill us."

We watched the flames silently for a moment, and then Katia asked, "Why didn't you just leave me there, when I told you to?"

"I don't know," I said honestly. "I guess it never really occurred to me."

She let out a sound somewhere between a snort and another sob. "I am a stranger to you." She worried at the napkins, and I saw a red scrape on the palm of her hand, probably from where she'd caught herself on the rock.

Absently, I turned my wrist over to look at the puncture wounds that Alice had left on me. Her teeth had been sharp, but the bite was shallow, and it had already stopped bleeding.

"Look, Katia...the circumstances of my birth brought me to the Luthers, and they're my family. But I was born connected to you, too." I held up my wrist, and pointed at hers with my other hand. "My blood is your blood. For better or worse."

I reached over and gently took her hand, keeping my injury away from hers. "And honestly, I could really use you. I have no idea what I'm doing most of the time, in terms of magic." I smiled. "I'd like you to meet Charlie, your great-niece, and I want to tell you about Sam. And I want to know more about Valerya."

Katia tilted her head for just a second, and then said, "She wants to know more about you, too."

My mouth dropped open. Holy fucking shit. "Are you...does she *talk* to you? In your head?"

"Yes, of course. She's my sister."

I grinned hard enough to hurt my cheeks. "Well, damn. Sam talks to me, too. I wasn't really sure if that was normal."

"I'm not sure it is for all boundary witches," she said. "Sisters might be special."

Fair enough.

Katia gently extracted her hand from mine. "Lex...I can't swear loyalty to your Maven. Not to anyone, ever again."

I rubbed my eyes. I was so fucking tired. "You know, I'm kind of getting that, yeah."

Katia let out a tiny, hiccuping laugh. "We'll figure it out," I promised. "I am going to find a way."

Her smile fell. "I don't deserve that."

I could have argued with her on that, but I knew enough about guilt to know that it wouldn't help. Instead, I told her, "Lucky for both of us, what we deserve isn't really a factor when it comes to family."

Through the windshield, the fire was beginning to die down, and I figured the sun would be up soon. I stepped on the brake and put it in reverse.

"Come on," I said to Katia. "Let's go home."

The Lost Girls

Chapter 1

My name is Corry Tanger, and I look just like every other college freshman. Blue eyes, blonde hair, athletic build, clothes from the nicer LA malls. If you passed me on the street, and you noticed me at all, you'd assume I was just another middle-class white girl from the Valley with too much privilege and no real-world experience. And up until a few years ago, you would have been right.

Scarlett says I shouldn't think like that. She says I was always special, but like her, I just didn't know about it for a long time. But I have become wary of seeing myself as an oh-so-special snowflake. I know too many other kids who see themselves that way, and can't see anything past it. They are special, therefore nothing terrible will ever happen to them.

I will never think like that again.

****

Late afternoon on a Sunday, and I was stumbling through my bedroom and living room, trying to remember where I'd left my phone. I'd only been in my new apartment, the bottom floor of a converted Victorian mansion near UC Berkeley, for about a month, and there were still a few boxes and stacks of unshelved books cluttering up the beautifully furnished rooms. Part of me was a little afraid to mess up the nice furniture with my junk.

I needed to call Scarlett, badly, but I couldn't remember where

I'd left my phone when I'd stumbled in at dawn, and it wasn't one of those fancy tracking phones that I could call from my computer.

When I'd passed out, a few minutes before sunrise, I had hoped I'd wake up with a new idea for how to avoid impending disaster, but I'd woken up just as stumped and worried as I'd been last night. And if I didn't call Scarlett and get a new idea, a girl's life was in danger.

The month before, while I was still living in the dorms, four female students at USC had been turned into vampires against their will. Because it happened on his territory, they became the responsibility of Dashiell, the cardinal vampire of Los Angeles.

They couldn't stay in town, where they knew too many people, but he wanted to send them somewhere he had influence—and a person who could keep an eye on them. There weren't a lot of places outside his own territory that met those two requirements, but that was where I came in. Like Scarlett, I was a null, meaning I existed in the center of a blank space in the magic world. Scarlett calls this space her radius, and hers was big and really well-defined, like a large perfect sphere, with her in the middle.

My aura was different, though: smaller, and sort of wispier, as though the shape of it was constantly drifting around a little like seaweed underwater. Because of that, I tended to think of mine more as an undercurrent, something that flowed around me, and was strongest in the direction of my attention.

The night Dashiell called about the lost girls—Scarlett's name for them, of course—my attention was focused on the question of whether I should drop out of school. I was in my freshman year at Berkeley, and although I liked my classes, life in the dorm was destroying me.

On the phone, Dashiell had explained about the new vampires, and told me he had the connections to get them set up in the Bay Area with older vampires who would mentor them. "But I'd like you to keep an eye on them," he'd added. "Meet up with them once a week or so, just to check in."

"Um…" Unlike my own mentor Scarlett, I had a hard time questioning Dashiell. Or being the least bit disrespectful, really. He scared the shit out of me. "No offense, sir, but…why? If they have their own mentors up here, why do you want to keep tabs on them?"

Even asking the question made my stomach do nervous flip-flops, but Dashiell didn't seem to think it was unreasonable. "New vampires are naturally loyal to their makers," he explained, "who in turn swear loyalty to the area's cardinal vampire. It is a sort of chain, where each link is a bond of loyalty. The chain is usually strongest at the first link."

"Oh." The four new vampires had been turned by an evil psychopath who was now dead, which meant the strongest tie in their brand-new lives had been severed.

"They will swear an oath of loyalty to their new fosters, but the cardinal vampire of the Bay Area will only allow them to stay there if they are my ultimate responsibility."

"Okay…" This didn't sound like a great gig, but I wasn't sure how to say so to Dashiell. He was helping with my tuition payments, and he'd been the one to get permission for me to stay there for four years. Was I even allowed to turn him down?

Before I could think of a response, he continued, "Of course, you are not expected to keep tabs from your dorm room. This offer comes with a new apartment near campus."

Those words felt like a boulder being lifted off my chest, and I barely heard the rest of what he said.

After that, everything had happened really quickly. The girls arrived and got settled with their hosts, and I was suddenly packing up my dorm room and dealing with the logistics of the move. The first couple of meetings with the girls went fine—mostly just getting-to-know-you stuff and small talk about how they were adjusting. We were all trying really hard to make it work.

And then the third meeting, just last night, had *not* gone well.

"Come on, phone," I muttered. I realized that I was standing in the middle of my living room, staring at a wall and breathing too fast. I crouched down, just for a minute, hugging my knees to my chest. I needed to find the *fucking* phone, but I also did not have time for a full-blown anxiety attack. Especially not today.

I'd gotten my official diagnosis of "generalized anxiety disorder" back when I was fifteen. Since then I'd lost track of the number of different techniques I'd tried to help manage it. Regular exercise curbed my anxiety overall, for example, but didn't do much for the immediate attacks. Medications made me too sleepy to concentrate on school, and I found that I loathed both guided meditation and yoga, which seemed to give my brain too much time to dwell on the past and/or spiral out.

Then there were the methods that were *not* recommended by my therapist, or any therapist. I'd tried drinking and smoking pot, but they made me depressed and paranoid, respectively. I could get some short-term comfort from sex, but I had some hangups, which meant half the time sleeping with someone caused me *more* anxiety. Or at least, *different* anxiety. The one thing that always did seem to help me was talking to Scarlett, and that wasn't even counting how much I needed her advice today.

I finally located the phone on top of a stack of clothes on my dresser, and called Scarlett on the video chat app without bothering to sit down somewhere. I had too much nervous energy.

The first five rings came and went, and I felt my stomach doing cartwheels. "Come on Scar, pick up," I muttered.

Just as I was about to give up, the little "connecting" message flashed, and I felt something unknot itself in my chest.

Scarlett's face appeared in the screen—and for a moment, I actually forgot why I'd called. She looked like shit: Her face was red and puffy, and there were new hollows under her eyes. She'd lost weight, probably from the flu.

She pasted on a smile, clearly making an effort to look together for me. "Hey, kid!" she said in her fake cheerful voice. "How's it going?"

I froze with panic. Scarlett had always seemed unflappable to me. I had literally seen her laugh in the face of mortal danger, and now she looked like the second act of a Lifetime movie and it was freaking me out.

"Corry? Did the screen freeze?"

"Nope, sorry, just zoned out for a second," I said, trying to sound calm. "How are you?"

"Oh, you know," Scarlett said, gesturing helplessly. She was sitting in her living room in the small guest cottage she used to share with Eli, and when I looked closer I realized that one of the side tables was missing, and the framed poster that had hung on the wall behind the couch was gone. I could even see a little outline of dust where it used to hang. Jesus. Eli must have come back and gotten all his stuff.

"Um…" The first words that popped out of my mouth were, "Where's Shadow?" The 180-pound, jet-black bargest that had adopted Scarlett was usually in the background whenever I called, panting happily and fogging up the camera on Scarlett's iPad.

"Jesse volunteered to take her her for a run, since I've been a little under the weather." Her eyes lost focus, and she looked lost for a moment.

Shit, shit, *shit.*

My first instinct was to hang up the phone and go hide in a blanket fort, but there was a life on the line here. I took a deep breath. "Scar, listen—I had my study group last night," I began. "Study group" was the hilarious code name Scarlett had chosen for the meetings with the baby vampires. The four of them weren't forced to come, and they occasionally missed a meeting if their new jobs dictated it, but there was a hell of a draw: being in the presence of a null, and getting to eat their weight in junk food.

"What happened?"

"There's this huge problem, and I don't know what to do—"

At that moment a text notification popped up at the bottom of the phone's screen. "Hang on a second," I told Scarlett, and checked the text.

It was from a number I recognized, though I hadn't programmed it into my Contacts yet. All it said was, "He's awake."

Chapter 2

The night before, three of the four girls had arrived at my house together, right on time: Taylor, Louisa, and Hailey. Taylor's host vampire lent her a car on Saturday nights so they could come to my place in Berkeley without messing with public transportation. It wasn't so much a favor as a precaution: the four of them were only supposed to take blood when they were with one another, or with their minders, since their control wasn't great yet.

Before the three of them arrived, I had been a little nervous, but also kind of looking forward to the evening. The Old World had been such a huge part of my life for the last three years, and now I was masquerading as a human college student most of the time. It was exhausting, trying to be College Corry. With the lost girls, I could be me. Or at least, a version of me that had less stuff to fake.

My doorbell rang at ten-thirty. As I went to the door I felt the three of them hit my aura, and even though they'd had practice being near me, when I opened the door they were still gasping with the shock of going from vampire to human.

Hailey was the first one through the door, wearing jeans and a rain jacket and her ubiquitous Bose headphones, her head bopping slightly as she entered the apartment. I didn't think I'd ever seen Hailey *without* the headphones. She didn't talk much, and I suspected she was adjusting to vampirism by tuning out the world with her music. I couldn't really blame her.

Louisa had been right behind her, smiling with relief as she became human again. Most vampires found this jarring to the point of pain, but Louisa always just looked grateful.

Taylor was the last one in. Unlike the others, she wasn't trying to look like a typical college student, which was good, because even though she'd been just twenty when she became a vampire, Taylor was one of those beautiful women who exuded confidence and poise. Tonight she wore a designer skirt, a trendy silk blouse, and ankle boots that probably cost as much as a month of my tuition. She nodded her head in greeting and breezed into my apartment, at least as much as anyone who'd just re-learned respiration could breeze.

I waited in the doorway for a second, but the night was still. Harper must not be coming, or she was getting dropped off by her minder. I closed the door and turned toward the other three, who had taken seats in the small living room. I'd bought and set out a huge amount of snacks, but none of them were even looking at the food. Or at me. Or at each other.

That was when I realized that something was very wrong. "Where's Harper?" I said to the room.

All I got was a variety of uncomfortable shrugs. Crap. I looked first at Louisa, who was picking at a loose thread on her jacket hem. She and Harper had been placed together with Odette, an Oakland vampire who owned two clubs and a restaurant. She required the girls to work shifts at the clubs, both to keep an eye on them and to give the girls walking-around money. "Did she have to work tonight?" I asked.

"She told Odette she couldn't work because we were coming here," Louisa said uneasily, still not meeting my eyes.

"Okay…" I looked from her to the other girls and back again. I was obviously missing something.

I turned my attention to Taylor, who had dropped into the armchair with her booted legs thrown over the side. She reached toward the coffee table and snagged a handful of popcorn, raising it to her mouth and absently catching a piece with her tongue. "Taylor? What's going on?"

The pretty vampire tossed thick blonde hair over her shoulder and a few kernels of popcorn into her mouth. "All I know is," she said, chewing, "she told *me* she had to work tonight."

"But you guys compared notes in the car," I said, thinking it through, "and realized she lied to both of you."

"Pretty much." Taylor gave me an unconcerned grin.

"She's been weird lately," Louisa added, her hands wringing in her lap. "I mean, this whole vampire thing is weird. Obviously we're still adjusting, but lately..." She shrugged.

"What?"

"She's been kind of moody."

Moody? I didn't really know what to do with that, so I tried to get back to the point. "But where *is* she?"

Taylor and Louisa both shrugged again, though only Louisa looked nervous.

I watched the two of them for a moment. This was something I'd learned from Scarlett: vampires are great liars, but it's because they rely on their ability to control their physiological tics. Take away the vampire magic, and many of them don't remember how to lie convincingly.

Taylor and Louisa were both pretty convincing, though. I looked at Hailey, whose gaze had dropped down to her cell phone with a look of intense concentration. Almost too intense.

What would Scarlett do?

I stepped closer to her and gently pulled the headphones off her head. She looked at me with surprise, but touched the phone, and the tinny sound of the headphone music died abruptly. "What?" she asked, her voice too innocent.

"Where is Harper?"

Hailey looked away from me. "I don't know."

I reached up and gently rested two fingers on her neck. She flinched, but didn't smack my hand away. "Your pulse is racing," I said calmly. "You're lying."

This was another Scarlett trick. I had no idea how fast pulses were supposed to go, but Hailey didn't know me well enough to realize that. "Can't say anything," she mumbled toward the ground.

Louisa had been a few feet away, but at this admission she came closer, looming over Hailey. "What do you know?" she demanded.

Hailey just shook her head. Even Taylor was watching with mild interest now. "Can you blame the poor girl?" she said, around another mouthful of popcorn. "We're supervised twenty-four-seven. She probably just felt like playing hooky for a night. Is it really that big a deal?"

All three of them looked at me questioningly, and I felt a stab of panic. I wasn't, like, *in charge* of them. Dashiell had told me to report any irregularities—he would be calling the following night to check in—but I wasn't an authority figure, or a leader.

In retrospect, this was the moment when I should have first called Scarlett. I was just too out of my depth to know I was out of my depth.

Then another thought occurred to me, and I looked at Louisa

again. "Did she feed with you before she left?"

Louisa shook her head. "None of us have fed yet tonight."

Shit. Harper was officially breaking one of her minder's rules, and that *was* a big deal. I had no idea how good her control was, but it seemed like a bad time to find out.

I turned on Hailey, trying to think of a way to convince her to talk to me. Scarlett would probably threaten her or yell at her, but I couldn't pull that off. Finally, I just told the truth. "Hailey, I can't force you to tell me where she went. And there's a chance that everything is fine. But if you don't tell me, and Harper does something reckless, or loses control, I won't be able to help her."

Hailey swallowed hard, her eyes filling with tears, and I felt like a bully. These girls weren't used to human emotions; she was having a lot shoved at her at once. Her lower lip trembled.

I hated to do it, but it was the only thing I could think of. "And if it's bad enough, Dashiell won't be able to help her either," I added. "Do you understand?"

Hailey nodded, the tears spilling down her cheeks. She whispered, "Harper went to Death Guild."

Chapter 3

I had no idea what that was, but of course Taylor did. Death Guild, she explained in a bored voice, was a "goth/industrial" dance club (meaning a loose organization of people) that swung between a couple of Bay Area clubs (meaning bars that had live music). "Once a month it's in Oakland," she added, examining her fingernails. "At the Uptown."

I looked at Hailey. "How do you know?"

"She invited me." Hailey shrugged. "I like live music."

Okay, that made sense. But there was live music all over the city. "Why would she go *there*?"

She chewed on her lower lip, looking longingly at the headphones, which I was still holding. "A few of the younger vampires we've met think it's funny to go to Death Guild and feed on the peakers."

Oh, I just knew I was going to regret asking this. "What's a peaker?"

"Club kids who get really, really high," Taylor put in. "Sky-high, peak, peakers, get it?"

"I get it."

"If we drink peaker blood we can supposedly get a buzz going," she added.

"*What?*" I stared at her in shock. I tried to remember the conversations Scarlett and I had had about vampire biology, but I'd never even *heard* of this. Once she had mentioned a vampire who'd fed on a human who was so drunk he'd had to go to the ER for alcohol poisoning. The vampire had gotten a little tipsy, but it hadn't even occurred to me that it might work for drugs, too. I suddenly felt very young, and very naive.

"It's a big thing here," Louisa said, almost apologetically. "Most of the senior vampires have forbidden us from going, though."

I raised my eyebrows at her. "Including Odette?"

Her shoulders slumped. "Yes."

So a hungry baby vampire had ignored her minder and gone to a club filled with goth kids on drugs. "*Fuck.*" Trying to appear as though I was sure about what I was doing, I grabbed the closest jacket-like item nearby—a quilted vest on a nearby stack of boxes—and put it on. "Louisa and Hailey, go home. Or stay here, or whatever. I don't care."

"What are you going to do?" Louisa asked, looking worried. It was her roommate in trouble, after all.

"Taylor and I are going to go get her."

"Why do I have to go?" Taylor complained, although there wasn't much heat in it. She just didn't like being told what to do.

"Because I don't have a car, and I'm nineteen. You're going to press a bouncer to get me in."

"Ooh, fun," she said brightly, swinging her legs off the chair.

Taylor was a surprisingly responsible driver…or maybe I'd just made unfair assumptions because she was, well, Taylor. In a way I was glad it was her, because she cranked up her music—an angry-sounding female singer I didn't know—and seemed to feel no compulsion to make small talk. Which was good, because I was lost in my own worrying.

What if Harper had done something really bad? I would have no choice but to tell Dashiell, and he might decide to cut his losses and put her down.

Most people would be horrified by the concept of exposing someone so they would be vulnerable to a killer. But the idea carried particular weight for me—because it wouldn't be the first time I'd done it. Before I'd really learned about nulls or the Old World, I'd made a deal with a very bad man, who had used to me to turn a bunch of vampires and a werewolf into humans so he could kill them.

Now, four years of therapy later, I knew that a lot of my past wasn't my fault. But I could not absolve myself for helping Jared Hess kill those people.

I closed my eyes and forced myself to take deep breaths, not caring if Taylor thought it was weird. I had to do this. I had to go into a crowded, noisy club and find out if one of my charges had killed someone. *Don't spiral, don't spiral, don't spiral,* I told myself.

Then I got distracted by a terrible *new* thought. "How many vampires will be there?" I asked Taylor.

"Real ones?" She gave me a mischevious side-eye.

I didn't take the bait. "Yes."

She shrugged. "Five, twenty, I don't really know."

Crap. The witches who ran Berkeley knew about me, of course, and the cardinal vampire in charge of San Francisco was aware that I was temporarily nearby. But I didn't think most of the local Old World was aware that a null was in their midst. Most of them probably would not appreciate it.

Taylor glanced over at me again, more serious this time. "Are you really going to tell Dashiell about this?"

"I kind of have to."

Dashiell called every Sunday night to find out how our weekly meeting had gone. Vampires couldn't tell if someone was lying on the phone, and I was a null anyway, but...I was very scared of him. I was pretty sure he'd hear a lie in my voice.

Taylor's face hardened, but she didn't try to argue with me. "What will he do to her?"

"That," I said grimly, "depends on what she's doing now."

By the time we arrived, found parking, and got past the bouncer, it was a little after midnight. I paused just inside the door, looking around. From Taylor's brief description I'd feared...well, Scarlett had once made me sit through the first two *Blade* movies, and there was this techno club at the beginning of the first movie that had struck me as super terrifying. But the Uptown was pretty mellow, with an "acoustic coffee house experiments with neon" sort of vibe. I wouldn't have minded hanging out there, if it were earlier in the night and less crowded. The place was packed, and very, very loud.

I'd expected everyone to be in all-black, with black lipstick and eyeliner for days, but although there were a lot of dark colors, there was no real uniformity to it. With the moving lights and the blaring music it was a kaleidoscope of thigh-high boots, fishnets, glitter, and piercings. There was also a lot of what Scarlett's friend Molly referred to as "vampire kitsch"—fake fangs, Nosferatu T-shirts, and jewelry made of silver coffins.

"It's kind of a labyrinth," came Taylor's voice in my ear, and I nearly jumped out of my skin. I hadn't realized how nervous I was getting until that moment. "Sorry," she added.

I nodded. "What do you mean, a labyrinth?"

"There are multiple floors and a garden court. Apparently some kind of goth market is happening upstairs, too."

A goth...market? *Don't get distracted,* I told myself. To Taylor, I shouted, "Where will be the biggest population of vampires?"

She gave a little nod, understanding. "Upstairs."

"Okay, you check the upper floors. I'll take this floor and the garden court. Meet me back here in twenty minutes, with or without Harper."

Taylor nodded, and I felt a stab of relief that she hadn't argued, though I didn't know if it was because my plan was good or she just didn't feel like shouting anymore. In seconds, she turned and disappeared into the crowd, and I realized with a jolt of anxiety that I was now on my own.

Chapter 4

So…many…people…

I wedged my way through the crowd with my body turned sideways, hating the constant brushes against my body. I'd already been through two rooms, one with a bar and one with just a giant television screen playing *The Lost Boys*, which would have been a little funny if I wasn't so uncomfortable. And vaguely lost. I wasn't worried about retreading the same ground, since the rooms all *looked* different, but I was starting to think I'd never be able to find my way back to the starting point.

The third room I entered was small and nearly square, with only a small bar on one wall and two doorways on either side. Crap. Which way? I started forward into the room, scanning the crowd—and then I stumbled to a halt, causing several people to bump into my back.

Harper was dancing on the bar.

A lithe redhead with slim hips and shoulders, she was fully clothed, in black leather pants and a skintight black tank top. There was a crowd pressed around her, watching and cheering. This wasn't really a dance-on-the-bar kind of place, I could tell, but there was also no sign of the bartender, and I figured Harper had probably pressed him.

Or killed him.

Don't panic, I told myself. *You've found her, she's okay, just get her out of here*. Right. I could work with a clear objective.

I reached the back of the throng of people and tried to work my way closer to the bar. A cluster of guys in Stanford gear pressed up against the bar, drunkenly yelling something at Harper. Their leader was a very tall pale kid in a backwards Call of Duty hat, and I could see him laughing as he stretched out one long arm, trying to touch her ankle.

Ignoring him, she took a couple of steps away, tossed her waist-length wavy hair, and kept doing body-rolls to the beat—and sometimes not quite to the beat. I'd spent enough time at Berkeley to realize she was high on something.

I'd reached the back of the Stanford group. There were five of them, and they all seemed to be at least tipsy. The tall one was still trying to reach for Harper, and the others egged him on. "Excuse me!" I yelled, trying to elbow past one of them, but they ignored me. "Excuse me!" I might as well have been invisible.

"Climb up there with her, Jax!" the one closest to me yelled.

The tall leader started to climb onto a bar stool, his movements clumsy, and I realized the risk if he actually laid a hand on on Harper.

"Please, let me through!" I shouted, but in that moment the music changed. The song sped up, and so did Harper—*too* fast, just a little faster than humans could move. Even with the loud music, I heard a murmur of awe go through the crowd, and I cursed inwardly.

"Harper!" I screamed as loud as I could, but if she could hear me, she gave no sign. Jax had gotten himself onto the bar now and was on his hands and knees. The humans between me and Harper began raising their cell phones, taking video of the superhuman dancing. I was reaching a point of no return here.

I *felt* like I was panicking, but for some reason my aura wasn't expanding like it usually did when I was upset.

You have to concentrate, I heard Scarlett's voice in my memory. I blew out a breath, closed my eyes, and concentrated on my aura, drifting and wispy. Scarlett and I had practiced expanding it on purpose, but even when I tried, I was still coming up short. She was too far away, and it felt like the more I desperately wanted it to expand, the less it would.

Someone jostled me so hard that I would have stumbled if there was enough room. I felt a wave of anxiety and despair, and on instinct, I gathered my frustration and my fear and discomfort around me and I *pushed*.

Like a pendulum, my aura swung forward. I couldn't be sure, but it seemed like it left my body for a second, though I could still feel it, still register what was happening. My aura hit Harper and swung back to me, but it was too late: Harper lost her balance and slipped, falling backward behind the bar.

If it had been a movie, the music would have stopped, probably after an elaborate record scratch, but of course this music was being piped into the speakers from somewhere else, and it just kept going. Jax sat back on his heels to laugh, but slipped on the bar and fell forward, toward his pals. They parted to make room for him, laughing, and I saw my opening.

"That's my sister!" I yelled as loudly as I could. To my surprise, the guys of people closest to me actually turned and looked at me, moving aside so I could get through. Encouraged, I started forward, screaming, "Let me through; that's my sister!"

It worked, or at least, it worked enough. I wormed my way through the crowd until I felt Harper come back into my aura. I reached the little fold-up door separating the bar from the rest of the room, and could see her on the ground, on all fours, her long, tangled hair covering her face. Lifting the door, I rushed toward her, dropping to my knees. I didn't want to identify Harper, so I used the first name that popped to mind. "Molly! Are you okay?"

Harper's head lifted, her hair parting just enough to reveal one eye, narrowed. "Oh, good. The fucking hall monitor is here."

I flinched back. Where was that coming from? But I needed to get her out of there, so I hissed, "Leave your hair in your face; they're filming."

The eye widened with fear, and I realized that entering my radius had sobered her. "Are you hurt?" I asked.

"No."

"We need to get out of here," I said, helping her to her feet.

"You're right," she said calmly, but before I could stop her, she grabbed a nearby bottle and threw her head back, chugging it.

"Don't!" I cried, but Harper fended me off with one of her long arms, continuing to glug. Finally I pushed the bottle away, and she let it fall to the ground with a crash and began coughing violently, probably from the taste.

"Hey!" I looked up and saw a large man with facial piercings raise the door and dart toward us.

"What the fuck do you two think you're doing!" he shouted. "Where's my bartender?" Great. He was a manager.

"He went home for the night," Harper said cheerfully. "He was looking a little pale." She hiccuped loudly.

Awesome.

The manager's brow furrowed with confusion, but then he spotted the broken bottle behind Harper. "I'm calling the cops," he announced.

I had just enough time to register another vampire in my aura before Taylor materialized beside me. "That won't be necessary," she said, holding something out to the manager. I saw that it was at least two folded hundred-dollar bills. "For the bottle, and the trouble," she went on, smiling. "My sisters and I were just leaving."

The man's mouth dropped open, and he stared at Taylor for a moment, while I put my arm around a rapidly disoriented Harper. Taylor didn't actually bat her eyes, but her demure, apologetic smile had the same effect.

The manager reached out and snagged the cash from her hand. "Yeah," he grumbled. "Okay, fine. Get her out of here."

Chapter 5

Between the two of us, Taylor and I managed to get a stumbling, ranting Harper out of the club. I knew I could probably sober her up instantly if I let her get out of my aura, but there was no good way to do it inside the packed club, not without giving her the chance to run away again. The crowd had lost interest in us, but I kept Harper's long hair in her face just in case.

"How did you know where to find us?" I said loudly to Taylor, looking over Harper's head.

"I was talking to the peakers upstairs," she yelled. "One of them got a text from a friend down here about a girl dancing on the bar."

"You were talking to the peakers?" I called back, raising an eyebrow.

Taylor grinned. "Don't worry, I didn't eat. Soon as I got close to you the high would be gone anyway."

I looked down at Harper. Was that why she'd grabbed that bottle of tequila? Because being near me had killed her high? She had to have slammed…oh, maybe five or six shots' worth of tequila. I wondered, as we worked our way through the crowd, what her tolerance would be like now that she was human. Was she basically starting from scratch with alcohol?

I got my answer when we finally made it outside, under the movie theater-style marquee advertising Death Guild. We crossed the sidewalk to the street—and Harper puked sour-smelling bile all over my shoes.

"Ewwww," Taylor said, rearing backwards. There were two drops of vomit on one of her pretty boots. "Gross."

Harper started to cackle. "Puked on the hall monitor," she mumbled. "Awesome."

I let go of her arm. "What the *hell* is wrong with you?" I screamed.

Both girls looked at me in shock. I felt tears of anger and frustration burn my eyes. "I am trying to *help* you!" I yelled at Harper. "I'm trying to get you out of here before—"

"Before what?" she said, her voice dangerously quiet. "Before I do something bad and you have to tattle on me?"

I looked around, suddenly scared that we were being filmed, or that another vampire might appear. I'd been lucky so far, but I was playing with fire just by standing out here.

Nobody seemed to be filming us, but there were plenty of people on the sidewalk who'd stopped to watch the college girls catfighting. Taylor, who'd been watching quietly from a few feet away, followed my gaze to the onlookers. "Anybody want to join our conversation?" she yelled, with the confidence of a long-term mean girl. "No? Then move the fuck along."

There was some muttering about the irresponsibility of millennials, but the sidewalk began to clear. I focused on Harper and tried to…what? Assert my authority? What a joke. I had none. "My job is to check in with you—" I began.

"No!" Harper's voice had risen. "Your job is to spy on us. And great news, hall monitor, you've caught me!" Her words were slurring a little. "I snuck out and ate a peaker, and now you get to tell Dashiell. Congratulations."

"It's not like I enjoy—"

"Of course you do," she snapped. "Because that's your thing. You pretend like you're our friend, but you're just a fucking prison guard looking for a pat on the head."

"I…" I began, but I had no idea how to finish the sentence. I could smell the vomit on my shoes, but I'd somehow lost the moral high ground. "He's my boss," I said weakly.

"Yeah, well," Harper's eyes filled with tears, which she swiped angrily. "Your boss can go...can go *fuck* himself." She stumbled, though she was standing still, and ended up plopping down on the curb. She did not entirely avoid what was left of the vomit.

I suddenly felt incredibly tired, and about seventy years old. I looked at Taylor. "I'm going to go ask the bouncer for some paper towels for my shoes," I told her. "That will sober her up. Do *not* let her leave."

Taylor gave me a lazy salute. I couldn't read her expression, but I didn't really care anymore.

I marched back toward the entrance—and ran right into Jax, the tall, drunk leader of the Stanford group. The rest of his buddies were right behind him. "Sorry," I mumbled, backing away with my eyes down. "My fault."

I tried to sidestep so they could get past, but Jax stepped into my space, laughing, and grabbed my wrists. "That's okay, jailbait," he said jovially.

I hated that word. "I'm nineteen."

It was, of course, the absolute wrong thing to say. "You hear that, gentlemen?" Jax crowed to his followers. "She's legal!"

"Let me get past," I said, trying to step around him, fighting against the panic of being trapped.

He stepped sideways with me, and when I tried to go the other way, he mimicked me. "Look at that, she wants to dance!" he yelled, to no one in particular. He finally released my wrists, but only to get a firm grip on my waist. "Are you a good dancer, like your slutty friend back there?"

Jax suddenly spun me sideways, pressing my back lightly against the building. He crowded in close to me, his hands going to my ass, and he craned his neck to whisper in my ear. "She's hot, but I prefer my girls a little more basic, you know? Makes 'em work harder in the bedroom."

He kept talking, while I stood there completely petrified. He was a foot taller than me, and stronger than he looked, and this was happening really fast. I looked over his shoulder for help, but all of his friends had either wandered off or were laughing at us.

I turned my head to look for Harper and Taylor—and like magic they appeared, at almost the same moment I felt them in my aura. In fact, one of them was standing on either side of me. "Let her go," Taylor said, her voice so hard it startled me.

On the other side, Harper was pressing against his arm where he held me. "Now," she said, so softly that only the four of us would hear.

Jax turned his head, assessing the two of them with a little chuckle. "Hello there, gorgeous and gorgeouser. Your friend and I were just having a little word."

"She wants to go home now," Taylor told him. "Let her go."

Behind him, one of his friends called, "Come on, Jax, this is boring! Let's go get food."

Jax lifted his hands, his eyebrows raised with exaggerated innocence. "I get it. You bitches stick together." He winked at me. "Until next time, Corry Tanger."

My mouth dropped open. "How did you—"

"Ta-daaaa." He made a little flipping motion with one hand, and between his fingers a small plastic card appeared. My school ID, which I'd stuck in my back pocket with my driver's license and some cash. Stupid, *stupid* Corry. "Berkeley, huh? What a shitty school." Jax lifted his lips in a salacious grin. "But don't worry, jailbait. I can teach you some things."

I completely froze up.

Taylor snatched the ID out of his hand, tucking it into her own pocket. I stepped away from him, and without being told Harper and Taylor moved in front of me, closing ranks. They were human, this close to me, but I could hardly tell by looking at them. They looked like predators.

"Taylor," Harper said in a low, level voice, "please take Corry to the car."

"No," I blurted. "You don't have to—"

Taylor was already pulling on my arm, leading me toward the street—and getting Harper out of my radius. "She's already fucked," Taylor was saying in my ear. "Just let her have this one."

We had stepped off the curb now. I dug my heels in and yanked my arm free…but I didn't run back to stop Harper. I didn't try to throw my aura at her again. I just stood there and watched, as she threw Jax headfirst into the side of the building.

Chapter 6

We ran before the ambulance and the cops got there.

Actually, I don't remember running to the car, or climbing into the backseat. All of a sudden Taylor and Harper were arguing in the front, while I sat there and numbly wished I could take a shower.

"Did you *have* to shatter his head on a brick wall?" Taylor snapped.

"You left me there," Harper countered. "What did you think I was gonna do to him?"

"Just kick him in the balls a little!"

"Well," Harper pointed out smugly, "I did do that, too."

"Yeah, once he was down, and that's gonna look even worse!"

"Pffft," Harper scoffed. "You guys will be fine."

Taylor smacked her palm on the steering wheel. "But you won't!"

Harper quieted, turning her head to look out the window. "I was never going to be fine, Tay. It's over for me."

"Don't *say* that!"

"I'm sure there were security cameras outside the club—"

They continued their bickering, but I looked out the window, dimly realizing that Taylor was about to pull onto the bridge. "This is wrong," I said absently. "This is the wrong way."

Neither of the vampires in the front seat seemed to even hear me.

What would Scarlett do?

"Hey!" I shouted as loudly as I could.

"Jesus Christ!" The car swerved in its lane, and Taylor threw a glare over her shoulder. "What the hell, Corry?"

"Turn the car around. We need to see if he made it to the hospital."

"Why the hell would we do that?" Harper demanded, as if I'd suggested we try to dig holes all the way to China.

"So you can press him," I said, surprised at the calmness in my voice. "If he's alive, and you press him, his buddies, the cops, and anyone else there who's talking about it, it goes away."

"We're not that great at pressing people yet," Taylor admitted.

"You're going to have to practice."

Harper and Taylor exchanged a look. "Will...will that actually work?" Taylor asked me. "It just...goes away?"

I started to giggle. I couldn't seem to stop. I laughed until tears were running down my face, soaking my quilted vest. "What's so funny?" Harper demanded, turning sideways in her seat to look at me.

"You...you thought you were in trouble for ditching study group," I sputtered, barely able to get the words out around my chortling. "And now you might have killed a guy!" I actually tipped sideways, laughing and laughing, until only my safety belt kept me from collapsing across the seat.

Taylor spun the wheel for a U-turn, shooting Harper a severe look. "Way to go. You broke our null."

Harper called both of the two closest emergency rooms, and found that Jax had been admitted to the second one. He was alive, but that was all the information the operator was allowed to give to strangers on the phone.

By the time we reached the ER, I had finally calmed down, my hysterics resolving into minor hiccups. Taylor parked in the emergency lot and insisted on going in alone to find out what was going on. Of the three of us, she pointed out, she'd been the least involved, and besides, she could press everyone to forget she'd been there. She assured me that she could handle erasing a short conversation from someone's memory.

Only after she'd left did I realize that Harper and I were now trapped in a car together.

We had been sitting in the car for several silent minutes when she said begrudgingly, "I'm sorry about your shoes."

I didn't glance down at them. It was too dark, and I didn't really want to see them, anyway. I had thought about slipping them off when we got in the car, but there was a good chance that I'd have to go into the hospital, and taking them off and having to put them back on again seemed much worse than just leaving them. "I'm getting used to the smell," I said in response.

Harper snorted. She was human, this close to me, and it was making her fidgety— she played with the seat belt and the glove compartment box, checked her appearance in the visor mirror, flipped it up, checked it again. I had the feeling that human Harper hadn't spent a lot of time with uncomfortable silences.

I decided to extend an olive branch. "I'm not your jailor."

"I know," she said. "That wasn't fair. Us being here isn't your fault. But you *are* our hall monitor."

For a moment I thought about arguing with her...but she wasn't exactly wrong. If I hadn't told her I would tell Dashiell about her indiscretion, would she have beaten the shit out of that kid? And why hadn't I stopped her from throwing him into the wall? He was an asshole, but he hadn't actually hurt me. He probably deserved a kick in the balls, but not...this.

"Why did you take this gig?" Harper asked abruptly.

"For Dashiell?" Duh, Corry. What else could she mean?

But Harper just said, "Yeah."

I opened my mouth to make an excuse—something about money, maybe—but stopped myself. If the asshole died, Harper might too. She deserved the truth. "It was the apartment," I confessed. "I couldn't handle the dorms."

For the first time, Harper turned herself all the way around in her seat so she was facing me. There was enough light from the parking lot for me to see her amused expression. "Your roommate was that bad?"

"Actually, I had a single." Scarlett had arranged it, telling Dashiell I needed to be able to have private phone conversations about the Old World. She always looked out for me.

"Then what?"

"The bathrooms," I said quietly. "I couldn't deal with the other girls seeing me naked. They were starting to talk about it."

"Why couldn't you?" Harper said, her eyes running up and down me in a straightforward assessment. "You've got a good body."

I let out a tiny snort. "That's not really the point, but..." I turned my head to look out the window. A new ambulance was pulling up, while two more were speeding away. "I was sexually assaulted a few years ago. By a teacher."

"Oh." There was surprise in her voice, and regret. "I'm sorry."

I shrugged. "Now I've got a thing about people seeing me naked."

Okay, fine: they were giving me regular panic attacks. My therapist called this "triggering." I called it really, really inconvenient to playing Normal Corry. When Dashiell called I had been thinking about dropping out of school, at least until the next semester, when I could look for private housing.

To Harper, I said, "I was really focused on getting away from the dorms, and I said yes to this without really thinking about what it might be doing to the four of you." I cleared my throat. "For what it's worth, I'm sorry."

Harper turned back around in her seat. "I'm sorry, too," she said quietly. "I just...I got tired of the club, of having to smile and toss my hair while guys grabbed my ass and whispered about what they wanted to do to me. I thought if I just took one night off, to blow off some steam..."

Before I could think of anything to say in response, I glanced through the windshield and saw Taylor hurrying back toward us. "He's going to kill me, isn't he?" Harper said. "If the kid dies, the vampires will kill me."

I decided to be honest. "Probably."

Taylor reached for the handle. "Don't tell her," Harper said, and then the door opened.

Taylor climbed back into the driver's seat. "The good news is, he's alive," she said. "But he's unconscious. I was able to press his friends and the cops that showed up to take his statement, but Jackson—that's his name—is out of it. The nurses don't think he'll wake up tonight. It could be days."

"Shit," I mumbled.

"What?" Harper asked.

I shook my head. "That's too much time to press someone to forget something."

Both girls turned and looked over the seat at me. "What do you mean?" Taylor demanded.

Their mentors hadn't explained this? Of course they hadn't, I realized. They probably didn't want the girls experimenting with pressing people. "You can only press someone to forget a big event within the first couple of hours. After that, it's too imprinted into their memory. You'd have to press them to forget the whole day, and the brain rejects that much interference."

"We could kill him," Taylor offered, in a half-kidding way.

I shook my head. "No, we couldn't. We don't do that, even to an asshole."

"She's right," Harper said, subdued. "I'm fucked."

I had been more or less numb since the thing outside the club, but now I felt panic rising inside. Dawn was only a few hours away.

Then it would be sunset, and Dashiell would be calling me, wanting a report on the girls. If this Jackson kid could identify Harper, she would have to disappear. Dashiell might be willing to just relocate her somewhere else, but I kind of doubted it. He didn't have many more places to send someone, and he'd already invested a lot of money and favors in setting the girls up here.

"Do either of you have any cash?" I asked.

"Yes," both girls said together. I smiled. Vampires.

I looked at Taylor. "Take some in, and bribe a nurse to text my cell when he wakes up."

"I could just press her to do it," she pointed out.

"Do both," I instructed. Vampire presses didn't usually just wear off, but I wasn't sure how skilled Taylor was. "Just in case."

"Then what?" Harper asked.

"Then we wait, and hope he wakes up before dawn."

I drifted off around six a.m., and didn't wake up until the car door opened next to me. "Corry," Harper said, standing there with her hand out to help me. "This is your stop."

I opened my eyes, looking around. We were pulled up to the curb in front of my apartment.

Reflexively, I checked the cell phone in my hand, but there were no missed texts. Jackson hadn't woken up.

Blearily, I looked at Harper's outstretched hand, and then to her face. "There's gotta be something else we can do," I said.

She gave me a sad smile. "There isn't. And I knew that when I decided to dent the kid's skull. Maybe this is for the best." She waved the hand. "Time to say goodnight."

I took it and allowed her to pull me up. When we were both standing, she was about three inches taller than me, but thin and fragile-looking, compared to the goddess who'd danced on the bar a few hours earlier.

She slipped something into my hand, and I looked down to see cash. "For the shoes," she said firmly. "Please burn them. They smell terrible."

I reached up and threw my arms around her neck, surprising us both. "Bye, Corry," she said quietly, and then pulled away, climbing into the car without another word.

I left the shoes outside on the mat and stumbled into the house. I took a quick, exhausted shower, and collapsed on my bed, feeling thoroughly defeated. My laptop was on my nightstand, and I automatically pulled it toward me. After a moment of thought, I began searching for Jax online.

It took a few minutes, but I knew where he went to school, what he did for fun, and what he looked like. Eventually I found him on Facebook, and got his last name: Rutledge. A few more minutes of research was all it took to learn that he was from just outside Napa, and he was a star athlete: there were a bunch of newspaper articles about his high school tennis career, suggesting he might be good enough to go pro after college.

The articles often mentioned his father, a prominent property manager who owned or co-owned seven vineyards. They were rich, and litigious to boot: Oliver Rutledge had sued several of his former partners over various business disagreements.

My head dropped onto the bed. This just got worse and worse. Harper's only chance now was for me to, what, convince Jackson that his assault had never happened? It would never happen, not without

Dashiell getting involved to pay the kid off, and then he would have to punish Harper.

I needed to talk to Scarlett, I realized. I had been trying not to pull her into my mess while she was getting over her breakup, but this was too big for me. The nurse had said Jackson might not wake up for days—there was time to get Scarlett to help me make a plan. I knew, though, that I couldn't do much without a couple more hours of sleep. I would just worry myself into circles. When my tired body sagged down onto the bed, I let myself drift off.

Chapter 7

He's awake.

I closed the text, sick with worry, and returned to my video call with Scarlett. It was too late. Jackson was waking up, and he was going to tell the cops about Harper and me.

My insides suddenly felt all sloshy; I looked at Scarlett in a daze. She was staring at a spot on the coffee table. "I'm back," I said, though my mouth was dry.

Scarlett blinked and seemed to shake herself out of her thoughts. She gave me a shaky smile. "Right. Sorry. What were you saying?"

"The lost girls came over for our meeting last night—"

"Yeah. Yeah."

I began to cry. I just couldn't help it.

This finally got Scarlett's complete attention. "Corry! Honey, what happened?"

I just shook my head. I wasn't strong or brave, like Scarlett. I was just a pile of anxieties that had walked into a bad situation—again—and now might get someone else killed because of it—again.

"One of them...did something...really bad," I sobbed. "Dashiell's gonna call...and—and—"

"He's going to expect you to tell him what happened," she finished for me.

I nodded.

"Honey, I know you think he's scary, but you don't have to tell him anything you don't want to."

I just shook my head, because we were so far beyond that particular problem. Jackson's injury was going to get out, one way or another.

A new, horrifying thought struck me: if I gave Scarlett the details, would she get in trouble, too? Could my actions come back on her?

It felt like the panic was going to choke off my air. I didn't want to pull Scarlett into *my* mess.

With enormous effort, I made myself calm down enough to say, "I keep trying to think, what would Scarlett do? And I have no idea, and the clock is ticking, and I just, I can't calm down."

"Corry…" Scarlett set her iPad down on the little stand she kept on the coffee table, and I could see her scrubbing her hands on her face for a moment, folding her legs under her. Then she looked directly into the camera. "Yes, you can," she said firmly. "You can do this. Forget about what I would do. The first step is to calm yourself down so you can think, and you *know* how to do that. Right?"

I found myself nodding along with her. "Good. And remember: in Dashiell's world, what happened is never as important as what *appears* to have happened."

Those words brought me up short, because she was right. I'd been trying to erase history, but what I really needed to do was rewrite it. "Okay," I said slowly.

Scarlett gave me her real smile, the one she reserved for only a handful of people, and just like that, I felt safe again. "I love you. You can do this."

I hung up the phone and ran to the bedroom to get dressed and get on my laptop.

The cab to the hospital was the most expensive single ride I'd ever taken in my life, but I barely registered the cost as I handed the driver the wad of money that Harper had given me for my shoes. I had an hour before sunset.

At the hospital, I marched up to the nurses' desk, trying to channel Scarlett's confidence, and announced that I was Vanessa Rutledge, and I'd come to see my brother. I gave her the room number, and she asked for my ID.

I reached for my pocket and then put a look of sharp annoyance on my face. "Drat. I left it with the driver. I was in such a rush to get here." I dug out my cell phone. "I'll call him to come back here. Hopefully he hasn't gotten on the bridge yet."

The nurse eyed the three people waiting for information behind me, and sighed. She clicked a few things on her computer, and handed me a sticky label that said VISITOR. "Make sure you bring it next time," she said sternly.

Taylor had said that a guard was outside his room the night before, but her press must have held, because the hallway was empty now. I took a deep breath and pushed the door open.

Before I went into Jackson Rutledge's room, I was expecting something out of a movie: machines all around him, maybe a breathing tube, doctors rushing in and out. Instead, there was just the douchebag from the night before, with a single machine on either side of him and a long bandage wound around his head. He was wearing a hospital gown, but his pelvis looked lumpy under the blanket, and wondered if they'd had to bandage his testicles.

His eyes widened as he saw me, and his hand began to move—but I was ready for it. This was a vampire tip, which I'd actually learned from Molly: get the nurse's call button away from the angry patient.

It's a lot easier when you have vampire speed, of course, but Jackson was slow and dulled by drugs, and I managed to beat him. "Nope," I said, lifting the cord and remote away from him. "We need to talk first."

His eyes narrowed, and I felt the fresh fear and panic, remembering his hands on me. "You," he said venomously. "You little *bitch*. Do you know what your whore friend did to me? I am going to destroy—"

"Shut up," I snapped. "You're going to listen to me, or I'm going to toss this remote on your genitals until you're quiet. Got it?"

His face shifted with fear, and he closed his mouth. "Did you talk to the police yet?" I asked. "Shake your head yes or no."

Glaring, he shook his head from side to side. "I'm waiting for my attorney to arrive tonight with my father," he said nastily, ignoring my order to be quiet. "Your stripper pal is going to be arrested."

"That's not going to happen," I said.

"Oh yeah? What makes you say that?"

"Because you're going to tell the police the same story that everyone else is saying: you were drunk, you stumbled, and you hit your head the wrong way on the wall. It was just an accident."

He scoffed. "What the fuck are you on? You might have paid off the nurses or whatever, but nobody stumbles and hits the *top* of their head. Why would I—"

"Because you care about appearances."

His brows furrowed. I'd thrown off his line of thought. "Huh?"

I tossed a sheaf of papers on his stomach. "What is this?" he demanded, picking them up. "A payoff?"

"No. Those are retainment contracts for the three private investigators I hired this afternoon."

"What are you talking about?"

I sat down in the chair, crossing my legs as I regarded him. "It's *painfully* obvious that you have a problem with women. And although I don't have as much money as you and your dad, I have enough saved up for a couple of weeks of the best PIs in San Francisco. As of"—I checked my watch—"forty minutes ago, they're devoting their considerable talents to finding every single woman you've ever even spoken to, and checking to see if you've crossed any lines. Sexual harassment, assault, rape—hell, if you told someone her butt looked fat, I'm going to find out about it."

"You wouldn't—"

"Of *course* I would. I consider it not just a personal investment, but maybe even pursuing the course of justice. If there's anything illegal, of course, I'm going to throw eveyrthing I have at getting charges filed against you. If there's anything untoward, but just on this side of the law, I'm going to start calling sports journalists."

His face went slack, and he looked numbly between me and the papers.

I smiled sweetly, pointing at the top sheet. "One of them is the same firm used by the last guy your dad sued. He lost that case, you remember? How do you think he'd feel about his opponent's investigators digging up dirt on his son?"

"You can't do that," he whispered.

"Not for very long, no. But I think I've got a budget for, oh, maybe three weeks of full-time investigation?" I swung the call remote around on its cord for a moment. "Of course, if you're innocent as a newborn lamb, I'm screwed. I'll have wasted my money. But something tells me I've made a good investment today. And if I can find even one credible witness who'll testify that you groped her, your allegations against my friend aren't going to hold up very well. How many people saw you reaching for her when she was on the bar last night?"

Jackson's mouth open and closed several times. I gave him a minute to think it over—after all, he'd had a head injury.

Then he thrust the papers back toward me. "Call them off," he said. "I'll tell the cops it was an accident."

I took the papers. "I'm not going to call them off, Jackson. Not for…oh, at least a week. But I *will* keep whatever I find to myself, as long as you never so much as speak of me or my friends, ever again. Are we very clear on that?"

He nodded. "Excellent." I stood up. "Wishing you a speedy recovery."

At the door, I paused and looked back at him. He was staring at the wall with a dazed expression. "Oh, I almost forgot," I said brightly, and when he looked at me there was actual fear in his face. "Thanks for the dance."

Chapter 8

Dashiell called an hour after sunset, right on time. "Good evening, Corry," he said, sounding as cordial as ever. "How are things with our four new vampires?"

I closed my laptop, curled my legs beneath me, and leaned back on the sofa cushions. I'd only made it back from the hospital forty minutes ago. "Honestly, Dashiell, they're having a hard time adjusting. What they're going through isn't easy, and I'm not sure their jobs are suitable."

"What do you mean by that?"

"Louisa and Harper are working at a club, where they're occasionally harassed by human men. You can imagine how that might make this transition harder, given what happed with Oskar."

"I see." To his credit, Dashiell sounded concerned. "I'll have a word with Odette about it. Thank you for informing me."

"You're welcome."

"Is there anything else I should know?"

Was I being paranoid, or was there an edge to his voice? I'd scoured the internet for evidence of Harper's indiscretions. There *was* a video of her dancing on—and falling off— the bar, but her face was obscured by her hair. If the club had surveillance video of the attack out front, they hadn't made it public, and as long as

Jackson played nice, there would be no reason to. "Everything is fine here, Dashiell. Thank you for checking in."

My boss wasn't an idiot—he knew I had answered the question I wanted to answer, rather than the question he had asked. But Scarlett was right—Dashiell cared about how things looked, and if I was telling him everything was okay, he sort of had to believe me.

"All right, Corry. Have a good evening. I'll speak to you next week."

I said goodbye and hung up, pushing out a deep breath of relief. Then I jumped, as I felt the phone buzzing in my hand. I glanced down and saw Scarlett's face on the screen. Smiling, I took the call.

Powerless

Author's Note

In 2014, I was invited to participate in an urban fantasy boxed set called *Shifters After Dark*. It sounded like a really cool opportunity, but I would need a new project to include. *Bloodsick* is set fifteen years before *Dead Spots*, and tells the story of how Will Carling became a werewolf.

I hoped that the project would do well, of course, but I was entirely unprepared for how many readers would fall in love with Sashi Noring and her relationship with Will. Sashi is a fun character to write —she's the only one of my narrators who is naturally cheerful, for example— and I found myself involving her in the main series more and more. (As it turned out, having a healing witch on call is a pretty useful story thread to pull.)

When the time came to brainstorm stories for this compilation, I realized that what I really wanted was a chance to write Sashi again, both for me, and as a gift to the people who frequently asked about her.

"Powerless" is during the events of *Shadow Hunt*. Because it is sort of a sequel to the earlier Sashi story, I strongly recommend saving it until after you have read *Bloodsick*.

Chapter 1

The day Scarlett Bernard changes my life again starts off as a perfectly normal Saturday. At least, normal for me, and for Las Vegas.

Six days a week, I wake up late, go to the gym, do the shopping. Sometimes I have an early dinner with one of the casual acquaintances I have cultivated since moving to Vegas: a couple of friends from book club, or one of the other mothers from the equestrian center where my daughter, Grace, took horseback riding lessons until she left for college.

In the evening I dress in my professional-looking but easily laundered work clothes, and at ten pm on the dot, my driver, Darby, arrives at my house in a discreet black BMW, and we go to work. For the next ten hours, Darby chauffeurs me between casinos with my medical kit, visiting injured humans who are too busy, rich, or criminal to seek medical care through official channels.

My bread and butter is, of course, hangovers. Among the one-percent of Las Vegas's biggest whales, it's known that for an exorbitant fee, you can have your hangover dissolved by Sashi Brighton within three minutes. From there, my services extend all the way to healing serious trauma like stabbings and gunshot wounds, although I'm a little embarrassed about how much my business partner, Teagan, charges for *that*.

On a busy night, I might visit two dozen people, ranging from a rich tourist with a migraine to a parolee who accidentally shoots himself in the foot playing with a gun he's not supposed to have. On those nights I often stagger into my house at six a.m. and collapse in the foyer, unable to make it to the bedroom without rest. This was rather embarrassing before my daughter left for college, but now there is no one in the house to catch me sleeping on the carpet.

Despite the occasional crazy nights, I don't mind the work, most of the time. Teagan handles billing and scheduling, so all I have to do is show up where and when she tells me, and do what I was literally born to do. Teagan is a human, with no knowledge of the Old World, but she's also a retired stripper. Fifteen years in that line of work taught her how to run a business without asking any questions. She's never asked me, for example, how I am able to heal people of their ailments, or why I have to take the occasional job from Silvio, the vampire in charge of the Old World in Las Vegas. Silvio mostly leaves me alone, wary of my connections in Boulder and Los Angeles, but every once in a while he has me come in to take care of a human hurt by one of his vampires— probably just to remind me that he can. That's the cost of doing magical business in his city, and when it happens I pay Darby and Teagan out of my own pocket.

Teagan and I have developed a reputation for total discretion, which keeps us safe. We have also agreed on one rule: in the case of domestic violence-related injuries, the injured party has to get in the BMW with me and take a ride to an all-night shelter for people trying escape abusive relationships. Most of these are women, and after riding with me they are free to return to their partners—and unfortunately, most of them do. Taking that ride, however, is mandatory.

It is the hardest part of my job, and a situation that comes up far too often. After I heal the woman and drop her off, I will often curl my legs up on the seat and cry—for the woman I just helped, and for the werewolf that I couldn't help, a long time ago. Darby, a quiet man by any standards, never mentions the crying, though he must hear it.

On this warm Saturday morning in early May, I am just getting off a surprisingly dull shift, for a Friday night: two cases of alcohol poisoning, one asthma attack, and a billionaire's son who drunkenly sliced his hand open with a broken glass. I consider that a slow night, so at six a.m. I have Darby drive me to the pediatric oncology ward at the children's hospital in Las Vegas, where the volunteer coordinator is happy to let me come and go as I please. I spend a couple of hours "visiting" the patients—coaxing their bodies toward health—so I can at least feel like I accomplished something with my night.

Darby drops me off at home, where I have no idea what to do with myself. Ordinarily I would be going to bed around now, but I foolishly drank a large coffee at the hospital, and I am wide awake and feeling restless.

So I wander around the house, still wearing my work clothes from the night before: black slacks and a dark floral blouse with modest hoop earrings. I gravitate toward the refrigerator and the living room mantel, where I at least have some framed photos. My home is beautiful and well-kept, but lately it has been feeling more than just empty—it feels impersonal. I miss my daughter, and the noise and mess that seemed to tumble after her whenever she was in the house.

Checking my watch, I decide I might as well get our weekly call out of the way. Grace is a freshman at CU in Boulder, and a much more dedicated student than I was at her age. It's after nine a.m. By now, she will be awake and studying, or going to brunch with the Luthers. I call her cell phone, and as I wait through the rings I am steeling myself for the conversation ahead. Grace knows she has to take these Saturday calls if she wants me to keep paying for school, and it infuriates her.

"Hello," my daughter's sullen voice says. I know immediately she is not with the Luthers—she would have felt the need to fake a nicer attitude.

"Good morning, Gracie." I am trying for just the right tone—not too chipper, not too mom-like, but friendly. "How was your week?"

"Fine," she replies in a monotone. "My grades are fine. I'm not dating anyone. I have enough friends and money."

I refuse to sigh into the phone. I'm getting better at these calls. "I stopped by the stables the other day and gave Andromeda some carrots," I offer.

Grace's voice perks up, just a little. "Really? How is she?"

"Good. Blair says that gash from last year is completely healed now. They're putting her back in the jumper class."

"That's great." Grace remembers that she is still punishing me, and modifies her tone. "Is there anything else?"

I force myself to stay calm. I was just as bad, if not worse, when I was her age. Grace can play a young version of me if she wants, but I refuse to be my mother. "Just that I love you more than anything, and I'm always here if you need me."

There is a pause, and then she says, "Bye, Mom."

I hang up the phone thinking that at least she didn't call me "Mother" this time.

When she was little, Grace thought I hung the moon. I was the cool young mom who always seemed to be home and available, since I hired a babysitter to stay in the house at night when I needed to work. Then, when she was fourteen, I got a phone call from a woman in Boulder, Colorado, named Lex Luther.

I've always done the occasional out-of-town freelance work for longtime clients—Teagan would just charge an even more absurd fee than usual, and call in an off-duty ER doctor to fill in for me in Las Vegas. The call from Boulder was unusual, though: it was the first time I had ever been contacted directly, rather than through Teagan, and the first time I had been been commissioned by another witch. My magic doesn't work on most people in the Old World, but the circumstances were interesting, and Grace, who was reading Stephen King novels at the time, wanted to visit Colorado. So I agreed to the job.

And it changed our lives. I made my first real adult friend in Lex, and her family welcomed Grace and me into their lives with open arms. And, perhaps most importantly, I began a long-term relationship with Lex's brother-in-law, John Wheaton.

John knew about the Old World, because his daughter was a null, but he was also human, and ninety-nine percent of his life was about human things. As long as the two of us kept our homes in our respective states, I never had to face the ridiculous fact that I was somehow still in love with a man I'd known for a few months almost nineteen years earlier. By all accounts, it was the perfect relationship for me.

For a moment there, it seemed possible for Grace and I to be accepted into a normal human family—the kind I had never had, as the purposefully-bred daughter of powerful witches. Then one night, a year ago, John offered me an absolutely perfect engagement ring, and I had to acknowledge that my stupid bloody heart refused to let go of the impossible.

I didn't know how to explain something so absurd, so I told John that I was hung up on the past, and he deserved to be with someone who was all in, the way he was. Words that sounded trite, but were absolutely true. And Grace never forgave me for them.

It's my own fault—I never brought Grace into the Old World, never let her become a witch, so I could never be honest with her about her father. I knew, when I made that choice, that I was sentencing myself to a certain distance between the two of us, but I never dreamed how much keeping secrets from my daughter would backfire on me.

Now Grace lives in Boulder, and thinks her mother is a selfish, cold bitch who threw away the best thing that ever happened to her. She prefers John and the Luthers, with their bright, noisy, interlocking lives, to our silent house in Las Vegas that is always empty at night. I can't even blame her, even if it breaks my heart. I learned a long time ago that you can live with a broken heart. At least Grace is happy, and I know John and Lex are keeping an eye on her.

After I hang up with Grace, I stand at the spotless kitchen counter for a moment, tapping my fingers while I try to think of something to do. I'm not sure I feel like socializing, but even if I did, my casual Las

Vegas friends will be busy with their families on a Saturday. The cleaning service was here on Thursday, so the house is spotless.

I know I should just go to bed, but I don't feel like sleeping yet, so I decide to drive to my favorite bookstore. I will find a new novel, bring it home, and curl up on the couch with it until I get tired. If I need to catch up on sleep I can always call Teagan and let her know I'll be coming in a little late. Feeling better for having a plan, I scoop up my keys and purse and am off again.

When I arrive at the bookstore, I accidentally leave my cell phone in the car and decide not to bother going back for it. It's hot outside, and besides, who would call? I have already talked to Grace today, Lex the day before, and Teagan knows better than to call me in for any work emergency before my shift that night. I browse the shelves for nearly an hour, and wind up purchasing a Susan Hill mystery, two different haunted-house novels—they've become much more interesting now that Lex can give me the real scoop on ghosts—and Katy Tur's nonfiction book on the 2016 election. The tiredness is starting to overtake me as I walk back to my car, and I muse that I might just go straight to bed when I get home after all. The books will keep until later.

I start the car to get the air conditioning going, and glance at my phone's screen as it lights up with the car charger. To my surprise, there is a missed call and new voicemail from Scarlett Bernard. I frown, picking up the phone. Like most people in the Old World, Scarlett mostly operates at night. If she's calling now, I wonder if something has happened to her and Lex's friend, Jesse Cruz.

I press the buttons and listen to the message. Scarlett's voice is shaky, and she speaks even faster than normal. I have been doing my job long enough to recognize the effects of adrenaline. "Sashi, it's Scarlett. Sorry, duh, you know that; you have caller ID. Anyway, listen, I've got a situation here. Jesse's brother Noah was, um, mugged at the park this morning. It's really bad. I don't want to say more on the phone, but will you come? Please? I know it's LA, but…please just come anyway. He's at Hollywood Presbyterian Medical Center. I will pay you literally *anything*. Please."

Her voice breaks on the last word, and I feel a cold wave of nerves. Scarlett didn't make any jokes at all—in fact, she sounds terrified. I haven't met Jesse Cruz, but both Scarlett and Lex speak highly of him. If his human brother was mugged on a Saturday morning in a public park, it seems likely that someone in the Old World was trying to get to Jesse—or to Scarlett. Something is going on in LA.

I call her back, but there's no answer. I chew on my lip for a second. My impulse is to go, of course. Yet I sit there in the parked car with the air conditioning blasting at me, torn.

Will is in Los Angeles.

I know, because my mother told me. I haven't spoken to her in almost twenty years, but she sends me an annual holiday card. I'm sure she would say she's just attempting to reestablish contact…but I know she also wants to remind me that she knows where I am. Shortly after I left home I changed my last name to distance myself, but she has plenty of money for a private investigator. She can find me anytime, and wants to make sure I know that.

The cards are impersonal—the sort of officious "Happy Holidays" greetings that also come from the bank where I got my mortgage. A few years earlier, though, she'd scribbled at the bottom, *Just talked to Will in LA.* Followed by her phone number.

It was bait, of course. I knew she was trying to tempt me back into her life, and I knew exactly where that would lead: to her getting her claws into Grace. It was almost certainly too late for Grace to become a witch, but my mother wouldn't hesitate to use her to manipulate me, or start figuring out how she could set Grace up with a male witch, so they could produce more little witch babies. Still, that was the closest I've ever come to giving in and calling my mother. Instead, though, I'd shredded the card.

Then, only a few months earlier, I met Scarlett in LA, and she told me a little bit about Will—that he was still a good person, and a good alpha to his pack. God, that conversation had rattled me. But Scarlett was kind, and she has kept her promise not to tell Will about Gracie— otherwise I would have heard from him by now.

I know it's LA, but please just come anyway. Scarlett knows how much I would worry about bumping into Will in Los Angeles, and she still asked me to come…which means it's urgent. Checking my blind spot, I pull back into traffic and turn toward the airport, calling Teagan on the car's Bluetooth speaker.

"You're heading out now?" she says briskly, when I explain that I have an out-of-town job. My favorite thing about Teagan is that she never complains when I need a sub at the last minute. Teagan knows how to massage our clients' egos, and if that doesn't work, she offers them a free hangover cure sometime in the future. If that still doesn't appease an irritated client, Teagan simply drops them. There are always more whales, always more casinos wanting to contract my services.

"Yes, I'm going straight to the airport." I have an overnight bag in the car, for exactly this sort of thing.

"Is it a paying job?"

I hesitate. Scarlett is a friend and I don't need the money, but I'll have to charge her, at least enough for Teagan and Darby's percentages. "Yes."

"Then I'll call and get you on the next flight," Teagan says. "You can get the ticket on your phone."

I thank her and hang up.

Chapter 2

I am too nervous to sleep on the plane, but I do my best to relax, hoping to restore my strength so I can do my job. Scarlett, and plenty of others, call what I do "healing magic." I've given up trying to correct them, because that's more or less the result, but what I actually do is use magic to communicate with a human body—the immune system, usually, but I can work with any of the body's major systems or organs. I speak to the part of the body that needs to be healed, and I encourage it to work faster, harder. When I was a child I used to call myself a "nudger," but that was mostly just to irritate my mother. "Thaumaturge magic" is the term she prefers. She was the one who trained me, who drilled me every single day of my teenage years, and I have to admit, she's the reason I'm as good as I am. Bloodlines matter, but much of magical strength is like muscle strength: it grows the more you work at it, and I am very strong now. Doing ten-hour shifts, six days a week will do that to you.

When my cab arrives at the hospital a little after one o'clock, I nearly bump into Jesse Cruz, who overhears me identify myself as Noah Cruz's girlfriend. Jesse is astonishingly handsome, and as tired as I am, I have to blink a few times to remember that he's not an actor. He speed-walks me to his brother's room, where I am too much much of a professional to gasp at the sight of the man's face. Noah, on the other hand, is probably a nice-looking man most of the time, but his face is currently a pulpy mess of contusions and abrasions. His ankle is broken, as are several ribs, but the doctors tell me they are most worried about the swelling in his brain.

When they've finished updating me, they allow me to sit at his bedside and touch his arm, which is all I need for now. The hospital staff comes and goes, sometimes talking to me, and I am able to murmur vague answers, but everyone takes the expression on my face for deep personal grief and leaves me alone.

I pull in my magic, and push it into Noah's body, first just to send out inquiries. I can't really verbalize this process, but it's more or less me sending a *What hurts?* message throughout his body, almost like bats using echolocation to find obstructions in a cave.

Some bodies respond better than others, and I am happy to discover that Noah Cruz has a very responsive system. It immediately begins telegraphing major problems in a number of systems. I start at the brain, where the doctors are most concerned. I push magic into the damaged cells.

Heal // grow // restore

Heal // grow // restore

The cells begin to perk up almost immediately, like a flower blooming in time-lapse photography. Sometimes bodies respond to me directly—*Interest // connection?*—but Noah's body doesn't need the reassurance that someone cares for it. I don't know anything about this man, but I can tell that he is loved, and he knows he is loved. It makes me think even better of Jesse Cruz.

And his parents. They arrive at the hospital at some point, and I have to pause to go through introductions. Carmen Cruz is eager to chat with her son's "girlfriend," but I need to stay focused on Noah's body, so I quietly murmur that I don't mean to be rude, but I'd like to pray over Noah. It is not that far from the truth. Carmen looks a little disappointed, but she and her husband take up chairs on the other side of the bed, and I forget they are there.

Time goes by, while I stay focused on my conversation with Noah's body. I have to pause two more times when a doctor or nurse insists on me moving away so they can check his vitals, but I am able to pick up where I left off. I clear the damage in his brain first, because that's most important, and then I close up the internal bleeding. I partially heal his ribs, but not all the way—an X-ray still needs to show fractures, or else the doctors will get suspicious.

By the time I finish taking care of the internal bleeding Noah's body is ready to wake up from the coma that the doctors induced—it seems I have accidentally caused the medicine to wear off. I coax the body to remain asleep. I am not ready to have a full conversation with Noah yet, and besides, this much healing, this fast is really going to hurt. I'm getting tired as I check over the ankle, but I'm glad I do, because it's worse than I thought: Noah has a compound break, with some tearing of muscle tissue and bones. I begin nudging the breaks and tears until I have convinced the body to knit up all but the fractures in the tibia and fibula. These small changes will show up in an X-ray, but they will be written off as a minor distortion in the machine.

Noah's body really wants him to wake up now, so I looking around, seeing that there is nobody else in the room at the moment. Noah's parents must have gone to get food, or run an errand. They probably even told me, but I wasn't listening.

No matter. I tell Noah's body, *Release / / awaken / / heal*

Then I pull back, becoming aware for the first time of the phantom pain in my own body. I am not injured, of course, but I have gone so deep into my conversation with Noah Cruz's body that for a few minutes I can feel his injuries as if they were my own. This happens fairly often, mostly for really serious injuries or diseases, and I have learned to let the aftereffects wash past me like the undertow returning to sea. I close my eyes and breathe deeply, trying not to clench up from the pain that is not real, not mine.

"Hey. Who're you?"

I open my eyes and find two clear brown ones looking at me. The bruising has faded from Noah's face. His eyes widen, and he croaks, "I've definitely never seen a nurse who looks like you."

"I'm not a nurse," I say, leaning toward him. "My name is Sashi Brighton. I'm a medical specialist from Las Vegas, and I came to check on you as a favor to Scarlett."

I keep it vague on purpose, partly to test his cognitive reactions. He blinks a few times, processing, and then says in his hoarse voice, "Jesse's Scarlett?"

I smile. "I suppose so." I can hear footsteps outside the door, so I add quickly, "Listen, I said I was your girlfriend so I could get in here. Just go with it, okay?" I give him a conspiratorial wink, just the slightest bit flirty, and take his hand. The poor man just nods, dazed.

It is nearly six when I leave the hospital, and I am exhausted. I haven't stayed up this long in years, and the combination of the children's hospital and Noah Cruz has worn me out. Scarlett has promised to send a vampire to guard over Noah when the sun sets, and if someone were to attack between now and then, there is nothing I could do anyway. So I say a quick goodbye to Noah's confused parents, knowing that the vampire will probably take care of their memories, and stagger out to a cab.

Teagan texted that she can buy me a ticket back to Las Vegas that night, but I am knackered. I don't want to stay in Will's city any longer than I have to, but judging from how distracted both Scarlett and Jesse have been, it's obvious that everyone is involved in some sort of crisis. I'm fairly confident I can slip to a hotel, spend the night, and fly home in the morning.

Twenty minutes later, I stumble into a chain hotel in Burbank, hand my credit card and drivers license to a clerk, and take the room key card he slides me, yawning practically the whole time. I have a small overnight bag I keep in my car for just this kind of last-minute trip, but when I reach the room I don't even bother to brush my teeth. I pull back the covers and fall onto my bed.

And my cell phone rings. Of course.

I check the display and see that it is Scarlett again. Groaning, I lift the phone to my ear. "Did something else happen to Noah?"

"What? Oh, no, not at all! I was calling to thank you."

I rub my eye with my free hand. It feels crusty, though I don't *think* I've fallen asleep yet. "You're quite welcome. I'll send you a bill in a few days, when things calm down for you."

"Yeah, listen, about that..."

I freeze, my hand still on my temple. Have more humans been hurt? If so, do I even have the energy to help them?

"Sashi...I want to tell Will that you're here. I think you guys should have a conversation."

I sit bolt upright as though I've been electrocuted. "With respect, Scarlett, that's not really any of your business."

"You're right, it's absolutely not. But I still want to tell him you're in town."

I try to force myself to think politically, something I rarely need to do. It's possible that this is one of those loyalty things, because of Los Angeles' unique power-share situation. Perhaps Scarlett has some sort of pact to tell the truth to the others? "Do you think that's really necessary?" I say, trying not to sound like I am panicking. "I'm going back tonight, soon," I lie. "He doesn't need to know I was ever here." I glance at my overnight bag. I can just leave the hotel room, right this moment, if it means not having to face Will.

"Sashi...I'm pregnant."

When Scarlett says that, I actually stand up from the bed and do a few squats, shaking out my legs. I'm that convinced that I must somehow still be half asleep. When I'm certain I am awake, I say,

"That's not possible." Scarlett is a null. I don't know much about them, medically speaking, but I do know they can't have children.

"Apparently it is. Do you remember the guy I lost in Vegas? The other null?"

The image of Scarlett, hurt and broken on an empty airplane, fills my memory. I was asking her questions, trying to keep her conscious and responsive as I cleaned her wounds. She'd been halfway in shock and visibly grief-stricken. "Oh," I say now, feeling stupid. "*Oh.*"

"Yeah. He died not knowing he was going to have a kid. And Will…there's a good chance we won't make it through this tonight."

No. The word screams itself in my head. Not Will. He's not allowed to die. But all that comes out of my mouth is a strangled, "I see."

"Look, I'm pretty sure I'm going to be the world's shittiest mom, and I have no right or place to give you advice," Scarlett continues. "But maybe if Grace met Will…maybe if she understood why you couldn't marry John…"

Bollocks. I stare at the hotel room ceiling for a moment, wishing…what? That Scarlett didn't know my secrets? That I wasn't still half in love with a man I can't be with?

I am just so tired. Tired of all of this—being alone, feeling these things for a man who really no longer exists. More than any of that, I realize, I am tired of being afraid of it. Of hiding from what happened to us.

"All right," I hear myself say. "What do you have in mind?"

Chapter 3

Half an hour later, I am pacing back and forth across the mouth of a long, winding driveway, while my Uber driver waits discreetly down the block. I have already forgotten if the driver is a man or a woman; I'm so distracted.

Will. I'm going to see *Will.*

I am also going to throw up in these very nice bushes, I think, as my stomach does another backflip. I open and close my hands, certain that if I tried to use them they would start shaking. What if he decides not to come?

I doubt Will has become superficial since we last met, but I can't resist looking down at myself. I'm wearing the slacks and wrinkled blouse I put on for work more than twenty-four hours ago, and my hair…I touch it, and my memory flashes back to another night that I was a mess, when I turned up at Will's apartment bloodstained and filthy.

Then I see the figure walking down the driveway.

I'd expected a car—doesn't everyone drive everywhere in LA, and aren't they all in a hurry tonight? Who has long driveways in Los Angeles?—but he is walking at a measured pace, hands in his pockets, giving me plenty of time to see him. He is silhouetted by the lights from the house, but I would know him anywhere, if for no other reason than he moves like Grace. Like our daughter.

I know I should wave or something, but I just stand there, wordless, and watch him come back to me.

There are streetlights down here, and two ornate lampposts like something out of a Victorian novel, and as he steps into the light I want to cry out. He is older—but not much. It's been eighteen years, but I wouldn't know it from the tiny crows feet at his eyes.

Then his eyes lift to meet mine, and I stop breathing. He *is* older. His eyes are full of it. "Sashi," he says quietly, looking away from me. He has stopped six feet away from me, an agonized look on his face. "I'm so sorry."

I don't have to ask what he's sorry for, because I know. Of course I know; I've thought about it every day for the last eighteen years. I cross my arms over my chest as the images overtake me again: Will, as a wolf, ripping apart the alpha werewolf who wanted to hurt me.

I want to tell him I understand, but I can't seem to speak. "It's not your fault," I finally manage to say. "I should never have trusted my mother. I should never have left you that night—"

"Sashi, no—" He takes a step closer to me, and I take an instinctive step back. The thought of him touching me isn't just scary; it's…distasteful. Species don't mix in the Old World, at least not often, and I grew up being taught to fear the pack.

Some of this must show on my face, because I see the hurt in his eyes. I also see him bury it. "I know what you did," he says.

I am genuinely confused. "What I did…?"

"That night…with Astrid. When Luke came to kill us, you stayed to protect me. With a screwdriver." He smiles, a little crookedly. "Against an insane alpha werewolf."

I look away. "I had some silver rings, too. And a wrist brace."

"A wrist brace?"

"Like for rollerblading, in case I fell? But it kept my wrist straight." I hold up my hand and mime a stiff punch. Great. Now I am babbling *and* I probably look like a homeless idiot.

When I risk looking up at him, though, his lips are pressed together in a line, and I realize he is trying not to laugh. Against my wishes, I feel a smile twitch on my face, which makes Will break out in that heart-stopping grin I know so well.

"You went up against an alpha werewolf…with a screwdriver and a wrist brace?" he chortles.

"And some silver rings."

I can't help it, I start giggling, and then we are both laughing, some of the tension seeping away. God, I had forgotten how much Grace's laugh is like his.

When we finally calm down, Will gives me a look of such sadness that I feel like I've been slapped. "I missed you," he says simply, shuffling his feet against the drive. "I tried looking for you a couple of times, but you'd moved on, you'd gotten married…"

I look up, startled. "I never got married." I manage to close my mouth before the words *I never moved on* can follow. I have at least that much dignity left.

He blinks. "Your last name changed. You have a child."

I hug my arms around myself again. There is no point in correcting him about my life, or the last night I'd chosen to distance myself from my mother. It doesn't matter, but Grace does. This is why I am here.

Tears are running down my face, but I think I can keep my voice together, and I have to do this. "Will," I whisper, forcing myself to look at him. "*We* have a child."

At first, he just looks confused. "You were on the pill," he says uncertainly. "I saw the package."

"I stopped taking them. Because…" I take a deep breath, and force myself to finish the sentence. "You needed bone marrow."

Comprehension crashes into him, and he actually staggers, his hand going to the lamppost. He is on his knees, and I rush to him, but I cannot stand to touch him, so I kneel down too, three feet away. "I have a baby?" he mumbles, looking at me with shock.

"You have a teenager," I correct, trying to smile. "Her name is Grace. Grace Jody, for your sister. She looks like me, but she moves like you. She has your laugh, and the way you smile…and…"

It's too much, it's *obviously* too much for him, and I force myself to shut up. Will just continues to stare at me, dumbfounded. After a moment, he manages to say, "Why didn't you *tell* me?"

"By the time I found out," I say, "you were…" I almost say "dead," because that's the way I've always thought of *my* Will. But that's confusing, because this werewolf in front of me…he isn't the raving lunatic I'd imagined, based on my experience with Luke. So I settle for, "gone."

"You could have—" he begins, but he stops himself and shakes his head. "No, you couldn't, because you'd just seen me rip apart Luke in front of you. Oh, sweetheart, I'm—."

I flinch at the word, and he shakes himself again. "I'm sorry. I'm really sorry; I shouldn't have said that."

"It's okay."

He lets go of the lamppost, easing back on his heels, and gives me a look of astonishment. "You came here tonight. For me." He raises an eyebrow and looks me over. "Without even a wrist brace?"

I give him a weak smile. "Scarlett said you're a good man. She said you might die tonight, and you deserved to know about Grace." I shrugged. "And I couldn't bring any weapons on the plane."

I was trying to keep my voice light, but his face hardens. "Wait, *Scarlett* knows about my daughter?" I don't answer, but he's smart— even smarter than I remember. "Because of Vegas. Dashiell said Clifford was healed in Vegas. That was you."

He stands up and begins to pace in tight circles, looking furious. I start to shrink away, but force myself to stand up to him. I am not twenty anymore. And I have so little to lose.

"It's not Scarlett's fault," I say quickly. "I made her promise."

"I'm her fucking partner," he snarls over his shoulder, not looking at me. "She should have told me."

"*I* should have told you," I snap at him, and my tone surprises him enough so he spins on his heel to look at me. "But you were a werewolf, like Luke, and I thought it would poison you, and I wasn't going to let that near my baby. *I* made that decision, and I'd make it again, and if you want to be angry at someone you can bloody well be angry at *me*."

We stand there for a moment, breathing hard, and I realize what I've done. I just challenged an alpha werewolf. I *yelled* at him. I have seen Luke beat the hell out of his own werewolves for a fraction of the disrespect I just showed.

It has been twenty years since I've had regular dealings with werewolves, but I remember the right moves: I should drop my eyes, lower my head, show submission. But I am too bloody tired and too bloody stubborn, and I stand my ground, my eyes blazing into Will's.

Then, to my total and utter shock, *he backs down*. Will turns away from me, lowering his head. "I'm not Luke, Sashi," he says wearily.

We stand there for a moment in silence. Will is facing the house, looking up at the lights. "I should get back up there," he says, almost to himself.

I am still in shock that he backed down, but I glance down the street, where my Uber driver is still waiting. I'm sure I owe him a small fortune by now, but I can afford it. "Right. Well. Scarlett has my phone number. You should call me in a few days. If you want to meet Grace," I add hurriedly, because whatever value there might be in clearing the air, nothing has really changed between us.

Will turns back to look at me again. "What did you tell her about me?"

I have to swallow several times, my cheeks burning. "That you were a summer fling, and I didn't know how to find you," I say quietly. That was quite an abridged version of the web of lies I'd had to spin over the years, but it was more or less accurate.

"She bought that?"

I can't help but smile, just a little. "For now, anyway. She has plenty of other things to be mad at me over; she hasn't gotten around to her paternity."

Will starts to say something else, shakes his head, and mumbles, "I'll call in a few days." Then he turns around and begins trudging up the driveway.

And I stand there watching him, alone again.

Chapter 4

After the confrontation with Will, I return to the hotel, cry for nearly an hour, and pass out on the covers.

When the phone rings, it feels like seconds later, though the clock says it's after midnight. The caller ID says Scarlett Bernard, but when I answer the phone I hear Jesse's panicked voice. "Something's happening to Scarlett," he yells into the phone. He sounds like he's standing in the middle of a movie theater that's playing a war film.

I sit up straight in the bed. "What do you mean? What's going on?"

"I don't know, she's...she's using all this power. Her eye is bloody, you know, like a subjunctal... subjunctive..."

"Subconjunctival hemorrhage," I say, remembering the pregnancy. My head hurts from crying, but somehow my brain is clearing. "She's hypertensive; her blood pressure is rising. Tell her she needs to relax."

"She can't do that!" He says something about riders and specters, but I can't follow it.

"I don't know what to tell you!" I say, frustrated. "She's too stressed. If she keeps it up, she'll lose the baby, and possibly even die."

"*Shit*. Call you back."

He hangs up, and I stare at the phone, flabbergasted. Then I throw off the covers and hurry to the bathroom, cursing myself. Scarlett and the baby are in real trouble. Why didn't I ask more questions about the situation in LA? She actually *told* me they could all die, and I hadn't taken her seriously.

The woman in the bathroom mirror is a mess: her eyes are puffy and bloodshot from crying and lack of sleep, and she's still wearing clothes from two nights ago. I splash some water on my face and throw my hair into a ponytail, yanking clean clothes out of my bag. It's only after I get dressed that I realize I have no idea where to go to be useful.

"Bollocks!" I call Jesse's phone, and then Scarlett's, but neither answers. Why would they, in the middle of a fight? I press my hand to my forehead. Think, Sashi, think.

I snap my fingers. There was a vampire still at the hospital, to guard Noah. What was her name? Scarlett said she was her roommate...Lex said Scarlett and a friend had visited Boulder. Dropping onto the bed, I dial Lex's phone.

It's very late, but Lex is almost as nocturnal as I usually am. "Sashi? What's going on?"

"Lex, I need the name of Scarlett Bernard's friend, the one who came to visit you in Boulder. I think someone told me earlier today, but I can't bloody remember."

"You mean Molly?"

"Yes!" I exhale. "Cheers."

I am about to hang up, but Lex says, "Wait! You only get this British when you're upset. What's going on?"

"Something big, I think, but I need to get back to you on that. I don't suppose you have Molly's mobile number?"

"I think I might. Give me two minutes and I'll text it to you."

I could try to go through the hospital operator, but I don't know if Molly has used a false name with Noah, and besides, my word will carry more weight if I call Molly directly. "Right. Bye."

I hang up the phone, turning it over in my hands impatiently and berating myself. Scarlett's baby is in trouble—*Will* may be in trouble, says a voice in the back of my mind—and I'm right here in the same city, where I could help, and I didn't get any details. Because I was mooning over Will.

Lex's text comes through, a number with an 818 area code and the words *Fill me in as soon as you can.* I dial the number, and a cool female voice answers immediately. "Hello?"

I need to be sure. "Is this Molly?"

"Yes, who's this?"

"My name is Sashi Brighton. We have some mutual friends?"

Her voice warms considerably. "Hi, Sashi; I know who you are. What's going on?"

"That's what I wanted to ask you, actually. I just got a call from Jesse that Scarlett is having medical problems, but he hung up, I have no idea where they are, and you're the only one answering their phone."

A longer pause this time. "I only have a general idea, but honestly, I'm not sure I should tell you. Scarlett says you're like me—not really a fighter."

I blow out a breath, feeling again the horrible impotence that comes with my magic. As strong as I am, it's only strong for a thaumaturge witch. In an actual physical confrontation, I can only stand at the sidelines waiting for someone else to get hurt. "She's right; I'm not. But I'm a licensed physician's assistant. I can help the people who *are* fighting." I want to help Will, but I'd seen him fight. Scarlett needs my help more. "And I can try to help Scarlett and the baby," I add.

"She told you about that?" Molly sounds surprised, and I realize it might have been a secret. Molly clearly knew, though, so I don't think I've done any harm.

I have a sudden thought. "Look, you said you have a general idea, right? Can you tell me the nearest hospital, where they might bring Scarlett?"

"In that part of town…it'll be St. Jude," Molly replies. "We've got people there."

"Thank you!"

"Do you need a car?"

I blink. "I can get a cab…"

"Better not," Molly says. "Cabs leave a paper trail. I can get you a car from one of the humans who works for us."

The way she keeps saying "us" and "we" is a bit unnerving, but I can't argue with her logic. I tell her where I'm staying, and she promises that a Toyota sedan will be out front in fifteen minutes with the keys inside.

I hang up the phone and collect my things, tossing them into the overnight bag. Downstairs, I grab a paper cup of stale coffee from the lobby and hurry out front. By the time I make it outside, the car is waiting. No one is inside. Impressive.

As I drive toward the hospital, following the navigation on my phone, I vacillate between worrying that I'm overreacting, and worrying that I'm underreacting. Should I have pushed Molly to give me the location of the fight? Would my presence there make any difference? Come to think of it, will my presence at the *hospital* make any difference? Molly said the Old World had people on staff there, so what exactly can I do that they can't?

I don't have an answer to that, but I am certain of one thing: I can't just sit in a hotel room doing nothing while Scarlett may be losing the baby. I'd rather be a redundancy on the sidelines than out of the match entirely.

I am half a mile from the hospital when my mobile rings, the screen filling with the words Caller Unknown. I haven't figured out how to link up the bluetooth with the car, so I fumble with the phone and finally get it set on speaker. "Hello?"

"Sashi Brighton?" It is a man's voice, deep and a little gravelly, but he speaks with urgency.

"Yes, who's this?" I say.

"My name is Hayne. My wife is Kirsten Harms."

I don't know him, but I know Kirsten Harms's name—and the fact that he knew I would suggests he's aware that I'm a witch, too. "I understand," I say. "Would you happen to be with Scarlett Bernard right now? I'm worried about her."

The man does not hesitate. "Scarlett is on her way to the hospital. I have a situation, though, that I need your help with. Jesse gave me your number. He said it could only be you."

I blanch, but isn't this exactly why I'm here? "Tell me where."

Hayne directs me to an enclosed parking garage only two blocks from the hospital, and I am relieved to learn how close I am. "I've taken out the security cameras; just go straight to the second floor," he tells me. "I didn't know where else to take him."

I don't know this part of LA, but I find the parking garage easily. It's part of an industrial-looking block filled with businesses that are closed for the night, and nothing is moving on the street. I pull into the garage and speed up to the second floor, turning right at the corner—and my car's headlights seem to flare red with blood. It is seeping out of the tailgate of a huge, dented pickup truck.

A muscled African-American man waves me to a stop behind the truck, opening my door for me. I throw the car into park and jump out without looking away from the pickup. "I'm Hayne, we spoke on the phone," he says as we hurry toward the back of the truck.

Hayne pulls the tailgate down, and a man is lying back there, writhing with pain. He's covered in blood, and more blood pools in the truck bed and drips down to the concrete. It isn't hard to see the source of the blood: his left hand and forearm have been sliced off near the elbow.

A blonde woman is crouched next to him, bedraggled and blood-smeared. I think it's Kirsten Harms, but neither of us stop for introductions. "We tried to put a tourniquet on but it's not helping," she calls as I approach. "We can't call anyone else."

I try to climb into the back of the truck, but the tailgate is slippery from all the blood. In the end Hayne simply lifts up my rear and deposits me next to the injured man. I approve.

I sidle closer to the injury. It's a clean cut, but still spurting blood, despite what's already in the truck bed. He must be a witch—a vampire or werewolf would be healing faster than this. "If he's a witch my magic's not going to help much," I say, though I am already rolling up my sleeves.

"He's not a witch. He's human...now," the woman says, her words coming out high and tight. "That's why we can't take him to the hospital." There's a certain tone in her voice, but I'm not listening—I'm analyzing my patient. The man has abrasions and cuts on his face, and one eye is swollen, but blood loss from the severed arm is what's going to kill him. He's breathing fast, his lips and fingernails blue. From my quick glance, I estimate that the amount of blood in the truck is nearing 40 percent of his blood volume.

"Hold him still, as much as you can," I say grimly, and I put both of my hands on his upper arm, reaching for my magic.

I don't bother asking his body where it is hurt. I plan to concentrate directly on stopping the bleeding, and then push his system to replace the missing volume in order to regulate his blood pressure. I can immediately feel, however, that he is fading quickly. The blood loss is even worse than I thought. He needs the hospital, but he's not going to make it there in time.

Seal // stop // heal is the message I send into his arm. It's crude, but I'm worried about how little strength I feel from him. I have seen serious blood loss before, but never this bad.

Ally // champion

Ally // champion

Ally // champion

My brow furrows. It's hard to explain, but the body isn't framing this as a question. It's as though it recognizes me. I've had that happen before, on some of my frequent flier whales in Vegas, but never with so much...familiarity.

There's no time to puzzle over it. I'm still tired from the previous day, and this man needs everything I've got. I push *Seal // stop // heal* into the arm until the blood slows to a trickle, and then I tell the blonde woman to re-tie the tourniquet. The man has gone still, and I worry that he's slipped into coma.

When the tourniquet is secure, I move to the delicate bit. Rebuilding lost blood volume was one of the first things I learned how to do, but it's always difficult, and a case this severe requires all my concentration.

Hayne and the blonde woman are talking about something in excited voices, but I tune them out. Instead, I remember my mother's voice lecturing me: "Bone marrow produces stem cells, stem cells make blood cells." Placing my hands on his chest, I visualize my way into the bones themselves, where the marrow is stored. *More* // *faster* // *create* I tell the bone marrow.

It responds immediately. *Ally* // *champion*

I expected to have to coax it harder, but within seconds I can feel the body struggling to obey me, to reverse direction. It's like watching an airplane try to correct its trajectory in the seconds before a crash.

As tired as I am, I don't understand how he's still able to fight, but that's exactly what he does. I can't let up on him for a second, though. I stay deep in his bones, following the sped-up production of blood. When it flags, I encourage it. When it hesitates, I nudge it along.

I am paying no attention to how much of my own power I'm burning through—until I feel myself tipping sideways. I have to let go of the patient with one hand so I can catch my fall.

"Ms. Brighton?"

Someone touches my arm, and I look up, startled. The blonde woman—Kirsten— is crouched next to me, looking worried. "Are you all right? Can you save him?"

I listen to the patient's body again. "I can stabilize him for a little longer," I say quickly. "But we need to get him to a hospital."

"I told you—"

"He needs oxygen, a skin graft, drainage tubes, sterile dressings to prevent infection. I can't do any of that here. Put him under a different name if you need to, but get us to a *bloody* hospital or he will die."

Kirsten and Hayne exchange a worried look. I open my mouth to argue further, but just then the patient's right hand rises, falters, and lands on my hands where they are pressed on his chest. I am stunned that he isn't in a coma, but even more astonished when he manages to speak. "Sashi," he mumbles.

I go very, very still, and look closely at the man's face in the lousy parking garage lighting. I try to erase the blood, the swollen eye and lip.

The truck seems to spin, and I can feel myself swaying.

"Will?"

Chapter 5

I won't leave him.

At the hospital, I run alongside the stretcher, and I hover outside the door during the surgery, my face pressed to the window. They try to pull me away—my pants are soaked in his blood, and more blood covers my arms nearly to the elbow—but I fight until they are convinced it's easier to leave me. Kirsten and Hayne disappear, likely to try and conceal Will's identity from the people at the hospital who are already on Dashiell's payroll. I don't even notice when they leave.

Other people appear and talk to me, lots of people, and most of them try to convince me of something: Go change, go eat, go sleep—something like that. I am not listening, because I won't leave him.

If I leave him, if I even let him out of my sight, I am sure I will wake up and none of it will be real. I will be in the hotel bed in Burbank, or back home in Las Vegas, pining for something I lost almost twenty years ago. Or maybe I'll be in bed at John's house in Boulder, wishing I could be grateful for the man right next to me, instead of dreaming of the one I lost.

So I won't leave him, and I won't listen.

Stabilizing Will has exhausted all of my magic, and the surgeons are still worried. I am so tired I have to lean against the wall and fight not to slide down to the floor. After the first surgery, when they move Will to recovery, I stumble along quietly, a little ways behind the stretcher, to show them how good I can be, how I will not interfere. My head is spinning. Everything is spinning.

In the recovery room, they don't know what to do with me, and maybe Dashiell or one of his people pull strings, because eventually they give up and bring me a chair. His blood is still drying on me, but I won't leave him. I have never been this tired, but I am afraid to sleep. Time passes. I keep my hand in contact with him whenever they'll let me. If they tell me to move back for a moment I do so meekly, because I will do anything to keep from being pulled out of the room.

I don't know how long it has been since the parking garage, but eventually a man crouches down beside my chair and takes my hands, ignoring the brown stains of dried blood. "Sashi," he says gently, and I see that it is Jesse Cruz.

"Is Scarlett okay?" I blurt, surprising myself.

Jesse's face tightens. "They're not sure. The baby's heartbeat is strong, but Scar's been unconscious since last night, and nobody really knows why. Molly's sitting with her right now. How is Will?"

"On the edge of a coma, I think." I look helplessly at Will, with his paper-pale skin and dark-circled eyes. My stupid magic may have kept him alive, but he and Scarlett aren't out of the woods. I am the most powerful thaumaturge witch in North America, but I couldn't help her, and I almost couldn't save him. In the grand scheme of this mess, I've done so little. And now I'm out of magic. I haven't felt so completely powerless since...well, since the last time I failed to keep Will safe.

"I should have come with you last night," I say faintly. "Maybe if I had been right there on the scene..."

Hesitantly, Jesse touches my shoulder. "Sashi, tell me the truth: would Noah have died, if you hadn't come?"

My brain is hesitant to switch gears, and I have to stare at him for a moment before I find the words. "Brain death would have been likely. The internal injuries were potentially fatal, depending on the quality and expediency of the surgeon."

Jesse smiles. "That sounds like doctor-speak for yes. And Kirsten and Hayne think you saved Will."

My eyes return to his closed, sunken eyes. "That remains to be seen." My voice breaks, and I clamp my jaw shut. I never wanted Will to become a werewolf, but at least then he was practically indestructible. Now he is so vulnerable, so fragile. And I am right back to kneeling beside him in my mother's garage at twenty-one, helpless to stop what's happening to him.

Jesse is studying me. "Are *you* okay?"

"He's human, but I'm out of magic. She said she could do it, but I didn't really believe her. Not really." I know that I am babbling, but I can't seem to put my words in a more logical order. "I think I wanted it to be true so much that I didn't let me believe it, or maybe I just didn't think he'd ever choose to…" I force myself to focus my eyes on Jesse and close my mouth.

"Hayne told me you didn't realize it was Will," he says. "I'm really sorry; I should have specifically told him to tell you. But Scarlett had just collapsed, and I was out of my mind—"

Jesse looks so guilty, I wave my hand to stop him. "Can you tell me what happened?"

He smiles.

The story is fantastical, even for the Old World, but that calms me, in a way, because it's too strange to be anything but true. There is a lot to absorb in the account, things I never knew about my own world, but I put it aside. I don't have it in me to process anything else today.

When Jesse finishes his explanation, he suggests, gently, that I take a shower in the hospital room's attached bath.

"I can't leave him," I say, as though this is perfectly reasonable.

Jesse doesn't ask me why I'm afraid to let Will out of my sight, which I appreciate. Instead, he offers to stay right there next to Will until I come back out. I know that he is just as worried about Scarlett, and I am so grateful I want to cry.

Instead, I grab the clean scrubs that someone has left me outside the bathroom door, and shower quickly, fighting the edge of panic that threatens me when I can't see Will. Jesse is still there when I come out, and so is Will, and my shoulders sag with relief. I touch Will's arm and listen to his body for a moment to make sure he is no worse off than when I left him, less than five minutes ago.

Jesse stands up and says with a touch of apology that he needs to return to Scarlett. I thank him for watching Will for me, and Jesse doesn't laugh at how silly that sounds. He does put his head close to my ear and reminds me to tell anyone who asks that Will's last name is Brighton. He's my husband, and he was in an industrial accident.

I nod. Jesse squeezes my shoulder briefly and leaves, while I settle back into the chair next to the bed, staring at Will. He's still so pale. He may wake up on his own, but the more likely possibilities are that I will either regain enough strength to help him heal further, or he will die before I can get enough magic to help him. Right now all I can do is wait, feeling almost nauseous with exhaustion and déjà vu. I sat next to Will's hospital bed so many times, when we were young.

I grip Will's right hand in both of mine, being careful of his IV, and it is only then that I can lean forward, rest my head on my arms, and fall asleep.

Chapter 6

All the patients in the cancer ward seem happy to see us, but this one's smile is something else altogether. It's light, warm, and welcoming, like he's been waiting his whole life for me to just walk through that door and say good morning. The room seems to glow because of that smile. I find myself smiling back at him before anyone has spoken, and I step forward and stick out my hand.

"Sashi," I say.

"Hello, Sashi," he says, aiming that charismatic laser grin straight at me. His hand is warm and rough in places, like he does the kind of work that creates calluses. I want to turn his palm over and run my fingers over it, inspecting. "I'm Will."

"Sashi…"

I open my eyes, straightening up. I have no idea what time it is. Actually, I have no idea what day it is. Someone has dimmed the lights, but I can feel my hand still holding Will's. Did someone actually say my name, or was I just dreaming of the day we met?

"Sashi," Will says again, and I realize that his eyes are open. He is still pale, with the dark circles and mussed hair, but he is *awake.* And staring at me in wonder. "Hello," he whispers.

I let out a sob of relief, which makes his brow crease with worry. I sniffle for a moment, rubbing my eyes on the shoulder of the scrubs to get rid of the tears. When I have it under control I say, "You look like shit," because I know it will make him smile.

I'm right. "I *feel* like shit," he admits. He looks at our linked hands, but does not move to pull away from me. His head is still sunk back on the pillow, like he's too exhausted to lift it. Quickly, I check in with his body, and find that the healing process is humming along. It is as though it is still obeying my previous orders.

"Can you talk?" I ask. I push a little bit of strength into him, using the magic I recovered while we were asleep.

"I think so."

"You're human," I say, stating the completely obvious. "Scarlett made you human." A sudden fear strikes me, and I have another word with his systems.

He watches my face, knowing what I look like when I am working. "What is it?" he asks.

"I was checking for illness," I admit.

"And?" Will doesn't look particularly concerned about the answer.

"Whatever Scarlett did to your body, it feels new now," I tell him. The scientific part of my brain wonders how far this purification goes: will he need vaccinations again, like a child? Then I glance at his arm. "Well, except for one thing."

Will nods and looks ruefully at the amputation. "This witch, he cut off my hand with a sword. He was going to kill me, and Scarlett shot this energy at him…but I was too close."

I nod, not sure what to say. Finally I settle on, "How do you feel?"

Will knows that I am not asking about his body. If I want to know *that*, I can just ask it directly.

His eyes go distant for a minute as he considers the question. "Sad," he admits, looking down at the place where his hand used to be. "Weak. And…" He presses his lips together, but somehow I understand.

"Relieved?" I whisper.

Will nods. "It was a lot of responsibility," he confesses. Then he lifts his right hand and absently kisses my knuckles, and there must be something wrong with my nervous system because I swear I feel it all the way down to my toes.

"What's going to happen now?" I ask.

"I can't go back," he says, seeing the fear on my face. He looks down at his left arm. "It wouldn't heal, now, and I can't be alpha with three legs."

Oh. "That's why they could only call me," I say, finally comprehending. It's all perfectly obvious, of course, but my head wasn't clear enough to put it together before. "Will Carling has to be dead, or everyone will find out what Scarlett can do."

He nods again. "She'd become a target to everyone in the Old World who's unhappy with what they are, and everyone who thinks she's too much of a threat. Even Dashiell wouldn't be able to protect her from that."

"And she's pregnant."

"Yes."

I look at our locked hands for a moment. I am not afraid to let go of him anymore, and I know that I probably should. It's been nearly twenty years; I have no right to him. But I don't move, and neither does he.

A cell phone buzzes on the small wheeled table near the bed, and I realize it's my phone. I don't remember putting it there, but someone else probably picked it up for me. I reach over with my free hand and pick it up, checking the screen.

"What is it?" Will asks.

"A text from Jesse. Scarlett's okay; she's awake."

Will returns my smile. "I think those two finally got together."

I hadn't given their romantic status any thought, but that certainly explains Jesse's devotion. I put the cell phone back on the table, and when I turn back Will is watching my face closely. "What?" I ask.

He blinks hard for a moment. "I just remembered seeing you last night. You were in the back of the truck with me. You...brought me back."

I look down at my lap. "I used up a lot of energy early yesterday morning, at pediatric oncology," I explain. "And then I healed Noah—

Noah Cruz, Jesse's brother? I'm sorry I was so weak by the time I got to you. If I were fresh, I could have done it faster—"

"Sashi..." Will squeezes my hand as he interrupts me. "I think you are the strongest person I've ever known."

Fresh tears prick my eyes, and there's a sudden lump in my throat. I have no idea what to say.

"Remember that afternoon, the day we met?" Will asks. I nod. It would be embarrassing for Will, or anyone else, to find out how often I think about that day. "I think about that all the time," he says now, echoing my thoughts. "That day, and the day you turned up at my apartment in Winona."

My cheeks redden. "Those stairs."

He smiles. "You were so—"

"Don't say cute," I warn him.

"I wasn't," he promises. "I was going to say 'lost.' And you came to me."

"I shouldn't have. I knew dragging you into that mess would put you in danger."

"If you hadn't, I would have died of cancer. And we wouldn't have Grace."

"But I didn't know that," I argue, because I don't think I will ever absolve myself for recklessly falling in love with Will.

"Sashi." He kisses my knuckles again. "I have never, for one instant, regretted meeting you, or falling in love with you."

The tears spill down my cheeks, dripping onto the borrowed scrubs. "Yes, well, they've given you quite a lot of drugs."

He smiles. My lower lip trembles, but I don't let myself smile back at him. Instead, I force myself to finally release his hand. I swipe at my eyes with a tissue from the nearby box and then smooth down my hair. It's completely dry now. I must have been out for awhile.

Will watches me without comment. "I'm not the same," I tell him, when I'm sure of my voice. I think of all the things I've done that I wouldn't want him to know about, because he'd be disappointed in who I've become. The abusive men whose money I've taken. The women I didn't help. All the compromises. "I've done so many things I'm not proud of."

A shadow falls over Will's face, and for a moment it seems like he can see the sins as I'm remembering them. But then he says, "Same here." He shifts in the bed a little like he wants to get up, but falls back, exhausted.

"And it would be foolish for us to jump into anything," I hear myself adding. "You're hurt, and your whole life just shifted under you, and...and..."

"*Sashi.*" He says my name with fondness—and a little exasperation. I mimic his tone. "*Will.*"

"You're right, my whole life just blew up. It was a pretty good life, most of the time. But it was always a consolation prize, because I couldn't be with you."

He reaches for me, and I take his hand again. I can't help myself. "Your pack—" I start to say.

"—Is going to be fine," Will interrupts. "I had a good beta; he'll make a great alpha." He squeezes my fingers. "Look, I'm not proposing or anything," he adds. "But I've spent almost twenty years now *not* getting over you."

I think of John, and everything I lost because I couldn't let go of Will. I whisper, "Same here."

Will's sunken, tired eyes are twinkling at me. "So what if we tried...*not* getting over each other? You know, just for a while."

I'm crying again—did I ever stop?—but manage to say, "I suppose I can try that."

Then I reach over and let myself touch his face. He has a five o'clock shadow that rather suits him, and his hair is longer than it used to be. He lets go of my right hand and reaches up to press my fingers against his face. His skin is warm.

"Sashi..."

"Yes?"

"I don't think I can sit up," he says very seriously. "But if you don't kiss me, I'm going to have to try."

Smiling through my tears, I bend forward, very gently, and kiss him like I'll never stop.

Nativity

Author's Note: Nativity is set immediately after the events of Shadow Hunt.

I.

"*Dude!* We can't be these people!"

Jesse barely heard me; he was very focused on navigating the hallways with the wheelchair. The hospital wasn't particularly busy at this hour on December twenty-fifth, but he insisted on keeping every single person in the hall at least four feet away from me, in case they…I don't know, began projectile vomiting typhoid or something. His task was made harder by the fact that I was approximately the size and shape of Violet, the gum-chewing girl in Willy Wonka and the Chocolate Factory, *after* she turns into the blueberry.

"Can't be…what people?" He was actually panting with the effort of running, but I was momentarily distracted. We had just rushed past a small family of witches.

I'm a null, a rare individual who blocks out all of the magic in a given space around me. I can feel magic in my radius—witches register as sort of a neutral white noise—and although I'm used to having people with magic go in and out of proximity all the time, in this particular moment it was off-putting. Maybe because I was about to do a very scary, very human thing: have a baby.

Then Jesse whipped around a corner fast enough for one of the wheels to momentarily leave the ground. "Jesse, slow dow—ah, fuckity fucking *pus bucket*—" I'd been clutching the wheelchair's armrest for dear life, but as the new contraction hit I had to let go so I could curl myself over my enormous belly. Yeah, I was pretty sure this was what Violet had felt like when the Oompa Loompas took her off to be squeezed.

Jesse, valuing his life, stopped doing zoomies around the hallway and came around to crouch in front of the wheelchair, letting me grip both of his hands. "Bad?" he asked.

I nodded tightly, squeezing his hands as hard as I could. I would have liked to explain my rad Willy Wonka analogy, but I was irrationally certain that if I unglued my jaw to speak it would make the contraction pain worse. All I could really do was wait for it to pass.

When I was sure I could talk, I gave Jesse the fiercest glare I could manage. "Get…me…*all*…the drugs."

He jumped up and hurried back to the wheelchair handles, and we were off again.

Half an hour earlier, the two of us had been enjoying a nice, low-key Christmas at home, along with Shadow, the bargest who adopted me a few years back. Jesse had taken over my crime-scene cleaning responsibilities until after the baby was born, and he'd been just about to leave for a call when my water broke.

If you'd asked me that morning, I would have been confident that all arrangements had been made: the hospital bag was packed, my sometimes assistant, Corry, was on call, and my best friend, Molly, had already paid an absurd amount of money for a stranger to install a car seat into my new van. I don't know if anyone is ever *ready* to have their first baby, but I certainly felt like we were as prepared as we could be.

But the moment I felt the warm gush of liquid, our little guest house erupted into frenzy. Corry had to be called, I couldn't remember where I'd left the damn overnight bag, and one of my shoes—the only flats that I could put on my swollen feet without any help—was inexplicably missing. At the same time, Shadow had decided that no, she should definitely be allowed to come into the delivery room with us after all, and she tried to force her way after me. It was hard to block a one-hundred-and-eighty-pound bargest from following you out the door when you're the size of a refrigerator.

221

All the baby books, not to mention the parenting class we'd taken, said there was plenty of time between the first contraction and the moment you needed to be in the hospital. I could feel Jesse working really hard to project calm as he found the bag and the shoe and hustled me out to the van—but everything inside me was saying *this is happening NOW*.

During the car ride to the hospital, my thoughts whirled around two terrifying fears: first, that by the time we made it there I would be too far along in labor to get an epidural, and second, that the baby would be born before midnight.

Finally, we made it inside the miraculously empty elevator, and Jesse pushed the button for the third floor maternity ward. "Can't be what people?" he asked again as the elevator rose. He was leaning on the elevator wall, trying to look nonchalant, but his leg was jiggling frantically.

"We can't be the people who have babies on Christmas!" I wailed, making Jesse do a double-take. I couldn't really blame him, but I found myself suddenly *very* upset about this.

I knew, of course, that it was probably just hormones pulling my strings, but knowing that didn't make it feel any less real.

"Would it really be so bad?" Jesse asked as the elevator dinged and he pushed me forward. "If the baby's born before midnight, that's less time in labor."

That's when I burst into tears. I'm not proud. "It would be *terrible*," I sobbed. Goddammit, why couldn't I calm the hell down? The frustration at being unable to regulate my feelings was only making my out-of-control emotions worse. "We'd be those *people*! And we'd have to name her H-Holly or Christina or some festive shit and everyone would laugh at her! And she wouldn't get to have *her own special day*!"

Jesse, to his credit, didn't laugh at me.

My radius, which expanded whenever I got upset, began to grow. Hospitals weren't a particularly popular place for the Old World, but I could suddenly feel two werewolves and a handful of witches on the floors around me, and the little blips in my radius vied for my attention.

The nurse at the desk took one look at my face and moved her gaze to Jesse. In this one single incidence, I couldn't even blame her. "How far apart are the contractions?" she demanded.

"About every four or five minutes."

"Okay, good." She picked up a clipboard. I was still crying, so I leaned sideways so I could free one elbow to dig into Jesse's side.

"Ow! Um," he rubbed his stomach and added, "She would really like an epidural, please."

"Don't worry, honey," the nurse said over the computer screen. "You've still got time."

"We made a reservation," Jesse told her. "Scarlett Bernard?"

The nurse checked her computer screen, and her eyes actually widened. "Yes, of course, sir," she said hurriedly. "We'll show you to the room right away."

I stopped crying long enough to crane my neck at Jesse. I felt like I'd missed something. My OB-GYN, Dr. Berghahn, had probably let the hospital know my due date, but "reservation" sounded suspiciously formal. Jesse, for his part, was looking suspiciously nonchalant.

Or was I just being paranoid? *Fuck* I hated this baby hormone shit.

Two minutes—and one paralyzing contraction—later, Jesse and I were ushered into a private birthing suite that was larger and nicer than any hotel room I had ever personally slept in, including the Venetian in Las Vegas. "Whaaaat the hell…" I muttered, staring. It *looked* like a hotel room, with a beautiful, elevated full-size bed. I didn't even see any medical equipment, although there were telltale panels on the walls that probably folded down or out or something.

The opulence made me uncomfortable—I'd never been great with displays of extreme wealth—so as the nurse and Jesse helped me out of the wheelchair and into the bed, I gave him an accusatory look.

"Dude. Why are we in a ridiculous place?"

Jesse made a fuss of adjusting pillows and blankets, avoiding my eyes. "Um, it was Dashiell's idea."

"Here," the nurse said pleasantly, producing a folded pile of extra-soft clothing. She set it on the foot of the bed. "When you're ready, please change into this."

She smiled some more, and I wondered if she would actually curtsy. Thankfully, she left the room without me needing to throw up on her.

I looked at Jesse, who looked a bit terrified to be suddenly alone with me. "Since when does Dashiell get to make decisions for my baby? Turn around." I'd gotten rather body-shy about my awkward new shape.

"Let me help—" he began.

"I can do it myself!" I snapped. Whoops. That had been a bit hasher than I'd intended.

"He's not making decisions for the baby," Jesse explained, facing the wall like he was in time-out. "But he knows a lot of people on the board of this hospital…"

I pulled my giant maternity top and bra over my head—that was the easy part—and picked up the top item of clothing. It was shaped kind of like a hospital gown, but kimono-style, and it was so outrageously soft that I instantly resolved to be buried in it someday.

I shook it out and gaped. "Jesse. This is fucking *monogrammed*."

"Uh…" he sounded embarrassed. "We had to book in advance."

"What the hell did you idiots do? She's not a royal baby."

"She's an *important* baby," he corrected.

This was sort of true. Up until—oh, about nine months ago—only a few people on the planet even knew nulls could have kids. Everyone else, me included, thought nulls were sterile.

We were wrong. Before Jesse and I got together for real, I'd had a brief relationship with another null, Jameson. He had been killed shortly after, and it wasn't until months later that I learned I was pregnant with a child who would become a powerful witch.

Still, I couldn't drop it. "Even if she *is* important, that doesn't mean you dummies should be spending the GNP of a medium-sized country on a hospital room!"

"Can I turn around now?"

"No!"

I got the kimono-thing on okay, but it took a little while to wriggle out of my leggings and underwear. By the time I flopped back on the bed I felt exhausted—and filled with dread. This already wasn't anything like I'd imagined. Or was I just being hormonal?

Aaaaaaaargh.

"Okay," I said weakly.

Jesse turned around and scooped up my clothes without being asked. He dropped the pile on top of my duffel bag, and came back to take my hand.

But I wasn't done yelling at him. I knew I was overreacting, but I'd spent eight months picturing this moment, and I had kind of been clinging to that vision for comfort. "Jesse, it's *too much.*" I gestured at the table of gleaming remotes next to my bed. I didn't see a television anywhere, but I suspected one of those would make it appear. Aside from the door we had come in, there were *three* other doors in the room, and I wasn't sure I even wanted to know where they led. "I think this suite might be bigger than our house. Do you know how many regular-sized hospital rooms could fit in—"

Jesse kissed me quickly on the lips, cutting me off. "Scarlett...this floor has the best security in the hospital."

That brought me up short. "Oh."

Outside of my partners, nobody in Los Angeles knew that the baby would be a witch—but because we can so thoroughly trash the status quo, nulls are considered both dangerous and valuable. I was a particularly powerful null, with the backing of some powerful people, so of course it had crossed everyone's minds that someone could try to use the baby to get to me.

"Did you bring my knives?" I asked anxiously. We had been

arguing for the last two weeks over whether or not I could bring weapons into the delivery room. Jesse seemed to honestly believe I might shank someone for being too slow with the ice chips or something. Every time I put some of my throwing knives in my hospital bag, he found them and took them out.

Now he kissed my forehead. "No, but I brought a Glock," he said, one hand waving toward the small of his back. "And the security here is top notch. *And* Wyatt is on his way to the waiting room. He'll stay there until dawn, and then Hayne is sending Cliff over." Wyatt was a vampire who for some reason had developed a particular interest in my personal safety, and Cliff was a human security agent whom I trusted. "You don't have to worry about either of your safety, I *swear*."

As he explained all this, Jesse's face was intensely serious, and I realized this was something he'd been really worrying about. I opened my mouth to apologize—well, I'd like to think I was going to apologize—but another contraction hit me, and Jesse pushed the button for the nurse.

She was there in *seconds*, and I began to change my mind about the extravagant hospital suite. "Another contraction?" she said. "I'll mark it on her chart."

"Epidural," I said between clenched teeth.

She smiled sympathetically. "I know it hurts, but you won't be dilated far enough yet."

I'd taken the birthing class; and I knew that the timing of my epidural depended on my dilation. And it sure as hell felt like I was ready for drugs. "Check me," I demanded, pointing at the hem of my gown.

The nurse scanned the clipboard. "Ms. Bernard, how long ago did your water break?"

Jesse checked his phone. To my shock, it was only 8:50 pm. "About forty-five minutes."

"I'm sure it's much too—"

"Check me!" I snapped. I acknowledge that it wasn't my finest moment.

The nurse clearly wanted to roll her eyes, but apparently I was a VIP now, so she just put on a dutiful smile and carefully lifted the hem of my kimono thing. Her eyes widened. "Oh, my."

"What?" I craned my head, but of course I couldn't see anything over my belly. "What's wrong with her?"

Jesse started to go look, but I held on to his hand. I had made it very clear to him that he would be staying near my head for everything that followed. If I was going to poop myself having a baby, neither of us was ever going to know about it.

"Nothing! Nothing's wrong," the nurse said quickly. She met my eyes, looking just a touch chagrined. "Um, would you like to know if your baby has hair?"

Yeah, I got the epidural really fucking quick after that.

II.

When you work in a secret supernatural underworld—and also watch lots and lots of television—you sort of expect drama in certain situations. Every wedding seems like it will have a surprise runaway bride, and every argument in a bar seems destined to turn into a brawl (though in my defense, this did happen a lot). I had worried that the Law of Drama would apply to my baby's birth, but when it finally did happen, everything was textbook. No emergency C-section, no forty-eight hours of labor, and, thank God, no masked gunmen trying to kidnap the baby or me.

First, I got my epidural. Once it kicked in I may or may not have proposed marriage to the anesthesiologist, but Jesse didn't take it personally. My OB-GYN, Dr. Berghahn—a sensible, smiling woman who projected a sense of we-can-handle-anything calm—arrived a few minutes later. She'd come in on Christmas, her night off, just for my delivery. For just a second I wondered if Dashiell had pressed or bribed her, and then the next contraction hit and I decided I didn't need to know.

The next few hours blurred by. Even a routine childbirth isn't particularly a good time, but I wasn't miserable, for which I give ninety percent of the credit to my epidural, and the other ten percent to Jesse. He knew me well enough to crack jokes instead of asking me how I was doing, and just to make me smile, he declared war on anything Christmas-related, tearing down decorations and yelling at nurses who said "Happy holidays!" When Christmas carolers swung through the hospital he shooed them away with threats of contacting the police. "I've never loved you more," I told him.

I kind of meant it.

By eleven-thirty I was exhausted and sweaty from the relentless contractions, and even though my lower half was numb, I wanted nothing more than to go to sleep. I wanted to hand off this whole labor thing to someone else, just for awhile. Since that didn't appear to be possible, I distracted myself by focusing on the clock. "We just have to make it past midnight," I told Jesse. "December twenty-sixth isn't so bad, right? At least she'll have her own day. She won't have to share with Jesus."

"I love you," he said with a weary smile. My impossibly handsome boyfriend looked tired and haggard. He'd been fetching me things from my bag, checking in with Wyatt in the waiting room, and communicating with my business partners and friends. I wasn't about to say his job was harder than mine, of course, but he did look wiped out. I reached up and rested a palm on his face.

I felt another contraction come, and he held my hands again. I gritted my teeth, forcing myself to keep breathing.

"Scarlett." Dr. Berghahn's calm voice came from the direction of my vagina. "She's ready. It's time to start pushing."

Shit. I had jinxed it. "No, let's wait," I said, as though I were just pushing back a meeting. "Just like, half an hour, okay?"

Yes, I heard how stupid it sounded.

"Scarlett," Berghahn said patiently, "I'm sorry, but the baby is ready *now*. Whatever the calendar says, it's time."

I knew she was right, but I looked at Jesse with tears again, as another contraction gripped me. Jesse's hands were crossed at the wrist so he could grip both of mine, and now he gave my hands a squeeze. "Forget the clock," he said softly, kissing my knuckles. "You've got this."

From beneath the kimono hem, Berghahn said, "Okay, Scarlett, here we go, one-two-three…"

And I pushed.

I pushed for forever. When I started pushing, I thought I was physically exhausted, but it turned out that was only the starting point of tired. It was like doing the entire LA bike marathon only to find out you have to run thirty miles to get home.

I was emotional, and my radius seemed to grow with each push, so that all the dots of magical activity buzzed in my mind while pain and exhaustion fought for my attention. Jesse talked to me, but I barely heard what he said, and registered none of it. I was sweaty and puffy and so, so tired.

And my stupid body, which had clearly chosen the baby over me, wouldn't let me rest. It just kept pulling on my energy resources until I was sure I had nothing left, and then it pulled some more.

After an eternity, I felt something loosen, and Dr. Berghahn said, "All right, Scarlett, the baby's head is out. One more good push should do it."

She was still calm, like that was a completely ordinary, doable request, and I would have laughed at the absurdity if I'd just had the strength. In that moment I had never felt so helpless, so completely empty. There was no way I was strong enough for another push, and I started to panic. What would happen if I couldn't get her out?

I rolled my head sideways to look at Jesse, whose warm brown eyes were so full of concern and love. There was suddenly just the two of us in the room, along with the endless noise in my head from my radius. "I can't," I sobbed. "I *can't*."

He smoothed sweaty hair off my face. "You *can*," he said very firmly.

I realized then that he was crying, silent tears running down his face. I wanted to touch him but I was too tired to lift my hand. "Scarlett," Jesse said, "your baby needs you."

"Come on, Scarlett, just one more push," Dr. Berghahn coaxed.

I didn't look away from Jesse. "*Our* baby," I corrected. I wanted to say more, but I didn't have the energy.

He nodded. "Our baby."

So I pushed again. I don't know how, but I did. And the doctor had been right: a second later I felt the massive release of pressure and pain. "She's out!" Dr. Berghahn crowed. I wanted to look, but I couldn't hold my head up. I wanted to ask Jesse to hold my head up, but I was too tired. So I just lay there for a moment, panting.

"You are extraordinary," he murmured, his lips against my cheek.

"Is she okay?" I managed to mumble. My radius was shrinking, some of the noise leaving my head, but now I had new worries. The baby wasn't crying. In movies the baby cried.

"She's great," Dr. Berghahn called from somewhere across the gargantuan room. "One moment, and we'll have her to you."

That had been part of my birth plan, I remembered—they would clean her up a little before they brought her to me. I think I nodded. I certainly meant to nod.

I was dazed, but a moment later Jesse stepped back from me, and then Dr. Berghahn was there, beaming at me with a white bundle in her arms. It was so small, I couldn't believe it.

"Here, Scarlett," my doctor said, gently transferring her to the crook of my left arm. "Here's your girl."

Everything else cleared away, and I definitely stopped breathing.

She let out a few angry squalls, obviously *pissed*. Her features were stretched into a scowl, and she'd already pulled her tiny arms free from the blanket and was waving them about with shaky rage, her little mouth moving like she was cursing us all for the inconvenience.

Jesse laughed, a beautiful joyous sound. "She looks just like you," he said. He'd resumed his place at my side.

"She's *perfect*," I whispered. Hesitantly, I put my index finger into her palm, and she automatically wrapped her hand around it. I snuggled her close, and she calmed down, though her brow was still creased with apparent irritation. We had clearly *ruined* her day.

"Seven pounds, twelve ounces, nineteen inches long," the doctor said, sounding pleased. "And look at the time."

I tore my eyes away from the baby to check the clock. It was 12:15. "Yessssss," I hissed. I didn't have the energy for a high-five.

"Scarlett, we do still need to get the placenta out." The doctor looked at Jesse. "Dad, will you hold the baby for a moment?"

Jesse looked up with almost cartoonish shock. "Me?"

Now it was my turn to laugh. "You *are* the dad, dummy."

Jesse took the little bundle with a look of awe and humility that would have touched me to my soul if a nurse didn't choose that moment to lean on my poor abused stomach. The placenta came out, which sucked, and my epidural had to be removed, which also sucked. Then the nurses managed to change the sheets without requiring me to actually get up, which was…okay, actually pretty impressive.

The staff obviously had a lot of practice with this routine, because within minutes of the baby's birth, the nurse helped me scoot over on the bed so Jesse could climb in with the baby between us, and then suddenly the room was beginning to empty. The nurse said something about resting and paperwork and breast-feeding, and everything seemed like it was happening really fast, like time was trying to make up for the hours that had dragged by earlier in the evening. I hoped Jesse was listening to the instructions, because I was busy holding *my baby*.

And then we were alone in the room. They'd dimmed the lights and left a padded bassinet for the baby, but I wasn't ready to put her down. Not when she was there, so real and perfect and holy shit, *outside of my body*. The baby had drifted off to sleep, still holding my finger, but both Jesse and I just lay there and marveled at her. As her face relaxed her angry glower was slowly replaced by exhaustion. I felt like I could probably spend the rest of my life just watching her face change.

I was in awe of this moment, one that I'd never expected to have, and never would again. "She still doesn't have a name," Jesse whispered, stroking her black downy hair.

"Yes she does."

Jesse looked at me, eyebrows raised.

"Esperanza," I said. It was the name of my hometown, and in Spanish it meant hope. Seemed pretty appropriate for a super-powerful witch baby.

A slow, wondrous smile spread over his face. "Esperanza Jamie Bernard," he pronounced, looking down at her. "I like it."

I felt a quick pang of sadness, but I shook my head. "Esperanza Jamie *Cruz.*"

Jesse looked up at me. He was trying to keep his expression neutral, but I saw the quick flare of joy before he got it under control. "You don't have to do that, Scarlett. I know how you feel about me."

I smiled. "That's good, but it's not just for you. Having a different last name will make it just a little harder for anyone trying to find her." I stroked her cheek with my thumb. "Besides, then her name represents everyone who made her. Esperanza for her mother's hometown. Jamie for Jameson, her biological father, and a good man who would have loved her very much. And Cruz for you, her dad." I kissed the top of the baby's head. "It feels right."

Jesse didn't speak for a second, and when I looked at him he appeared to be fighting to swallow. "You're all choked up, aren't you?" I teased.

He shook his head.

"You *are.* Your eyes are all misty and you can't talk. This is the end of the Iron Giant all over again."

As an answer, Jesse leaned across Esperanza and kissed me gently on the lips. "Shut up, Scarlett."

So I did.

The baby fell asleep first, and Jesse transferred her into the bassinet, wheeling it right up to my side of the bed. I lay on my side so I could still look at her, and Jesse curled in behind me, his arm over my side. After a few minutes, I felt him relax into sleep. My lady parts hurt now, and I was so tired—no one in the history of life had ever been more tired— but I found myself holding on, staying awake, so I could gaze at my baby.

I had made a baby.

Finally, just before two a.m., I drifted to sleep.

III.

A little under four hours. That's how long I got to be a normal— and I can't believe I'm saying this word—mom. Then, just before six a.m., my life came knocking. Literally.

I dimly heard the sound, but I didn't really wake up until I felt Jesse move, and then he was sitting up with his arm extended, his Glock pointed at the doorway. I lurched myself up, too, feeling a vampire in my radius.

"Whoa." Wyatt held up his hands, his mildly absurd handlebar mustache twitching with amusement. "It's just me, Miss Scarlett. Hello, Jesse."

Jesse put the gun back in the holster at his back, and dropped his head back onto the pillow in annoyance. I heard him mumbling a few choice phrases in Spanish, and I caught the word "heart attack" in English.

I pulled myself into a better seated position, wincing at the ache, and smiled at the cowboy vampire. I didn't bother to hide my exhaustion—Wyatt would have been able to tell, anyway. "Hello, Wyatt. Is everything okay?"

He shifted his weight a little, looking uneasy. "Ma'am, there's someone here who would like to see you. I tried to turn her away, but…well, I'm having a hard time with it."

I blinked, and for one second, my heart leapt. Could it be Juliet, my sister-in-law? Had Jesse or someone told them about the baby? "A human?" I asked hopefully.

"No, ma'am. A vampire. Never met her before. She says her name is Maven."

"Oh, *shit*," I said out loud, and then winced, glancing toward the baby. She stirred in her sleep, flailing her arms a little, but didn't quite wake up.

I looked at Jesse, whose face mirrored my concern.

I looked down at myself. My breasts were aching under the kimono—I was going to need to try to feed the baby soon. My hair was a mess, and I probably had sleep marks all over my face from the pillow. "Did she say what she wanted?" I asked nervously.

"No, ma'am." Wyatt still looked uncomfortable. He hadn't brought his big cowboy hat along, probably wanting to keep a low profile at the hospital, and I could see his hands open and close as if he was desperate to fiddle with it. I looked at Jesse, who gave a tiny shrug. *Up to you.*

"Send her in," I said, smoothing my hair down as best I could.

A few seconds later, a petite, beautiful girl with neon green hair poked her head into the dimly lit room, looking uncertain. She wore an oversized red sweater dress and an untold number of necklaces piled around her neck. In my peripheral vision I could see Jesse's confused expression—*this* was the superpowered vampire?—but I could feel Maven in my radius, and I knew exactly what she was. Her eyes found us, and she broke into a smile. "Hello."

"Hello, Maven. Come in."

I had kept my voice low so I wouldn't wake the baby, and as she crossed the room toward us, Maven took the hint. "I'm sorry to drop in unexpectedly like this," she said softly.

Carefully, I said, "May I ask why you're here?" There, that was diplomatic AF.

She answered me with something like reverence in her voice. "I've been alive a very long time, and I've seen all kinds of life come and leave this the world," she said, her hands clasped in front of her. "But I have never been able to greet the daughter of two nulls on her first night in the world. I never expected to have the chance. I'm afraid I couldn't resist."

I felt some of the tension leave my stomach. I had no way to tell if she was lying, of course, but when I'd met Maven in Colorado, the idea of a witchling—as she'd described the child of two nulls—had seemed to thrill her.

Jesse shifted a little beside me, and I belatedly remembered basic human manners. "Maven, this is Jesse Cruz." I didn't say "my boyfriend" or "my partner" or anything. I figured our relationship was pretty frickin' obvious at the moment.

"Hello," Maven said to Jesse, but her eyes flickered to the crib. Without taking another step toward the baby, she looked at me for permission. "May I see her?"

Jesse went tense behind me, and I knew he hated his current positioning, with me and the baby in between him and Maven.

Mainly to appease him, I told Maven, "You should know that if I put some effort into it, I can take the magic away from this entire building. And Jesse is armed."

Maven's lips twitched, but she said very seriously, "On my honor, on my life, I mean no harm to any of you."

I felt the tiniest buzz of magic at her words, although it fizzed out against my radius. I gestured toward the baby. "Go ahead."

The ancient vampire stepped up to the plexiglass crib, and her expression softened as she looked down at the sleeping baby. "Have you picked out a name?" she asked, her fingers touching the top of the crib.

"Esperanza."

Maven looked up then, smiling at me with obvious pleasure. "How perfect."

"It's a little on the nose," I admitted.

"Nonsense. The right name is the right name."

Silence settled over us, as she gazed down at the sleeping baby. I felt awkward, sitting in bed with a fancy kimono and giant painful breasts next to the closest thing to a goddess I was likely to meet, so by way of making conversation I mumbled, "How is Lex?"

Maven looked up at me with surprise and a hint of wariness. I wouldn't have recognized it if I hadn't spent so much time around vampires.

"I'm not trying to make some kind of dramatic secret point," I blurted. "I just haven't talked to her for awhile."

"Ah." Her features relaxed. "There was some…trouble…a few weeks ago. Someone fairly close to her died. She may have told you."

"No, she didn't mention it. Is she okay?"

Maven nodded. "We've got some changes on the horizon, but I think she'll be fine."

"What kind of changes?" Jesse asked. I shot him a look, but he didn't withdraw the question. Always the frickin' cop.

Maven smiled at him, and I knew no force on earth was going to get her to answer the question. She turned back to me instead. "I've brought a gift for you. For the baby."

"You did?" I said without thinking. "I mean, that's not necessary."

Amusement lit her eyes. "Oh, how could I not? It's Christmas, you have a baby, I'm a visitor from afar…"

I eyed the sweater dress with skepticism. "If you've got gold, frankincense, or myrrh hidden in that thing, I'll eat this kimono."

She threw back her head and laughed. The cardinal vampire of Colorado had a very nice laugh. "I'm afraid I couldn't get any of that on short notice. No, my gift doesn't come in wrapping paper, or even a card. But I've spoken to Dashiell, and I'm contracting one of his security humans to keep an eye on the baby, for the first year of her life."

"You got us…a security guard?" I repeated.

"Just during the day," she said. "He won't interfere with your lives, but he'll keep an eye on your home, and go anywhere the child goes.

Esperanza," she added, as if trying to get used to the name.

I looked at Jesse, not sure what to think. Even with the two of us and Shadow, I knew we'd both lost sleep worrying about the baby's safety. If we became the usual sleep-deprived new parents, would we notice someone about to throw a Molotov cocktail through the living room window? Would we be able to react in time?

But Jesse looked doubtful. "As much as we trust Hayne," he began, "I'm just not sure about a stranger—"

"Oh, I'm sorry," Maven broke in. "I should have mentioned. Dashiell said you already know this gentleman. Augustin Clifford?"

I looked at Jesse and grinned. "That's very thoughtful, thank you," he said to Maven, but he was smiling back at me.

"You're quite welcome." Maven dipped her head respectfully and turned toward the door.

Aw, what the hell. "Hey, Maven?" She turned, enquiring. "Merry Christmas."

Bonus Materials

Nightshades: Deleted Scene

This scene was the original opening to my Nightshades trilogy by Tor.com. I ultimately decided to cut it to get to the meat of the story faster, but it still serves as a good introduction to that world. The trilogy is available in bookstores or on Audible.

****

Bethesda, Maryland, 2018

At two in the morning, a halfhearted patter of rain began on the roof of Demi's little cottage. She grunted with annoyance and stopped typing long enough to rub her eyes, smearing makeup across her fingers. The gutters were full of last fall's leaves, which meant the rain would soak into the lawn and flood the basement again. She'd meant to go buy a ladder and clean them out herself, but she'd gotten distracted. Again. God, she missed the city.

Demi glared down at her black-smeared fingers, grabbing a tissue to wipe off the makeup. Now in her late thirties, Demi was aware that her days of black eyeliner and combat boots were numbered, but she was stubbornly holding onto the lifestyle as long as she could.

And to her baby, one of any number of dirt-poor, idealism-heavy "real news" sites that had sprung up in the years after The Smoking Gun and its ilk. Technically her site was third-gen ATG, after the gun, as her Darknet friends called it. Unlike TSG or many of her contemporaries, Demi refused to sell her well-respected but aways on the verge of bankruptcy business.

She went back to her email, a message to her favorite LA reporter, who was about to break a midlevel story about the California governor's political kickbacks. He wanted to go live with only one source, but that was There was a loud clapping outside, and for a moment Demi's hind brain just dismissed it as thunder. Then the sound came again, and registered it for what it was: someone slapping a frantic palm against her front door.

Demi froze, her fingers resting on the much-abused keyboard. Her real name was out there, if anyone looked hard enough, but this house was never connected to her in any legal sense; it belonged to a friend of her favorite aunt, who preferred the climate in Tempe. No one but her parents and the aunt knew exactly where she was.

There was a thud from her bedroom, and her deaf Chow mix Carl came plowing into the living room, barking furiously at the door. That was weird, too - he rarely woke up from noise, even vibrations in the house. For the first time, Demi wished she had taken her aunt up on the offer of an inexpensive shotgun "for protection."

The clapping sounded on the door again, and Demi pushed her chair back hesitantly, cell phone in hand. She couldn't call the police just for a knock. There was nothing to do but go answer it, and hope that Carl would eat anyone who threatened her.

In the foyer, Demi went up on tiptoes to squint through the peephole. A wet and irritated-looking man in his early fifties stood on the other side of the door, wearing a cap and one of those denim jackets with shearling on the inside. As Demi watched a thick line of blood oozed from a long cut on his forehead, and was washed away by the rain, which had picked up. The man shot a nervous look over one shoulder. Demi relaxed an inch. He'd probably been in a fender bender or something and needed a phone. Carl was still barking his head off, and she made no attempt to silence him, glad for the threatening sound. Holding onto the Chow's collar, she cracked the door open. There was a pickup truck in her driveway, with a massive dent in the front grill, which certainly lend itself to her theory—as did the man's hand, which he was clutching at the wrist as though he'd sprained it. "What is it?" she shouted over Carl's barking. "You need a phone?"

"That's up to you," he shouted back. Without another word, the man turned and began trudging back toward his truck, jerking one impatient hand for her to follow.

Demi was pretty sure she'd seen this horror movie, and there was no way in hell she was going out there in the rain to be ax-murdered. Journalistic curiosity or not, she would call the police, thank you. Demi moved to close the door again, but sensing her intention, Carl bellowed and twisted out of her grip, sticking his nose in the crack and wiggling out before she could do more than flail helplessly at him. "Goddammit, Carl!" she yelled, but of course he couldn't hear her. She swung the door open to see the dog flashing around the side of the pickup truck, and a moment later a man's loud yelp.

Oh, shit, did Carl bite the guy? Cell phone in hand, Demi ran outside in her bare feet, hurrying as much as she could across the gravel driveway. As she reached the pickup truck she opened the flashlight app on her phone and held it up, hoping the rain wouldn't get past her hard plastic case.

To her relief, the man was just standing there, still holding his injured wrist, at the corner of the truck. He was fine. But Carl was losing his shit, barking and scrabbling furiously at the pickup bed, trying to climb the narrow ledge and get inside, where there was a tarp draped over something large. She'd never seen him so worked up. Had the man hit a deer or something? Demi rushed to grab the dog's collar, but Carl saw her coming and dodged away, spinning to make another attempt on the truck bed. Still reaching for the dog, Demi shouted, "What's in there?" to the man, who just rocked back on his heels, shrugging. Curiosity got the better of Demi and she gave up on corralling the dog in favor of holding up the glowing cell phone. She leaned over the gate and tugged the tarp aside.

And screamed. There was a man in the truck, bucking wildly against the thick cords of climbing rope that encircled him from just beneath his nose all the way down to his ankles. He snarled at Demi, who fell back, intending to race in the house and call 911, Carl or no Carl. But then lightning really did light up the night sky, and in the instant brightness she saw the thing's eyes. They were red.

Not like the irises were red; that would have been weird enough, but everything inside this guy's eye socket was a dark, terrible red, like a congealed puddle of blood. He bellowed at her, bucking supernaturally hard against the climbing ropes, and even over the sound of the rain Demi heard them creak against the pressure. She shrank back, turning wide eyes to the truck's driver.

"I didn't know where else to take it," he yelled.

"What is it?" Demi said again, her voice gone empty with fear.

The man shrugged. "I have no idea," he called back, "but it really wants blood." He held up the injured hand, and for the first time Demi could make out the blood staining his free hand. When he took it away a worm of red blood immediately surged out of the wrist, running down the man's arm.

The thing in the pickup cab began to writhe. Like a man possessed was the phrase that popped into Demi's head, and she realized how appropriate it was. The guy —the thing?— looked like he'd stepped out of one of those old exorcism movies.

Demi turned back to the injured man. "Who are you?" she shouted. "How did you find me here?"

The man's face crooked in a half smile. With his good hand, he reached into a pocket and showed her a small leather item. Despite herself, Demi stepped closer and held up the cell phone light so she could see. It was a badge, with the words Federal Bureau of Investigation carved on the top. Demi gave the man a puzzled look.

"I won't tell you my name," he yelled. "Don't bother asking. But if I give this" —he kicked lightly at the tail gate— "to my superiors, it'll just disappear. That what you want?"

"No," Demi said instinctively, then again, loud enough for him to hear. "No." She bent down and grabbed Carl's collar firmly. "You'd better come inside."

The Long Good Morning

Before Scarlett Bernard jumped into my brain and kicked off the Old World series, I wrote a hardboiled PI novel called _The Big Keep_, which very few people read. I had originally intended for the book to serve as the beginning of a series, but it simply hasn't found the audience I had hoped for. I think readers were put off by the way the book defies genre categorization: I think of it as my hardboiled PI novel, but those don't usually include pregnant, happily married women. Since it clearly wasn't a cozy or a "women's fiction" novel (the two categories where pregnant, married women _are_ allowed), no one knew quite what to do with it.

Now and then I am asked when there will be another Lena Dane book, and the answer is: I'm not sure there will. During the planning phase of the series, however, I did write the first three chapters of the sequel, _The Long Good Morning_, and I wanted to include them here as a thank-you for those readers who have kept Lena alive when I wanted to give up. I hope someday I can deliver the rest of the book to you.

[These chapters have not been copyedited.]

Chapter 1

Maternity leave is not for the faint of heart.

That's what I was thinking, anyway, as I stood at the kitchen counter at 6:30 am on a cold Friday morning in mid-November, blearily watching coffee drip into the pot. I was so tired that the coffee pot actually looked sort of hazy, like when a character in a movie has a brief, well-lit trip up to Heaven. I'd already set out my favorite mug, a cafe-style cup with a picture of Benedict Cumberbatch as Sherlock Holmes. "The case of the missing REM cycle," I said to Benedict, because I was basically punch-drunk at all times these days. "The mystery of the interrupted-"

The construction plastic draped around the kitchen doorway rustled as my fifteen-year-old ward, Nate, bounded through it with the dog at his heels. Without anyone asking, Nate had taken over dog walking duties since the baby was born. "Good morning," he chirped. Then he made an apologetic face as he took in my appearance. "Uh-oh, you look terrible."

I glowered at him, too tired to reply.

They warn you, of course. Everyone says there will be no sleep for the first six months, and I'd known going in that I'd be tired. But understanding that you'll be exhausted and actually *being* exhausted, for every moment of every single day, those are two different things. During my time as a cop, and later as a PI, I'd faced down a serial rapist, a professional killer, and a pack of very judgmental prostitutes who *never* liked how I did my nails, and I'd happily go up against any one of them again if it meant nine hours of uninterrupted sleep.

I thought of Matt Cleary for a moment, the expression of crazed hatred on his face before I'd killed him. Okay. Maybe not.

"Lena?" Nate asked. "You okay?"

"What? Yeah."

"Then can I have the peanut butter?" he said patiently. He was holding a piece of dry toast.

I looked down at my hand and saw that it did indeed contain the peanut butter. When did I pick that up? "Sure." I handed it to him carefully.

My husband, Toby, came through the plastic too, and for a few minutes I leaned against the counter with my coffee —I was afraid to sit down lest I fall asleep; it had happened before — watching the two of them buzz around the kitchen, eating toast and packing up their wallets and textbooks and legal files, chatting about their busy schedules that day. Both of them had showered and combed their hair. They were dressed in clean shirts and pants with zippers.

I was so jealous I thought I might cry.

"Any plans for the day?" Toby asked me as he poured coffee into his to-go mug.

I shrugged. "It's really more of a goal than a plan. I thought I might actually take a human shower. Wash my hair and everything. Like humans do."

"I didn't want to say anything," Toby replied in a grave voice, stepping over to rest his forehead against mine, "but you do stink of sour milk and unwashed clothes."

"That," I said loftily, "is only because I am partially covered in both of those things."

He grinned at me, straightening. "Is the contractor still coming today?"

I stared at him for a long moment before my brain kicked to life with the right answer. We were remodeling the apartment to create a small bedroom for Nate off the kitchen. All three of us were eager for the additional space, but whenever the contractor came over he and the baby ended up in a sort of noisiness arms race.

"Right, yeah, at two," I managed. "I'll take the sprout over to my dad's store."

Nate looked up from his comic book, his eyes sparkling. "Not your office? It's your last week of leave; I thought for sure you'd be clawing at the files by now."

A moment of awkward silence passed between Toby and me, and Nate's teasing expression fell as he looked back and forth between us. I cleared my throat, unclipping the baby monitor from my yoga pants and fiddling with the volume switch. "Henley doesn't need me hovering over her. I'll be back when I'm back," I told Nate.

This was true. Henley, who was taking care of my private investigation firm while I was on maternity leave, had once been in my mother's class at the police academy. She'd taken early retirement from the CPD a couple of years earlier, and it had taken a full month of begging before she'd grumblingly agreed to take care of my cases after I had the baby. If I ever tried to micromanage her she would shoot me through the eye socket.

Nate was studying me, but Toby just put an arm around me and kissed my head. "Say hi to your dad and Rory for me," he said. "And be sure and bundle her up, okay? It's only supposed to be like thirty degrees today."

For a moment I wanted to smack him for insinuation that I didn't know how to keep the baby alive, but I was so damned tired that I wasn't sure if I was being overly sensitive or not.

He read my thoughts on my face and shrugged sheepishly. "I worry." His cell phone went off and frowned down at the screen, rolling his eyes in a way that definitely meant it was work calling. Toby was an associate at a big Chicago law firm. He gave me one last wave and answered the phone, taking it with him out into the hall.

Nate came up to say goodbye, too, and I pointed him toward the brown paper bag on the counter, which I'd filled with two turkey sandwiches, an apple, and a granola bar. Nate wouldn't mind packing his own lunches, but I'd said I would take care of it while I was on leave. It helped to keep moving while the coffee brewed.

"Ten more days," Nate whispered, giving me a conspiratorial wink. I smiled at him, but I couldn't help the rush of panic that flooded my bloodstream.

I gave Nate a little push toward the door, but he paused in the doorway.

"Forget something?"

"Um, kind of." Swinging his backpack around, he dug in the front pocket and pulled out a crumpled piece of paper. He thrust it at me, eyes lowered.

"What's this?" I unfolded the note, which was from his guidance counselor. My stomach plummeted as I scanned the typed lines. "Again?"

Nate was still avoiding my eyes. "I didn't do anything, I swear."

I sighed. "I know you didn't."

Mrs. Kapov —she had corrected me three times when I'd tried to use "Ms."— had listed three potential meeting times, each with a little box I could check off if I was available. I marked the time for tomorrow afternoon and scrawled my signature on the bottom, feeling dread settle into my belly. I gave Nate the paper. "I hope she doesn't mind babies," I said.

His face was very solemn. "To the best of my knowledge she

dislikes children of all ages."

I reached out to give him a playful smack, but he ducked it and darted through the doorway.

When the boys had left, silence descended on the apartment, and what little energy I possessed seemed to rush out of me like it was swirling down a drain. I practically floated into the living room, where I unclipped the baby monitor from the waistband of my yoga pants and put it on the coffee table, collapsing on the couch. Before I could topple sideways onto a throw pillow, however, the dog saw his opening and hopped up to drape himself across my lap. Which would have been fine if Toka were a Yorkshire terrier, instead of a sixty-pound pit bull. "Yeah, I still love you, buddy," I mumbled, my eyelids already dragging. I scratched his back a little, but it felt like the strength was just draining out of my fingers. "But I just gotta close my—"

The baby monitor hissed and then erupted with the peal of an angry, five-week-old baby.

I shook myself awake and beelined for the bedroom, the dog racing happily ahead of me. Toka assumed we'd brought the baby home as a gift for him, which was pretty much how he'd felt about Nate, too.

In the Bedroom Formerly Known As My Office, my daughter Viviana Dane Forsythe was wide awake and pissed as hell, kicking her little legs furiously as she glared at the puppy mobile above her crib with unfathomable rage.

I had to smile. "Were the puppies taunting you again, baby?" I said as I scooped her up. Viv squealed with surprise and joy, rubbing her face against my shoulder. Cuddling her to me, I marveled once again over how light she was. A sort of frantic fear gripped me every time I realized how squishy and fragile she was. I kissed her on the head and carried her back toward the living room, to the chair we preferred for nursing.

While Viv was feeding, my cell phone began to buzz from the pocket of Toby's oversized hoodie, which I'd taken to wearing around the apartment as a combination sweatshirt and bathrobe. I fished it out with my free hand and checked the screen. The caller ID read DANE INVESTIGATIONS, LLC.

My hormones were rampaging, and just seeing the name of my PI firm spurred a rush of emotions: joy and longing, guilt and dread. I checked my watch. It was only seven-thirty, but I figured my assistant Bryce must be calling to complain about his temporary boss again.

I sighed and answered the phone. "She made you come in early again, huh? Look, we talked about this. I'll be back in just-"

"Lena, listen," he interrupted. Bryce is almost always perky and cheerful, even when he's complaining, but today his voice shook with anxiety. "Something's happened. Something good, I think. I mean, I'm not really sure what to do here, or if there's anything for you *to* do-"

"Bryce, *stop*," I ordered. Whoops. I'd forgotten to keep my voice low, and Viv squirmed with irritation, making me wince. "What happened? Is it Ruby?" I had bailed Bryce's little sister out of trouble before.

"No, she's fine. Sorry, I'm not-" He paused to take a breath. "Okay, I just got to the office and there's this frantic message from Alicia Emerson on the voicemail."

I winced. I'd been half-expecting that call for awhile now. Alicia's sixteen-year-old daughter Carolina had been in a coma for over a year, since she'd barely survived a brutal assault.

"Carrie passed away, didn't she?" I said quietly, suddenly very aware of holding my own, perfect daughter.

"No, see, that's the thing," Bryce said, his voice tripping with excitement. "She woke up."

Chapter 2

I must have reacted physically: stiffed or yelped or something, because Viv sensed it and squealed with annoyance. But the sound seemed to come from miles away.

"Lena? You there?" Bryce said, and I realized he'd been talking.

"Sorry, what?"

"I said, the Emersons took her back to the hospital, but they're really anxious to talk to you."

That wasn't surprising. The Emersons had hired me to find out who had beaten their daughter nearly to death, the beating that sent her into the coma. I'd never been able to find the bad guys, but one thing we knew for certain was that Carrie had gotten a good luck at them. Which meant that she was now in very real danger.

"Okay," I said automatically, looking down on myself. Viv on my lap, and my gross clothes, and... and...

"Lena?" Bryce was asking. "Should I send Henley?"

"No," I said immediately. "I need to do this myself. Tell them I'll be there in an hour."

Viv's little brow seemed to furrow as she studied my face. "Come on, tiny human," I said to her. "Time to go see Grandpa."

It wasn't that easy, of course. I had to finish nursing, and then take a quick shower, with the baby strapped into her car seat in the bathroom where I could see her. Viv bellowed with rage for the first few minutes, then passed out, which gave me time to get dressed and pack up the diaper bag. I was stuck in my maternity jeans until I could drop another ten pounds, but I threw on a long t-shirt and a gray cardigan over them, figuring the Emersons probably wouldn't even notice what I looked like.

Hell, I probably could have arrived unshowered in Toby's pajamas if I'd wanted to. Against all of the doctor's predictions, Carrie had woken up.

When I first took the Emerson case, I'd learned a lot about comas very quickly. There is something called a Glasgow Coma Scale, which uses certain criteria to measure the severity of a patient's coma, on a scale of 3-15 (don't ask me why those numbers). Patients who score a three or a four are very likely to either die or be considered in a permanent vegetative state. Those who score eleven or higher are likely to make a good recovery. Carrie, when I was working her case, consistently scored at around a seven. Her prognosis was not good, and would probably slowly deteriorate over time. If she ever did wake up, the doctors doubted that her motor functions and memories would be intact. Most people who wake up from comas do so in the first four to six weeks, not after more than a year.

But apparently Carrie was different.

It was very unlikely that she would be able to remember the men who'd beaten her, but unfortunately we couldn't count on the bad guys to understand that.

After a moment of consideration, I reluctantly left my Beretta in the new gun safe in our bedroom. I was not back to work yet, and Toby and I had agreed that I wouldn't carry the gun unless I was actively working. I didn't want him to think I was trying to sneak back into things a week early. This was a one-time, professional visit due to very extreme circumstances. I felt confident that even Toby would understand that much. Mostly confident.

An hour after Bryce's call, I held Viv's carseat in the crook of my elbow while I tapped on the glass door at Great Dane Comics. My dad bought the store before my sister Rory and I were born, and now Rory helps him run it, along with a commando unit of grateful, nerdy teenagers. The store didn't open for another half-hour, but someone would be in by now. I cupped my free hand around the glass so I could peer in.

I'd been hoping for my dad, so of course it was Rory. She was moving toward the door, her look of irritation changing to puzzled delight as she recognized us. Throwing open the deadbolt, Rory squealed, "Vivi!"

The baby, who had woken up when I took her out of the car into the cool air, blinked dubiously at my sister as Rory ushered us in and gestured for me to put down the car seat so she could get Viv out. Rory was a near copy of me, only with a couple extra years, brunette hair, and terrible fashion sense. For some reason she dresses like a stay-at-home mom from 1994. Today she was wearing high-waisted jeans and an ancient boatneck sweater that did nothing for her.

When she had Viv cuddled to her chest, Rory stopped cooing long enough to remember I was there. "Hey, Lena," she said offhandedly. "I thought you guys were stopping in this afternoon?"

"Something came up," I said, trying not to sound brusque. "Can Viv stay with you for an hour or two?"

Rory's eyebrows went up, and she gave me the "you're not taking this seriously" look I knew so well. "This is my place of *work*, Lena," she said, keeping her voice pleasant for Viv's sake. "I can't just babysit whenever you need me to." Her expression shifted to a suspicious glare. "Are you sneaking into the office?" she demanded. "I thought you had another week—"

"This is different, Ror," I interrupted. "Carrie Emerson just woke up."

Her face went slack with shock. "Oh," she said after a long moment. "Oh." I admit, I may have enjoyed it a little. I so rarely get to see my sister completely taken off guard. I couldn't really blame her, though: Everyone in my life knew what the Emerson case had meant to me: it was my greatest failure, simple as that.

"Yeah, I'm pretty much right there with you," I said, to move things along. "The Emersons just called this morning, and they'd like me to stop by the hospital. I assume to discuss safety measures."

Rory nodded slowly. "Right. Okay." She looked down at Viv, bouncing her a little on one hip. I envied the easy, comfortable way Rory had with my daughter. When I held Viv I always felt like I was right on the verge of breaking her. "That's different then," Rory said at last. "Just this once, I'll call Aaron and see if he can come in a little early." She held out a hand for the diaper bag.

I handed it over gratefully. "She'll be hungry soon, but there's half a bottle of breast milk in there, and a four-ounce bottle of formula if that's not enough." I pretended not to see Rory's glower disapprovingly at the suggestion of giving a baby *formula*. "I'll be back as soon as I can," I promised, kissing the baby on the top of her fuzzy head.

"Lena-" Rory began, and I paused in my escape, raising my eyebrows at her.

She looked uncharacteristically unsure of herself, and I was expecting some kind of question about taking care of a newborn, maybe something Rory had forgotten in the years since her youngest was born. The last thing I ever expected to hear from my sister was, "Listen…when you *are* back, maybe we could talk. About, um, a case."

I stared at her for a long moment. Why the hell would my sister need a private investigator? Then a horrible thought occurred to me. "Is Mark-"

"Oh, no. God, no," Rory said quickly. "He's not having an affair."

My chest unclenched a little. "Oh, good. It would suck to have to shoot him."

She smiled, but it was thin. "No, it's about one of our employees. But it's not urgent; it can wait until you get back next week." She made a shooing motion with one hand. "Go."

A flood of emotion hit me as soon as I was back in the car: Exultation first, followed by plenty of guilt. My parenting books all said I would be devastated the first time I went somewhere without the baby, but I was actually sort of...delighted. That was wrong, right? Had I fucked up the whole parenting thing already?

Also, what had Rory meant, they were having a problem with one of the employees? Up until the baby was born I usually stopped by the store at least two or three times a week. I knew everyone who worked there, and over time, well...I had never told Rory or my dad this, but I'd quietly run background checks on all of them. Everyone came out clean. Had I screwed that up, too?

I shook it off. Right or wrong, I needed to put my game face on. The Emersons deserved my best work.

I started the car and pointed it toward the hospital, my thoughts turning to Carrie.

When I'd agreed to take on the case, the facts had seemed fairly straightforward. Fourteen months earlier, fifteen-year-old Carrie had walked two blocks from her apartment building to visit a movie rental store that was going out of business. They were selling off all the stock, and Carrie had browsed for over half an hour, chatting with the teenage employee. Eventually she had purchased DVD copies of *Love*

& Basketball and *A League of Their Own*. Her day was supposed to end with going home and watching one of the movies with her parents.

But while Carrie was paying for the films, two men in ski masks were in the middle of robbing the adjacent liquor store. They ran outside just as Carrie exited the video store, and she had the misfortune of seeing them as they pulled off the masks. The suspects had beaten Carrie badly enough to send her into a coma, and rushed off before the first responders arrived on scene.

Two months after the attack, the CPD case had stalled out, and Carrie's parents Alicia and Roland brought me in. I'd spent the following four months obsessing over the case: reinvestigating everything the police had done and following extra leads on my own. I'd talked to the owner of the defunct video store, the video store employee, the family of the liquor store guy, all of the other employees at both businesses, and most of the past employees who still lived anywhere near Chicago. I'd canvassed the neighborhood for other witnesses, spent days researching similar crimes, harassed the hell out of every CPD evidence contact I'd ever made. I'd even talked to Carrie's friends, teachers, and classmates, although the attack had to be random.

And after all that legwork, I had found a whole lot of nothing– except a bunch of maddening little details that didn't add up. The police had never found Carrie's cell phone, though there was no reason for the suspects to take it. The two men had been removing their masks when they ran out of the store, which implied that maybe they knew the parking lot cameras hadn't been working— but I had painstakingly eliminated all the past or present employees who might have had a motive to commit the crime.

This kind of robbery was also usually part of a pattern: drug addicts or gang members who needed cash desperately enough to kill for. Those kind of people didn't just *stop*; they always needed more.

They either kept going, or they turned up dead. And yet there were no unsolved crimes that could be linked to Carrie's attack, and the people who'd been arrested for armed robbery since then had all been cleared.

More than anything, though, the brutality of Carrie's beating bothered me. You rarely see that kind of violence without a personal motive. And if their motive was just not wanting to leave a witness, why hadn't they just shot Carrie? Why the beating? There were too many elements that just didn't make sense, but try as I might, I couldn't push my way through to the answers. I'd run every idea straight into the ground and come up with nothing.

As a cop, I could have left the investigation open and followed more leads as they arose, but as a one-woman PI firm I just didn't have the resources. Plus, even on a sliding scale I knew my work was draining the Emerson's very limited funds. So I'd asked my few remaining contacts in the CPD to keep me posted on similar crimes, counseled the Emersons on how to keep Carrie safe in the hospital, and walked away.

It was one of the hardest things I'd ever done, and only the distractions of Nate and the pregnancy kept me from sinking into depression over it. But now Carrie was awake, and with her the potential for answers. Maybe I would get another shot at keeping her safe. Or, to put it another way, I might have another chance to fuck it all up.

Chapter 3

Roland Emerson was waiting for me at the nurse's station, a wide grin plastered to his face. He was a portly African-American man who looked like he'd dressed hurriedly in patched jeans and a button-down with a coffee stain on one cuff. Before I could hold out my hand to shake he darted forward, with speed that didn't match his size, and wrapped his big arms around me. "She's back," he said, his voice thick with emotion. "She came back to us."

I pulled back, unable to resist returning the smile. "I want to hear the prognosis, but is Alicia around? Can we talk?"

He bobbed his head enthusiastically, the smile still on his face. I could ask him for the deed to his house right then, and he'd probably hand it over. "Come this way."

I followed Roland into a small, dimly lit private room with two people grouped around a hospital bed, where Carrie was propped up with pillows. She was a pretty, athletic girl, with her mother's willowy limbs and a perfect replica of Roland's nose. I'd seen her a half-dozen times when I'd been working the case, but this was my first glimpse at her eyes, which were liquid and luminous like Alicia's. She looked pale and drawn, shrunken, but those eyes were fixed determinedly on the middle-aged woman in a white lab coat who sat next to her bed, flipping through white cards.

"That's very good, Carrie," the woman was saying. "Can you point to the picture of a *dog*?"

She held the card close to Carrie's hand, and the teenager slowly lifted her index finger to touch one of the four black pictures. It must have been the right answer, because on the opposite side of the bed her mother beamed, squirming with pleasure.

"Alicia," Roland said softly, "Lena's here."

Several emotions flooded Alicia Emerson's face: pleasure, anxiety, and then fear as she remembered why I was there. She looked from me to her daughter, biting her lip. Seeing her hesitation, the woman in the lab coat said reassuringly, "We have a number of cards left, if you want to step out for a couple of minutes."

Alicia looked at her daughter. "Is that okay with you, baby? If I step out for just a minute?"

I watched Carrie closely. The teenager's pale face tilted toward her mother, then blinked, her head moving slightly in a ghost of a nod.

Alicia Emerson followed Roland and me out of the room, closing the door behind her. Her beautiful skin was flushed and excited.

"Isn't it incredible?" she asked, beaming. "We knew with the new medication there was a better chance, but I hadn't really let myself hope…."

"It is wonderful, Alicia," I told her. "Can you give me a rundown of what happened?"

"Well, you probably got my email last month," she began. I had a vague recollection of getting something in my inbox right around when Viv was born. It might even have been while I was still in the hospital. But I had no idea what it said.

Alicia must have seen the guilt on my face, because she reached over and touched my arm. "Oh, that's okay, Lena, you just had a baby didn't you?" She smiled fondly. "I remember how crazy those first weeks were. Anyway, a couple of months ago Carrie was doing a little better, and they reclassified her as in a 'persistent vegetative state.' She finally got to have the chest tube out, and they let her come home."

"I stayed with her during the day," Roland put in, picking up the story with the easy fluidity of the long married. "And a home care nurse stopped by every morning."

"And then we got a call from the university, about a study," Alicia continued. "They'd developed this drug for other reasons, but thought it might have some application for coma patients."

"When was this?" I asked.

"Four weeks ago. They thought it would be months, at least, before Carrie showed any change, but that's our girl." Alicia beamed. "She's a fighter." I saw that one hand was wrapped around her necklace, a small gold cross. Roland reached over and hugged her, as though he couldn't stand not hugging anyone in that moment. I couldn't even blame him, really. If Viv…

I pushed the thought aside. "What's the prognosis?" I asked. "Will she regain her memory?"

A shadow crossed their faces nearly simultaneously, as though something had just moved over the light. "We don't know yet," Alicia said quietly. "She knows who we are, and she seemed to recognize her name, but she can't speak, and her cognition is slow. Some of that will be temporary, but it'll be awhile before we know how much damage was done during the coma."

I saw Roland's arm tighten around her again. "But she's awake," he said simply. "Whatever she needs now, all that matters is that she's awake."

I nodded and took a deep breath. "Alicia, Roland, I'm so happy for you both, and for Carrie. But we need to talk about what happens now."

Alicia visibly flinched, like I'd slapped down a leaping puppy. I swallowed the lump in my throat and pushed on. "We knew that the risks for Carrie would increase if she woke up. You need to be prepared for that."

"No, you're right, but… what do we do?" she asked.

"First things first," I said firmly. "I know you're excited, but do *not* tell anyone yet. Not friends, not family, not her school."

Alicia frowned, her hand dropping from the necklace so she could hug herself. "Her grandparents…" Roland rumbled in his deep voice.

I shook my head. "Only if you trust them completely. If this gets on the internet, or even just spread around the community, the men who did this to Carrie could find out she's awake, and then she's in danger." There was also the possibility, however slim, that someone in Carrie's life had been involved in the attack somehow. I wasn't going to mention that, though. Not when they were celebrating.

She nodded slowly, though I could still see the reluctance. "Have you called Detective Beaumont yet?" I asked in a low voice. Kate Beaumont was the cop who'd worked the case, and the person who'd given the Emersons my name when the police investigation stalled out. She and I had always been cordial to each other, but never particularly close. I'd actually been a little surprised when she'd recommended me.

"Yes," Roland supplied. "She said they'd have an officer drive by the house several times a day, and we should let her know if and when Carrie can be interviewed." His brow creased with anxiety. "But that doesn't seem like enough, right?"

"That should be fine until she's out of the hospital," I reassured them. Roland and Alicia exchanged another joyous smile. Now that Carrie was awake she'd be going home. "Just don't leave her alone here, keep it quiet, and let me know when she's going to be discharged. At that point I'll come and do a check of your home security. Free of charge," I added, as Alicia bit her lip uncertainly.

"Thank you, Lena," Alicia said. "But we can't hide her forever. Eventually she'll need to go back to school–"

"One step at a time," I interrupted, touching her arm. To be honest, I wasn't quite sure what to do myself. The Emersons couldn't afford to pay me, but they needed someone to figure out who had attacked Carrie, and fast.

My office was more or less on the way back to the comic book shop, so I made the decision for a quick detour to pick up the Emerson files. I told myself that re-reading the file wasn't going to hurt anything, and I sounded really convincing. To further assuage my guilt, I called Toby's office to tell him about Carrie, but he was in a meeting. I texted Rory to check on Viv, and she reported that the baby was sleeping behind the counter. That probably meant I wouldn't get my late-morning catnap, but the news about Carrie was still pumping adrenaline into my system, waking up the tatters of my brain.

My office did not, unfortunately, look like anything you'd see in a Humphrey Bogert movie. It was in color, first of all, but your pretty basic small-business office setup: a large room that served as combination reception and waiting area, a door that lead back to my small office, a couple of closets. I had my own little bathroom in my office; that was something. Overall, though, it looked a lot like, say, a small custom book-binding office, which was what was on the floor above us.

The second I walked through the main entrance, Bryce leapt up from his desk to hurtle toward me. "Lena!" He threw his arms around me, doing a wiggly little happy dance. Bryce was in his mid-twenties, Asian, a little plump, and cheerfully gay. I hadn't seen him since he'd come to the hospital to meet Viv, and I had missed his positivity. "Tell me you're back to stay," he whispered into my hair. "Tell me the dragon lady is going home."

I hugged him back, but shook my head. "Sorry, dude. Just picking up a file."

"Who's that?" came a loud, nasal voice from the office. *My* office.

"It's Lena," I called back, pulling away from Bryce.

There was a squeak as a wheelie chair scooted back, and soft footsteps on the carpet. Then Louisa Henley, formerly of the Chicago Police Department, was leaning in my office doorway, frowning up at me. She was a short, squat black woman in her early fifties, with the general demeanor of a bridge troll. "I thought you weren't back til next week," she grumped.

"Hello, Henley," I said lightly. I wasn't allowed to call her anything else. No one was. "It's good to see you, too." She harrumphed, giving me a pointed look. "I just wanted to pick up a file," I told her.

She grunted and turned back toward the office. "Might as well come in and get an update then." She stomped back to my desk, leaving me to follow.

I raised my eyebrows at Bryce, who began humming a funeral dirge. I rolled my eyes at him and followed Henley into my office.

The moment I crossed the threshold I felt a great wave of longing. This room wasn't decorated with an eye toward reassuring clients. It was done with an eye toward reassuring *me*. A big, comfortably worn desk, a framed still from The Maltese Falcon, the rug I'd picked up for a song at a flea market. This was my space, and although I would be back soon, it still hurt to see another woman looking so comfortable behind my desk. Especially since it seemed so shockingly clean.

She motioned me to one of the two available visitor's chairs, and I sat down, trying not to feel resentful. "How's the kid?" Henley said, abrupt.

"Huh? Oh, she's good," I said stupidly. "Not sleeping much, but she's pretty happy when she's awake, so it evens out."

"Lawrence was like that. My third," Henley said, in a tone that left no room for further discussion on the matter. "I've done a bunch of those background checks, plus there are six active cases," she said, pointing toward a neat stack of file folders on my desk. It was practically the only thing on my desk. "Three claims for that insurance firm you work with, one marital, and two missing persons. I should be wrapping up most of it before you get back, except for the insurance." I nodded, not even trying to absorb all of it. Bryce would walk me through everything when I got back.

"What's this case you're looking at?" Henley demanded. "Something you don't think I can handle?"

I blinked. "Whoa. That's not it. It's just complicated, that's all." I briefly sketched out the Emerson case, up to the part where Carrie woke up that morning.

"Huh," she grunted. "Unusual."

"Yeah, tell me about it." A sudden wave of despair descended on me. I hadn't been able to find Carrie's attacker when I had nothing else on my plate. What could I possibly accomplish now that I had a fourteen-year-old ward and a newborn?

ABOUT THE AUTHOR

Melissa F. Olson is the author of ten Old World novels for 47North as well as the Tor.com novella Nightshades and its two sequels. She lives in Madison, WI with her husband, two kids, two dogs, and two jittery chinchillas. Read more about her work and life at MelissaFOlson.com.

48287242R00163

Made in the USA
Lexington, KY
15 August 2019